Making a Siren
A Cruel Twist of Fate
Cheyenne Dragon

To Petey and my forever sidekick, you always believed in me. To all the dreamers out there, believe in yourself and your dreams, and never let anyone discourage you.

Content May Include

Alcohol

Family Issues

Violence

Mature Content

Depression/Grief

Death

Sexual Context

Suggestion of Sexual Assault

If you are still in for an adventure buckle in and enjoy the ride! Pirates, Sirens & Mermaids, oh my!

Contents

Preface

Welcome to *Acropora, where the old world clashes with the new,* and that pesky patriarchy rears its ugly head. Do not fear; we buck against those beliefs. In a world dominated by the human race, the supernatural lurks in the depths below. After all, what is a good story without Pirates, Mermaids, and Sirens? A dash of danger, a sprinkle of forbidden romance, and a heaping serving of betrayal await you.

This story evolved from a writing prompt and took on a life of its own. I hope you fall in love with it as much as I have writing it.

Prelude

*W*hat had I done?

That was the only thought consuming my mind as I shuffled down the length of the plank. This was my personal brand of hell, carved out just for me. The whole 'walk the plank' thing wasn't typical for pirates; it was a folktale exaggerated throughout the years. How did I get so lucky as to experience it for myself? The crew grew restless, crowding behind me, cheering—actually cheering—spewing their vile thoughts about me. So much for brotherhood. What else did I expect? I knew the risks of this life, I just hadn't expected them to catch up to me so quickly. Thick jute ropes bound my body; I could only move in small shambles. The scrape of the cannon against the wood grated against my ears.

I felt the tip of a sword against my back, the cool metal biting into the cloth of my tattered shirt. Ice clutched my body; the fear of impending doom made my entire being frigid and setting my body into pre-rigor mortis. I couldn't flex my fingers. Terror seeped through the numbness that had overcome me. This was the first time I looked at the sea below and panic barreled through me, instead of the peace I usually claimed from it. My heart shredded into a million jagged pieces, I felt hollow. I gazed down into the murky expanse of open water, gulping what was soon to be my last breaths.

"Move! Faster down the plank, yer fate awaits ye," Marduke bellowed, his voice booming like a gust of wind at my back.

I winced reflexively and felt the sword nip at my flesh, just enough to send a wave of pain down my spine. A little yelp escaped my shivering lips, and the crew roared with laughter. The warm trickle of blood running down my spine made me want to scratch it.

"Down goes the whore!" another crewmate yelled ferociously. Rage crept back in, locked in a deadly battle with the panic seizing my soul.

My gasps quickened as I stared into the depths. No matter how hard I tried, my lungs wouldn't fill with sweet, salty air. I worked around the lump in my throat, the barrier for me to take in the oxygen I desperately needed. My knees trembled as I stood frozen, forever rooted to the spot. This had not been my plan. Everything had gone wrong, so, so wrong.

How did I not see this coming?

The plank bowed beneath the captain's foot as he brought it crashing down with brute force. As the plank sprang back, I felt myself knocked off balance, then I plummeted to my awaiting doom. The drop was in slow motion; the choppy water lapped at the bottom of the ship, and dread raced up my spine as I plummeted into the sea's cold embrace. I was bound and helpless to their mercy.

The icy waters swallowed me whole. I sank rapidly, the weight of the ball and chain dragging me to my watery grave. An overwhelming pressure began to crush me as the sea sought to enter my lungs. Salt water burned my eyes. My body betrayed me, forcing me to cry out and allowing the last of my air to escape to the surface. A billowing trail of bubbles marked my path as I descended further into the depths.

Oh, how my lifetime friend has forsaken me.

A dark haze crept into my vision as black seeped into my peripheral. My lungs burned with the desperate need for oxygen; if I breathed in, I would drown. My body bucked against my binds in a desperate attempt to save itself. I gave myself over to the darkness wholeheartedly, welcoming the sweet embrace of death. With a final acceptance, I took a breath, ready for this to be over. Death was a sort of freedom, right? Only, it didn't come. My body seized and a change took hold. The soul-wrenching pain that overcame me was more imposing than the crushing of my lungs. The haze in my mind went up in flames, crashing into me in hot flashes like the waves of a relentless storm.

My lungs seemed to burst, yet I could breathe again. I took a deep, shuddering breath as I screamed in agony. My flesh cracked as if it were made of marble and peeled away from my body in rivets, revealing a murky gray complexion. I writhed and thrashed like a wild animal against the ropes that bound me. They seared into my legs, so hot my skin morphed around them. They glowed as they sank into my skin, lashing them together. A new silver skin formed around my binds, elongating into a joined tail. Fins pushed their way out of where my thighs had been, bulbs tipped the flared ends of them. My feet elongated, curving as they went. Spines formed and webbing bound them together into a large fin that dipped into two equal lengths. Little bulbs adorned each of the swooping ridges, glowing purple in the dark water.

Agony seared through my arms as spiked fins pushed out of my flesh, blending with the silver of my tail. My eyes were the last to morph; I could see into the darkness now...as clear as the waters of the Caribbean. I took a few ragged breaths, recovering from the pain my body had just endured. As if my body knew what to do by instinct, I flipped my tail, and rushed back up to the surface. I broke through the water, flipping my hair back and gasping for any air my lungs could swallow. My body was still in shock, pain rushing through me in currents. Slowly, the earth-shattering agony eased away; the bite of the cold water worked to numb it. I already noted the water didn't feel as chilling as it should have. I saw the ship sailing in the distance, a black mark on the horizon. She was one of the fastest ships in the sea.

"Fuck the lot of you!" I screamed, my voice coming out hoarse and alien to my ears.

I bobbed up and down with the movement of the ocean, my tail flicking languidly through the current to keep me upright. I noticed my fingers were webbed, and sharp claws took over my nail beds. I slid my hand through my wet hair. It was no longer golden-brown, as it had been, but the color of seaweed, such a dark green it was almost black. I looked over myself in wonder, feeling my new slippery skin. Silver scales glistened over my tail and fins.

What do I do now?

Just as the thought crossed my mind, heads rose out of the water. I looked around, astonished at the crowd of beings that looked like me. Their eyes glowed yellow against the dying light. I knew then, this was where I belonged. Slowly, they began going under one by one, without a sound, and I knew they wanted me to follow. Not by any thought of my own, only instinct to guide me, my body turned with them, and with a flip of my tail, I followed them into the depths below.

Chapter 1

Hard Lessons

"Naida, can you pay attention when I am talkin' to ya?"

I snapped my head around focusing on my father, his chest puffed out as he inhaled in frustration. For the fifth time in thirty minutes, might I add.

"As I was sayin', ya need to grip the ropes tight. Unless yer plannin' on not catching the wind in the sails and not movin'... Are ya even listenin' to me?"

A smile tugged at my lips as my eyes wandered around the bay port where my father kept his boat. The water lapped at the dock lazily, and the faint sound of seagulls filled my ears. I spotted a few other ships bobbing in the distance. My father was one of the many fishermen in our little village of Greymouth. The name was fitting of our dilapidated town. Most of the buildings past the bay were rundown. Fishing brought most of the earnings in. We all suffered when the nets came in empty. Thick trees lumbered along most of the coast, dotting around the buildings in town. The mountains led straight to the bay; we just carved a little haven out of it.

"Yes, something about ropes..." I mumbled as I gazed at the sea.

I heard my father huff impatiently, muttering something about the new generation not respecting authority. When your life is ruled by a lead fist, you tend to put cotton in your ears. I had no genuine interest in learning how to work a fishing boat; my real reason to be out here was simply the sea, not listening to my father talk himself to death. It was comforting floating on the ocean, more than I have felt on any land. Here, the waters were a deep blue, so deep it seemed bottomless, like sapphires. The exact hue as my father's eyes—most of the townspeople, in fact. I'm unsure if that's a sure sign of inbreeding or simply great genetics, but almost everyone had the same deep, blue, captivating eyes.

Then, there was mine: a vibrant emerald green.

The eyes of my mother. One of the only things she left me. She passed away when I was six years old...much too soon to lose a mother, much too soon to have any existing memories of her. I can only remember glimpses, like a passing image in a wave rippling out around me. Only there briefly, never around long enough for me to fully grasp.

Since her passing, my father has struggled to keep us afloat. He traveled abroad in his youth to gain his education. I envied that about him; he got to escape. Meanwhile, I had never left this village once in my seventeen years. What made Father come back here, I would never understand. Without Mother's extra earnings, he had no choice but to fish. Education was a rarity in Greymouth, there were mainly jobs of trade in the village. He never cared enough to share his reasons for staying here after her passing. Not that we had the means to leave if we wanted to.

As the years went on and my yearning for the sea grew, I would beg every time he went out in the water, pleading to go out with him. Anything to see more than our four walls, I had mesmerized every crack and flake of paint. He argued for years against my relentless whining. I feared he would never give in, keeping me from the one thing I loved the most. Eventually, he grew tired of hearing me moan about it and gave in. I couldn't help but smile, behind his back of course, as I watched the man of stone crumble ever so slightly.

"Fine Naida, ye may come with me, but no foolin' 'round. The water is a dangerous mistress. Ye never know what she might do. Ye will be learning how to man the boat. So ye will have to learn to keep the boat as a man would. Someday, you will not have me and ya may need these skills to survive." my father spoke, a warning in his tone.

Not only was it unheard of for a woman to board a boat, but it was also a superstition that has bound our village to this day. The tale goes: women bring storms, and storms bring destruction. The voyagers were so super- stitious about this that no women were even allowed to do work near the water. Women were expected to hold work such as cooking, cleaning, and sewing. Meager jobs for meager people, if you ask me. Where is the ad- venture? This fate never suited me; in the confines of my home, I spoke about it often, yet never when my father was around. I yearned to explore, just as my father had. I simply didn't want to journey the land. The land has been mapped and marked; I long for something new, undiscovered.

Much to my father's disappointment, I longed for the sea with every fiber of my being. She held so much wonder and mystery; I wanted nothing more than to know her depths and discover the secrets she held. The ocean was my only friend after my mother passed, with my father being away for days sometimes while trying to make extra income.

Other children kept their distance from me; it was no secret in our town that I was strange, at least in their eyes. Mothers swept their children away as I passed. Even if they occasionally threw me a pitiful glance every now and then. My father's tinkering didn't help that fact. The only one that comforted me was the one I was forbidden from ever truly knowing. I could have sworn sometimes the ocean speaks to me in my mind. How impossible does that sound? I never mentioned that to Father; he would have me committed for insanity.

When he finally broke, my father told me to dress in baggy, bulky garb—trying to make me look as much like a boy as possible. My long golden-brown locks were tied up under a fisherman's cap. Dirt rubbed into my face helped hide my soft features. Brown, fingerless gloves protected my unworn hands from the rope's wear. I kept my daily leather boots, the sole slowly degrading from the bottom. I begged my father for a new pair but we didn't have the money. Altogether, it was believable for the first attempt at my disguise.

I glanced at my surroundings. The bay we were in was a crescent surrounded by our village. It earned the rather obvious name *Crescent Moon Landing.* The bay was a sight to behold; not even a painting could capture its fullest beauty. That was, until one got close enough to smell the people. The stench of fish permeated the air like a layer of film on skin. Our village was made up of noise, boats, and a population of about fifteen hundred people. Most ships have been updated to metal; some older wooden ones still dot the docks. My father's boat, *Maiden of the Sea,* was the smallest— barely holding the two of us—and the rattiest of the others by far.

He adored that boat though, and it was all we could afford. Honestly, I'm surprised he could manage to buy a metal one, even in her dilapidated state. Ripped and patched sails, rust, and more barnacles on the sides than I could count. My father said it gave her character. I thought she looked schlocky, but I would not dare tell him that.

He was not a brute, but he wasn't the kindest to others' thoughts, primarily if they differed from his own. Unfortunately for me, mine usually did. Sometimes, I wished Mother was still alive for the simple pleasure of watching them interact. Was it every woman that offended him or just me? Come to think of it, he never got into disagreements with our elderly neighbor. Maybe it was just me.

The sapphire water lapped at our boat as it gently rocked in the sea. The sun was rising, kissing the ocean out on the horizon. Peaceful. The growing reds and yellows spread across the glittering water over to our dull village. It was beautiful, enough to steal the breath from my lips. Light spilled over the water on the horizon, the golden ripples stretching toward our boat.

I faintly heard him drone on and on about securing the mast, readying the ropes, and letting the sails down when the winds picked up, but honestly, I couldn't be bothered to listen. The scenery was too distracting. Seagulls called out, swooping overhead. I had never been up this early to see the sunrise and I wanted to soak up every moment of this. This was what freedom tasted like: the open water, the sun shining on my face, and the taste of the salty breeze on my lips. I was enraptured in complete bliss.

I heard my father call out just in time to be swept in the stomach by the boom, which had not been adequately secured. All the air promptly left my lungs in a guttural whoosh.

A yelp escaped me as I was knocked overboard. The icy water gave my body a shock. I jutted up from the surface, flailing about, trying to keep above water. I inhaled water, my head dipping under as I thrashed my arms around. Panic was trying to grip me in her cold clutches. My father handed me an oar over the side to grab onto.

I grasped desperately for the lifeline. My fingers were numb, but I managed to grip the oar enough for him to pull me back onto the boat's safety. I sputtered water, desperately hacking to clear my lungs of the invasion as I lay on the deck. My heart was causing havoc in my chest; I could swear it would burst out at any moment. Try as I might, my lungs won't inflate as much as I wanted to suck in the sweet, salty air.

"Tis' why ye need to pay attention and secure the ropes!" my father laughed as I looked at him astonished.

"You did that on purpose?" I shrieked, my teeth chattering uncontrollably.

He tossed me a scratchy wool blanket but refused to answer my accusation. He was well aware I didn't know how to swim.

Chapter 2

Learning the Ropes

I made sure from then on to listen to my father. We secured the boom together as I cursed him under my breath. I tugged my sopping clothes closer to my body; the early morning breeze cut through me like a knife. The early spring weather was not forgiving out on the boat when I was dry much less when I was soaking wet. Goosebumps lined my flesh and my teeth chattered of their own accord. Trepidation lingered along my spine, fearing I may fall into the water below again. On more than one occasion, I caught my father smirking at me, stroking his mutton chops lightly to play it off. The lingering amusement in his gaze could not easily be hidden, to which I glared at him.

I was quick to learn the ropes were challenging to tie back. They were heavy and unusually thick, almost not fitting in my hands. My strength was not well suited for labor. Who am I kidding? What strength? He loved to mention how the very ropes I was tying may be bigger than my arms. To which, I rolled my eyes. I finally managed to secure a pitiful knot, my chest swelling with pride. My father took one look at my work; his lips cracked under the smile, and his thick brow raised assessingly.

"Oi, we got lots of work ta do." He rubbed his forehead with his rough hands, smoothing the sides of his mutton chops.

The heat of defeat clawed up my neck as he redid all my hard work. My hands were aching and blistered. He showed me how to properly tie the fisherman's knots, his arms bulging under the pressure as he tightened them. His arms and hands were thick with veins that protruded the more he worked the ropes. I glanced between his hands and my own; he dwarfed my dainty ones. His were rough with callouses from the wear of the ship, a pat on the back from him was like sandpaper against your skin. Not that I received any pats on the back.

How am I ever going to do that?

"Ok, the ropes got the best of ya. Let us see you work the nets, eh?" He suggested as he showed me how to lower them, making sure they were adequately weighted to go low enough to get some fish. "Now, the part that'll get ya is pullin' her back up." He was not lying.

I tried and struggled with all the strength I could muster. Grunting, I heaved the net a bit out of the water. I braced my feet against the side, grunting with all my might. The fish inside flopped around trying to get free. One squirted water in my face and I squealed, momentarily dropping the net.

"Naida! You 'gon let the fish get the best of ya?" I winced at my father's harsh tone.

"I'm sorry, I will do better." I bit my bottom lip and swept up the netting from the water. With all my might, I pulled it up and onto the deck. I swiped a hand over my brow, sweating from the exertion. The droplets of water rolled down my face, getting salty water into my mouth thanks to that stupid fish. I threw a glare at the net, ha that will show 'em.

"There ye be." My father smiled. "Now daylight is burnin', get those fish in the bucket."

I scooped up the net in both hands, heaving it over to the other side of the deck. A smidge of satisfaction warmed my belly as they wriggled and flopped around the deck before I dumped them into our fish barrel. They flipped and splashed around in the water, not having much room in the crowded barrel. Serves you right for making a mockery of me in front of him, of all people, I thought, I do that easily enough on my own thank you.

The day went on just like this, me attempting and failing to show my father I would make a good crewman. Silly me decided I wanted to impress him after the rough start to our day. By the time we were done, I could barely move my limbs. Every jostle from a wave felt like fire was racing through me. At least the pain was working to warm me up again. My clothes had finally dried some- what, the warm air around us kissing my skin with its playful breeze.

We docked at the bay, tied up the boat, and my fa- ther grabbed the barrels of fish, hoisting them onto his shoulders. I marveled at the fact he could carry them both. My legs were wobbly just thinking about it. I could barely walk up the dock with him, much less carry any- thing while doing it. Again, I swore I caught amusement in his eyes; if I wasn't so damn tired, I would be bristling at that.

I followed him to the market but kept my distance while he talked business. Fearful, if I did, someone would watch too closely and notice I was not a boy at all. The market was currently alive with the hustle and bustle of fishermen selling their catch of the day. The entire place smelled of fish, the salt almost palatable. With the crowd, it quickly grew too small for comfort, feeling like a school of frenzied fish. My throat tightened, my senses were overwhelmed and it was getting uncomfortably hot. I tugged at my collar, the material feeling restrictive. Suddenly, I was very thirsty and there were too many eyes around me. I was sure someone was watching me, I could feel the gaze like ice on my neck.

Trying to catch my breath, I moved to the shadows. The clamor of the market was overwhelming. Usually, I made it my mission to avoid this place. Over the growing chatter of the market, I overheard two other fishermen talking about a lady in the sea.

They cursed and spit on the ground, as was a tradition when talking about them. My interest peaked and all the other noise fell away as I tuned into their conversation. The one speaking was a rather burly fellow, looking like he had thrown a few rounds in a fighting pit before. His bushy mustache completely covered his upper lip, he looked like a cow chewing cud as he spoke. I wrinkled my nose. They were talking about spotting one sun-bathing on a rock, and were focusing on the way her uncovered bosoms looked. At that point, I tuned them out, rolling my eyes to myself.

The superstitions of this town never ceased to amaze me. I never understood how others lived their lives in fear. Many tales traveled throughout the town like a lingering foul smell. With our home being a fishing village, most myths include ladies of the sea. If it wasn't them, it was the dastardly pirates that liked to visit our little haven. I never understood why anyone would choose to come here, of all places. When it came to the ladies of the sea… two vastly different tales circled around.

One told of the beautiful creatures with skin that glistened like the sun itself shown from within them, long bright locks, and big tails in colors of the reefs. These were mermaids; it was told they would rescue sailors after their boats had been claimed by storms of the sea. These mermaids were admired by all; fishermen hoped to spot one when out on a voyage. As I got older and wandered around the village while Father was off on his boat, I would overhear tales of a shipwreck or two. When the survivors returned from them, they would recall alluring voices bringing them to safety and riding on the backs of giant sea creatures, only to find themselves on the safety of the shore with little memory otherwise.

Mermaids were a tale of beauty, but where there is light, there is always its counterpart. Darkness.

The other tale spoke of a darker creature of the sea, Sirens. The evil sisters of the mermaids. They feasted on the flesh of sailors. Following the tune, their song lured men from their ships into the water. The sailors' minds became mad; they wouldn't stop till they found the one the song came from. Then, the Sirens swarmed like a pack of sharks on their prey. Where there is one, there are many. These creatures were as dark as the murk they came from. Sharp spines in their fins instead of the elegant soft tails of the mermaids. Their eyes were a piercing yellow to see in the depths.

Theirs were the tales the drunkards tell in their stupor, daring only to speak of them when they won't remember in the morning. The village mothers warn their children about them when they misbehave, threatening to throw them into the sea. Sirens were used as the boogeyman, a way to keep the children in line. It was a darkness the village tried to keep buried far below the surface. Used as a fear tactic. An unspoken rule no one was to mention during the daylight hours.

These tales, however, had the opposite effect on me. I was ever curious when it came to the sea. What drives these creatures? Where do they come from? Are they born...or something else? Is there more to them than the beasts everyone claims they are?

I was abruptly brought out of my thoughts by a firm hand grasping my shoulder. I gasped my heart fluttering in my chest and turned to see my father looking at me impatiently. Jeez, what crawled up his ass and died?

"Work is done. Best be gettin' home, light is dyin'." His voice was stern.

I looked out to the sea once more, longing filled my body. It was too soon to say goodbye, but when the sun fades, it gets dangerous in our village. That is when the creatures come out.

We have another unspoken rule that no one is supposed to be out after the sun goes down. I glance around me toward the buildings, women are already closing the shutters; I hear the faint sound of locks clicking into place. People here take extreme caution to keep the songs out. I found it silly that they thought vented shutters would do anything against the lure of the song. Maybe the real reason was to keep the townspeople complacent. That was far more believable.

We trudge home through the quiet town, and I feel so small. The gray stone buildings felt daunting, even if they only towered two stories high. Smoke billowed from copper pipes on the roof, covering the village in a haze. It was eerie. My thoughts began to muddle with the dread of returning home. When my mother died, I spent too many days, and oftentimes nights, alone—with only the whispers of the ghosts haunting our house to keep me company. I don't believe it was actually haunted but it sure felt like it. It was maddening. I felt like eyes were always watching me, it was always worse that they never spoke though. On those days, time stretched on forever.

I, therefore, loathed the dark. I felt trapped in the four walls of our house. At night they were constrictive, a cage that was too tight. All I dreamed of was to be truly free, to simply exist as I yearned to. Wind swept across my face as I sailed my beloved sea. It seems to be a dream always out of reach, something my father would never understand. Maybe there's a part of me that secretly scares him, a part that is much like my mother. I blew the candles out with a deep sigh. Thoughts of swimming endlessly in the sea lull me into a deep slumber.

Chapter 3

Come to the Sea

I awoke the following day to dawn's light shining in my eyes through my shutters. Wiping lazily at my eyes, I tried to blink the sleep away, the outside world slowly returning to me. The faint sounds of the village waking up carried on the wind through my window. I dragged my stiff body out of bed, groaning when I almost fell over. Yesterday's labor had set in overnight, and I cursed my father under my breath. Almost tripping over my blanket strewn across the floor, I caught myself on the windowsill and unlatched my shutters once I regained my composure, throwing them open with an irritated huff. Only then did I see the sun was much too high.

Shit, I overslept!

Sloppily throwing on some clothes, I rushed downstairs to greet my father. The smell of stew clung to the air, but the house was still. I rubbed my forehead in frustration as I made my way into the kitchen. On the table, there was a note, full of chicken scratch and a ring stain of coffee.

Naida, I thought I would let you sleep in today. Yesterday proved rough for you. Stew is in the crock. I will see you when I return at dusk break.

-Dad

"He'll never keep me as a crewmate at this rate." I groaned into my hands.

He didn't even save me any coffee, nothing like more bitterness to wash down my own. Trudging over to our large cast iron cauldron, I peered inside. The "stew," as Father liked to call it, is whatever was made the night before for dinner being warmed into slop by the fire. Grabbing the wooden ladle and a bowl, I scooped it up. Plopping into the bowl was a vast amount of liquid with some unknown chunks.

Since this is done every night till the pot is empty, who knows what could be in the grayish slush by now. My stomach turned at the thought of actually putting it into my gut. I should be thankful, there were plenty of times the cauldron was empty for a few days. Pushing the bowl away, I decided to venture into town instead of staying indoors with the company of my misery.

I was a mess, and most likely smelled the part. The remnants of yesterday's catch wafted around me when the wind blew, making me gag. Oi, a quick go-over was indeed needed. Making my way to one of the streams that fed the sea, I tested the water.

A quick startled yelp escaped my shivering lips, the water was colder than a Kraken's heart. I took a sharp inhale and splashed my face. The shock was horrible, my body cringed and spasmed as I tried to wash myself down. I took off my shirt to help wash the rest of me as well as the cloth itself. My pale flesh was covered in goose pimples.

I made it quick and got the deed done. I looked down at myself, taking note of my thin frame and long nimble arms leading to slender fingers. Not the build for a fisherman, a body not meant for hard labor. Maybe in another lifetime, I could have been a half-decent dancer, if I knew how to dance.

In times like these, I longed for a friend, someone to talk to who would talk back. That was the only downside to my books. Sure, they could take me away to magical places, but they couldn't speak to me. I brought my hands up to my face, noting the blisters that had formed. All I wanted was Father's approval, to feel like he was proud of me for something. After yesterday, all I felt like was a letdown to him and how do I fix that? A pity party for one, please. I couldn't hold back the dominating voices of doubt in my mind.

You are weak and pathetic. You could barely work the boat yesterday, what do you expect Father to think of you?

Tears streamed down my face; I could taste the salt on my lips. An outward show in the bitter disappointment I was feeling inside. I had a feeling he always wanted a boy; I'm sure that would have made his life easier—someone to share his hobbies with. I either had my nose shoved in a book or my feet forbiddenly in the sand. I made sure to keep that little hobby to myself.

Who loves the sea, no, needs the sea like the very air they breathe and can't even swim? Nothing but a fool, that is who.

Anger overcame my sadness, and I threw my fist into the water. It sent what felt like waves of icy cold over my body as if to yell back at me. I was cold and alone but at least I didn't have to stare at that damned reflection anymore.

I see nothing but a girl who cannot do anything for herself.

Tears slipped down my face at a rapid pace now, my breath heaving as I tried to gasp for more. A heavy pressure settled in my chest, making it harder to inhale that sweet air I so desperately craved. I was useless. My stomach turned on itself, if I had a full belly, I would have spewed.

"You are not worthless...you are beautiful. We see nothing but love and light radiating off you, as if you were made of the sun itself."

"Who said that?" I whipped around, looking at my surroundings, my shoulders tight and the hairs on my neck rising to assess the danger.

The sweet almost lullaby voice whispering around me. They giggled, a childlike titter filling the air around me.

"We are not of land but of the sea, therefore we can see your beauty. Follow your tears, where they fell. Follow them where they will join us now."

I rose from my knees, even as they trembled, and did as they said; I followed the stream to where it let out at the sea. A moment of sanity filtered through the haze. Why on earth was I following this call? I brushed the remaining tear lines off my cheeks; I should turn around. Yet, their call begged me to keep going; my curiosity peaked, and I was it's willing victim.

Taking in my surroundings, I noticed big redwood trees dwarfed me at least ten times, with large boulders hiding me from sight. I carefully picked my way through them, watching my step as the soil gave way to loose sand and treading lightly around one of the more enormous boulders. I took in the sight of the ocean opening around me. I peered into the water, trying to catch a glimpse of whomever I was hearing.

This was crazy. I was crazy. I was following voices in the woods. Voices I had sworn I had heard before, memories of my childhood were being plucked from my mind. Why couldn't I just be the normal one? I bet my father would like me more then.

"Where are you?" I took a halfhearted step. A slippery rock had me unbalanced, and I fell into the water.

Dazed, I sputtered and wiped the sea water from my eyes that were now burning, my body shocked from the cold. For the second time in two days, I was unwillingly tossed into the water. Thankfully, my shirt hadn't dried yet. I cursed and tried to pick myself up, the sand suctioning my boot. Yanking on my boot, I wanted to get it loose from the quicksand effects. The struggle only caused me to fall off balance again. A movement out of the corner of my blurry eye caught my attention. There, in the distance, a figure poked up from beneath the surface. My eyes tried to focus through the tears forming from the assault. As she drew near, I could see a head with golden brown locks emerging, coming closer till shoulders appeared above the water. Her skin was fair, almost shimmering gold in the light, and her eyes met mine, a deep, piercing green. My heart lurched in my chest.

Do you not recognize me, young one?

A melodic voice spoke in my mind. Maybe I was too stunned to appropriately react to this situation; having someone speak in my mind was a peculiar sensation. Like an itch I couldn't scratch. My gaze slowly wandered over her, taking in the sight before me. She was unbe-lievably beautiful, simply majestic.

A tear broke loose, leaving a wet trail down my cheek. This was the voice, the one I recalled from over the years. A guide in my time of need. It drew me often to-ward the sea. I thought it was a pure figment of my cre-ation, something I latched onto when I needed a friend who would speak back. Her face... it pulled at the far recesses of my mind. A glimpse. A faded memory.

"Mom?" Just a whisper, it was all I could muster.

Chapter 4

A Mermaids Tail

The sea sprayed my face as I sat in stunned silence. I licked my lips nervously, the salt coating my tongue. There she was, only a figment of my faded memory. Memories seemed to come colliding in vicious waves now, washing over me. Her warmth, the glow of her smile, her eyes, the way she sang, how she held me. I was overwhelmed with the sudden rush of long-forgotten memories, ones that were now fully unlocked. Tears glistened on my cheeks, no longer from the salty spray.

"You died." My voice came out like the small sob of a child.

She came as close to me as she could with her tail. I forced myself up unsteadily, slowly edging deeper into the water. I ignored the fear rushing through me. The fact that I could be swept away by the current. I waded in until I was a little over waist deep, the water lapping at my belly button. By this time, my lower half was numb to the icy cold. The distance between us was swallowed up; even then, all I could manage was to stare in stunned silence.

Oh, little one. Her voice took a sorrowful tune in my mind. *I am so sorry I had to leave you. I got sick; it was time for me to leave my old life for a new one, but I could never let you go.*

"How is this possible?" My body shook as I tried speaking through the silent sobs that shook my shoulders.

I remembered her burial; Father insisted she be sent out to sea. We couldn't afford much, so he cut down some saplings and lashed them together to make a raft just big enough for her body. We sent her into the water as the sun set over the horizon, the purple hue caressing and encompassing her body as she floated out of our sight. I could almost taste the salt of tears on my lips as Father offered me a simple hand on my shoulder.

She reached out and gingerly wiped my cheek. Her fingers sent chills over my skin that wasn't yet numb to the effects. I winced from the foreign feeling of affection.

We are made, young one. When a woman who truly and fully loves the sea dies, they are granted fins. We come back as mermaids, my darling. Her voice of honey soothed me, even as my mind whirled at the statement.

So, it is true, mermaids do exist.

My mind was having trouble keeping up, succumbing to the truth before me. Not only was my mother alive but the rumors that flooded our village were true. Mermaids were real! Deep in my belly, I had believed it, but my father always told me not to believe in that rubbish.

As a child, I recalled my mother telling me stories of beautiful ladies of the water. I never wanted to give up hope that they existed somewhere out there. Even growing into my teenage years, I never gave up hope. Father, on the other hand, never wanted to hear any talk about them—scolding me to not get carried away in my fantasy books. He chastised the villagers for believing in the nonsense, even as he took part in their superstitions. It never made sense why he would work so hard to deny the existence of these sea creatures yet work even harder to keep me bound like the rest of the women. We locked the shutters every night, just like the rest of the town's folk. He was a hypocrite for denying me, for years, to board his ship.

She brought me out of my spiraling thoughts, keeping the irritation that was doing somersaults in my blood at bay. Instead, she lured me with the tales of her kind. She gave me glimpses of what happened to her; I saw her get sick through her own eyes. My heart broke alongside hers as I watched her grow fragile. Father hadn't let me into her room very often. She changed over a few months, which felt like the blink of an eye. She no longer recognized herself. Until, one day, her body gave out.

Another flash of a memory, and I opened my eyes to find myself right where we were in real life. I tried to stand, only to find I had a tail instead of legs. I flexed my toes, and my fins flipped leisurely through the air. Bright orange scales glinted in the sun, speckled throughout with a coral color. The edges of my fin rimmed in the same coral tones. The edges feathered out, tapering off into jagged spikes. My heart felt like it would pound out of my chest. I didn't know what was going on or what had happened. I remembered dying. How was I here? Confused and alone, fear pricked my skin, causing my hair to rise. My memories were mushed together, foggy.

I couldn't pull them apart to try and sort through them. All I knew for sure was a tug in my stomach, a desperate need to return to someone.

The next scene to flash before my eyes was heads popping out of the water, much like she had. A warmth came over me. Voices spoke in my head, much like she was doing now. An understanding, a call home that settled deep within my very bones. Instincts called me to join them. Ones that overrode every other feeling I had. I crawled through the sand, pulling myself to the water. My muscles strained with this newfound weight from my tail. The movement was much more complicated; my arms were not used to doing all the work. I tried to speak, but nothing happened; no words escaped my throat. I was momentarily thrown off, panic taking over the need to get to these beings. I gripped my throat, trying to speak, scream, anything, but only silence greeted me. They spoke in my head again, the odd sensation soothing me as they told me everything would be alright, and everything would be explained in time. I nodded; it was the only thing I could do, and I continued trying to pull myself to them. To the answers.

Once I felt the cool water embracing me, my heart raced in my chest. My body knew what to do and with a slight flip of my tail, I was surging toward the woman before me. They soothed and urged me forward, telling me my body would take over naturally—and it did. I felt like I was home, for the first time in a long time. It didn't hurt, it was enough to bring tears to my eyes. They crowded around me, brushing their tails against my own, sending electrical currents through me. It was a warm feeling, a greeting. A welcoming. One of them with long flowing hair approached me. She grinned, her face lighting up with warmth.

"Welcome home, come with us and we will explain all there is to know. Our elders will answer any questions you have. I am sure you have a few." Her voice carried on a melody of amber, rich in tone.

After the flashes of her life ended, my mother continued to explain to me who they were. I had so many questions and her laugh flitted through my mind like a bird. Her face set with an amused grin at my impatience.

She told me they were a race of women bound by sisterhood. All the love they had for the sea radiated from them in waves. They were the keepers of the water and they helped those in need. They were the ones to help sailors they rescued after a storm, guiding them to safety. It was their duty to help the sick in the water with remedies taught by the elders. She spoke of her home in the coral reef—these were cool water coral that their group called home. She showed me the animals she could communicate with much like dolphins did with a chirping dialect. They were unable to speak above the surface of the water. A curse of their race, she would not expand on the explanation of.

My mind swirled with all the information she over-loaded me with. Seeing her experience firsthand was remarkable. I couldn't believe this was all true. My thoughts spun helplessly, thinking of the other myths that could be real. The stories of great sea monsters that hunted in the depths. More than that, though, was the simple fact that my mother was there in front of me, more beautiful than I remembered. She seemed happy. She cupped my cheek in her palm, now warm as the sun beat above us.

I'm sorry I had to leave you so soon, young one. My heart breaks for your sorrow, for the time stolen from us. The melody that was her voice was soft and sad.

"Why have you come now? Why didn't you show your-self to me sooner?" Anger tinged my voice. It didn't make sense.

She winced but nodded to my accusation.

You were only six, much too young to show you the truth, my love. You would not have understood. Now, being seventeen, you are strong, strong enough for the truth. I am so sorry, my love. I have mourned you every day since my rebirth.

She dropped her hand from my face and wrapped her long arms around me in an embrace. My body melted. It was unlike anything I remembered: to have a mother's love and her embrace. Since she passed, Father's ways had been brutish—not completely unloving but not warm either. My world has been ice, much like the very waters surrounding it. She was his flame; without it, his heart had grown cold, with me being the only semblance of her left. I wiggled out of her embrace, keeping her an arm's-length away.

"Does father know?" I looked into her sad eyes. She shook her head, water droplets glistening off her long strands before falling back to the sea.

I have not shown myself to him, I cannot bear it. I loved him so much, it pains me to live without him. It is for the best that I have kept my distance. I watch. Looking from afar, I have seen you grow up. You both have changed so much. I am afraid, if I show myself, he will never let me go. I could feel a sob wrack in my mind. *He needs to go on with his life on land, and mine in the sea. It wouldn't be fair.*

She watched me as emotions passed over my face. Anger for the secrets, for keeping him in the dark. Sadness at the life we all had lost. Understanding, as she was trying to do what was best for us. I settled on curiosity as to why she showed herself to me.

"Why me, then?" I winced at the throbbing beginning in my head, a brutal headache sure to come.

She straightened, reaching to wipe a strand of hair that had fallen back behind my ear. *You've started to doubt yourself, young one. It pains me to see you in such misery. You have always come to the sea for comfort. I know you heard my whisper before.*

I had, indeed. Whenever Father left me alone, I ventured, my feet always seeming to bring me to the sea. I loved feeling the sun radiating off the water onto my cheeks. Every now and then, I would dare dip my feet into the dark waters, being sure to never go too far, since I couldn't swim. Occasionally, I could swear I would hear a whisper like a song on the breeze. I wrote it off as me being crazy, a simple explanation of an overactive imagination, turns out I am not.

It was then I noticed other heads started rising from the water below. As they came above the surface, each was as beautiful as the next. A variety of golds, browns, and reds broke the surface. Their skin glistened in the light just as my mothers had. I gasped in awe as more came from below. There was easily over thirty of them, and all stared at me. My face heated under the intensity and I shifted uncomfortably, shielding myself from the view behind my mother.

I must go, young one. My mother looked at me mournfully, even as her sisters beckoned her back to the sea. *I will always love you.*

With a swift turn and flip of her tail, she was going back, back to them and to the sea—away from me. I felt raw, as if someone had cut me open with a scalding hot blade to instantly cauterize it, only to slice into me again. A wound that had long since healed, ripped open and oozing.

Chapter 5

Siren

I stared after their disappearing forms as they went back into the waters below, their tails glittering in the light as they were swallowed up once again. Backing slowly out of the water, my sopping wet boots soon found dry sand, and there I stood alone, cold and broken. Everything I had known was a lie. Mother being alive changed everything. I crumpled into a pile of blubbering mess on the sand, my fingers digging into the cool layers below.

How could she leave me alone for so long?

Her unnaturally dazzling face etched itself so deep in my memory that all I could see was her. My mind was swirling, a spiral that set the world around me into vicious motion. My breath was caught in short panting spurts as I gasped for air between each soul wrenching sob. Soon, my vision felt fuzzy, black dotting my perception and I fainted in the sand beneath me.

Maybe it was the fact that I had no food. Perhaps it was the world-shattering news my mind could not fully wrap around; all I knew was the sun had changed positions when I awoke. By the look of it, it was half past noon. My stomach let out a fierce rumble, cramping from hunger.

I slowly rose from the sand, rubbing the grogginess from my eyes with the back of my hand. My head felt as if it were trying to split in two, no doubt I was dehydrated. Swiping the sand off my clothes, I was happy to note they dried out in the time I was unconscious. I ventured back into town to scrounge up some food.

The village was buzzing with chatter. Sounds of children's laughter filled the air. It almost brought a smile to my face. I wondered if, at one time, I had been that carefree. Fresh baked bread, smoked fish and other delightful smells wafted to my nose, causing my mouth to instantly water. My stomach lurched, giving a low rumble in aggravated agreement. I dug in my pockets, seeing what money I had to buy something and pulling out a few copper coins.

"Great, looks like I have five coppers..." I muttered to myself, trying to think of what I could get. I walked up to one of the many fish stands, looking at what the soup of the day would be. "Might I get a bowl of the, um, daily special?"

The man behind the stand hmphed his response and snatched the money from my hands. He mumbled something under his breath and grabbed a metal bowl to fill. The stew sloped into the bowl; it looked much more appetizing than what we had at home. He shoved the bowl across the wood, scraping its way in protest. Truthfully, the last thing in the world that I wanted to eat right now was soup. It was the only thing I could afford though and honestly, most likely the only thing my stomach could tolerate with all the upheaval I experienced.

Usually, I would be bothered by his apparent disdain for me, but I was too hungry to deal with his pisspoor attitude. My stomach growled loud enough for him to hear. At least I shouldn't have to apologize as I shoved the heap-full into my mouth. He grunted in surprise at me feverishly shoveling the stew into my gullet. I only turned my eyes back to him once I was done. One furry brow arched as I slid the bowl back to him. I nervously wiped my mouth on my sleeve, cheeks turning rosy as I exited the stand.

It was still too early for Father to be home any time soon; I had at least five or six hours. I wandered over to the library without knowing what else to do. My home away from home, even if it was creepy. I would happily pass the time with my nose shoved in a book; I could already smell the delightful scent of old books. It has grown to be a comfort smell, as much as the ocean—minus the fish, that is.

The building was a gothic monstrosity, a cross between a church and a mausoleum. Two giant torches lit at all hours posted outside the entrance. It was intimidating. Built long before Greymouth was deemed a fishing village, back when it was meant to be more. I heard once it was planned for logging, but that was just speculation. It surprised me that the building was somewhat intact after all these years, preserved even with age. I would sneak in here often as a child and spend my days amongst the books. The worn, stained pine flooring and wrought iron accents were a security blanket to me. The bookkeeper, not so much. He always creeped me out; I usually kept from speaking to him more than necessary.

The old wooden door creaked under my weight as I pushed it open. It gave some resistance, a puff of dust billowing into the sunlight in a thick cloud. I coughed; the amount of dust made my nose run and eyes water as I waited for the sneeze to come. It never did, leaving me with an idiotic look on my face, my mouth partially open and nose scrunched. Inside it was cold, at least ten degrees different from the warm spring air outside. Dim light streamed through the yellowed windows. It was musty, to say the least.

I suppose no one yearned to read in this village. Most people don't know how, proper schooling is not required nor expected. My father was one of the few who valued education; the higher power of knowledge leading to his presumed higher self-worth. He used to be quite the tinkerer, making little things around the house for convenience. They looked worse for wear now over the years. Since Mother's passing, Father cared less and less to tinker with anything. The only reason I was taught how to read in the first place was the value he held in knowledge. The fact that I wasted it on fantasy tomes most of the time was one of my many failures in his eyes.

A lot of good that knowledge is doing us now.

After the reunion with my mother, everything in my being screamed at me to learn more about these ladies of the sea. Mother told me about the mermaids, yet she made no mention of their darker counterparts. In my youth, even though these tales always intrigued me, I never sought out those kinds of books for fear my father would find out. Unfortunately, my growing curiosity—bordering on obsession—needed to be settled. My mind still spun with the fact that she had been alive this whole time. The thought made the soup in my stomach turn sour.

My footsteps scuffed across the wooden floor; it was so quiet in here I swear I heard a mouse fart. The bookkeeper peered at me behind thick bifocals as I made my way to the check in. He almost looked like a lost spirit behind his large oak desk, forever charged with haunting the cobweb-ridden tomes. His wiry gray hair stood on end; his frame was so thin that the breeze on a stormy day could snap him in two.

"How might I assist you, madam?" he croaked, his voice sounding like raspy leaves.

"Do you happen to have anything on mermaids?" I inquired, wincing slightly as my voice echoed.

He continued to look at me as if I was a figment of his imagination, until a slow grin of amusement cracked his dry lips.

"Section five, row three through eight, my dear," he replied, licking the blood gingerly from his open wound.

I turned on my heels to find the section I needed, glad to escape the unsettling man before me. It was not hard to find; there must have been forty books on the subject. I noted it was the most extensive section in the building. The top books were well cared for; surprisingly, the bindings were worn but not torn or cracked. These rows were clean, not a speck of dust to be seen. The few townsfolk who came here checked out these books often.

After the first four rows of mermaid tales and "history" of the creatures, the last row was dark, hidden in shadow. Dusty. Warped and untouched in what seemed like ages. One tome piqued my interest, I looked at the worn leather binding, and in faded silver lettering read: *Siren*.

My heartbeat sped up slightly as I plucked the book off the shelf. It was covered in a thick layer of dust; all but one large handprint. I sized my hand up to it, and my interest peaked. The size of the handprint was strangely familiar. Who had checked this out? There was a light smattering of dust over the handprint so it must not have been too recent. I blew it off gently, the dust billowing in the air. The title read:

Siren, Monsters Lurking in the Depths Below.

Chapter 6

Making a Siren

My lungs hurt, and my throat itched desperately from the thickness of the air. I shuffled over to a table that was just as grimy. Plopping the book down caused a thud to ring throughout the building. I looked up, wide-eyed over my little stack of books, only to see the keeper peering over his thick bifocals, grumbling to himself. This book was three inches wide; I could tell of its wear by running my hands over it. It was as long as my forearm. The leather face was cracking, the silver lettering fading with age. It looked as if no one had ever tended to this book, not caring enough to fix it.

It felt old. Ancient.

"The rule of Good and Evil is as old as time itself...w here there is light, there is its counter—for one cannot exist without the other. There are creatures in the waters that surround us. One a savior...the other a nightmare. Created by injustice, they hold the lust for the flesh of men. Driven by revenge. Gleaming in silver, no gold to be seen. Their long locks are cursed to be a seaweed green. Shark-like teeth to rip through flesh, piercing yellow eyes to see in the murky depths."

Chills crept along my spine. The lyrical way in which the tome was written turned the chills to ice. The thick yellowed pages radiated a sense of dread. I cringed at the dog-eared page tips. The disrespect. If ever a book were to unleash a curse, it would surely be this one. I was surprised, with the superstition in this town, it was available to be read at all, not locked under the restricted section. I scanned over the pages, feverishly trying to find any mention with *Siren* in the paragraph.

These are the monsters mothers warned their children about when they misbehaved...unlike the tales of mermaids that spoke of beauty, the siren was a tale of terror.

Sirens sang a sweet melody that enchanted those it reached, often sending sailors into a spiraling madness. Some would call it love. Others knew better. Once someone hears the sound they are enraptured, doing whatever means necessary to get to the siren singing. This has caused many casualties at sea. At least, those are the whispers that come back to shore—even when the men do not.

"It is told throughout the seas of great tragedies. Women who love the sea die peacefully, bringing unknown beauty...

The rest of the section had been torn away. I fingered the ripped edges in the spin, feeling like there was a rock in my gut. Why would someone tear these pages out? Frustration built within me, I could have pulled my hair out. Why is there never any godsdamned answers? I turned the tome in my hand and spotted the faded lettering on the spine: Cross Blackwood. The chair scraped across the floor in an ear-splitting screech as I picked up my book and hurriedly shuffled over to the bookkeeper. I audibly huffed as I slapped the book on his desk. He turned around wide-eyed in surprise, turning a shade paler—as if that was even possible.

"Do you know where I can find this Cross Blackwood?" My voice rang loudly in the quiet space.

"It is only me in this building, why are you yelling?" His gravelly voice grated over me.

"I apologize." A blush creeped over my cheeks. "Do you know them?"

"My dear, do you know how old that tome is?" He scoffed, like rattling leaves in the wind. I merely shrugged in response. "That was written before your many great grandpappy was born."

I arched a brow at his sass; I didn't believe he was capable of it. "Well, do you know who would have looked at this book?"

"Does it look like I have many regulars here?"

"Pardon me, but I didn't exactly have to fight to the counter to speak with you." I was just about done with the attitude I didn't ask for.

He wheezed out a rattling laugh. "You are quite right. I apologize, I'm not used to talking to others."

"Ah, you're just used to gliding through the stacks moaning and groaning about? You know, you do look rather ghoulish."

He leaned forward, a wry smile breaking his lips, "I know. I rather like it that way. Keeps the riff-raff out."

"I see," I shot back, setting him with a glower, "Do you mind if I take this book out?"

"I don't see why not. Just make sure not to damage it."

"Well, you were doing a mighty fine job of that before I even got here." I wounded him with that blow. "Did you notice someone had the audacity to dog-ear the pages?" My voice raised an octave with how appalled I was by that fact.

"Well, if you are quite done madam, I have other business to attend to," he muttered, raking his eerily long digits through his knotty white hair.

If I'm not mistaken, a spider dropped out of it and scurried across the desk right before my eyes.

"Yes, I see you have dusting to do." I wrinkled my nose and turned back to the shelves.

I scoured the shelves to see if there were any more tomes on Sirens. It seemed there was only this one. The tales died along with the sailors. If any happened to escape, to make it back to shore, they are more often passed by word of mouth. Which was less than reliable.

I thought back to the mysterious handprint on the book. Who would have checked this out? I knew very few that could read, besides me and my father. My father, the well read outcast. Could he have come across this tome? What purpose would he have to check this out, was he just as curious as I was? I never took him for the type. In fact, he refused to talk about the creatures that take our little village captive. They were just a myth, after all. He taught me to read so I could question the world around me...except when it came to him. His word was law.

My mother was much like me from the little father spoke of her. He said she was foolish for her obsession, yet I could see, even now, his love for her was unyielding. Father said he would catch her often at the cusp of the ocean, letting the water wash over her feet, sweeping away the sand underneath. That action alone was forbidden; women were not meant to be in contact with the sea. I believed he feared that in me— that he saw too much of my mother reflecting back.

It was difficult trying to find my own memories of her, they had become so faded over the years. She had almost been a lost memory, someone I knew of once but was cast away to the void. I spent years of my childhood not fully understanding the loss of a mother, since I barely remembered a time when I had one.

The weight of the information was heavy on my soul. Meeting my mother, the fact that she was back. She was alive. This new knowledge about the Sirens. That damn bookkeeper and his creepy aura. My mind kept flinting back to the one core thought, the one that was consuming me in a slow fire.

How dare she, she left us! She left me alone all this time. Now she decides to come back?

I knew in my heart that it was wrong to be angry, but the overwhelming weight was turning into a slow rage of desperation. I couldn't help the feeling of abandonment that clutched at my soul. More like the vice of its claws shredding at my soul. It was not fair that she got sick. That she was taken away from us, from me. Now that I knew she was alive...in some form anyway...my world was flipped upside-down. Not a care in the world for the life that was stripped from me, the one I could have had with her.

She loved the sea...

The thought circled my mind in a slow vortex, building speed. She died because she was sick. I suppose that was a peaceful death. She was now a mermaid. My throat was dry as I tried to gulp, seemingly having no moisture left to do so.

These creatures are not born, they are made...

Whatever does that mean? My mother loved the sea almost as much as herself and died of natural causes...

"I bet the other pages would be really fucking helpful."

I muttered, slamming the tome closed in frustration. The bookkeeper peeked around the corner, gazing at me with a curious look on his face.

"Sorry, sir," I mumbled softly, almost to myself.

I sat dwelling in my thoughts, feeling like I was drowning, my mind whirling with a hoard of questions—none that could be answered. At least not yet.

Chapter 7

Fairytales

The sun was beginning to set by the time I left the library. I hadn't realized it had gotten so late. The sky danced with color, blood orange light spilling over our village and glistening through the thicket of trees. It sent golden light bathing over the little buildings throughout the town and led to a bold red sky in the horizon speckled with purple hues. Puffy clouds sat happily dotting the azure.

Red skies at night, sailors delight.

Something my father often quoted, the memory of it brought back some childhood memories. When he had just taken up fishing to start supporting us, he would bounce me on his knee and repeat that quote soothingly before he left for the day. How did I survive most of that time alone? I recalled an older lady that would come and check on me every now and then to make sure I was fed and bathed before Father returned.

Most of that time, though, I was left with silence. Books were my only comfort. They transported me to places beyond my imagination—where I was a princess, a queen, a huntress, a warrior slaying dragons. Father never understood why I would rather have kept the dragons for pets. He scoffed at my argument about keeping it safely under my bed and feeding it mice. When life got hard, my books never let me down. They were stability when I had none. Always a happy ending, that much I could count on.

I smiled at the sky, the warm glow caressing my cheeks. The air was still crisp under the sun's heat. I took a deep breath, fresh air and the ever present smell of salt and fish. Ah, home sweet home. My hair swirled around me, tickling my neck as it carried on a soft breeze. I lingered for a few moments, wanting to soak in the radiance of the sky. I tugged the book closer to my chest, the weight of it comforting in my arms. One last deep inhale and I set foot back to my little abode.

As I crested the top of the hill leading to my shack of a home, my nerves were getting the better of me. I knew what was waiting for me there: my father's stern look and a lecture on responsibility as well as being away from home so late in the day. I sighed deeply through my nose as my lips pressed into a thin line once the tiny house came into view. I crackled my knuckles nervously while trying not to drop this damn book, which seemed to be gaining weight the longer I held it. My insides turned uneasily, the sourness of nerves taking hold.

Our house was nestled at the peak of the most prominent hill in our village; nothing but Red Alders surrounded its small stature. The towering trees dwarfed our home; they could grow up to fifty feet tall. I recalled trying to climb those beasts more than once as a child, only to fall and scrape my elbows and hands on the fallen debris below. Our abode was an A-frame, though not the most centered. It had wooden siding with a copper rooftop that was turning green from years of wear. It held tiny windows to let some outside light in and a door small enough that my father had to bend and sidestep to walk through it or he would knock his head.

Our even smaller yard was unruly, without Mother's touch to care for it. A memory surfaced of a once lush garden, some little flower beds adorning the front of our house. Father had no time for such tedious tasks, and I was more of a black thumb than green. Soon enough, the wilderness reclaimed the groomed land. With the weather finally warming up, he would soon set off into the thicker woods where the smaller dogwoods grew to chop wood for our furnace. I loathed when he would ask me to bring the tarp and drag the logs back home. He enjoyed laughing as I struggled to pull it over the roughterrain. Maybe this year that would play out differently.

I breathed in the scents of the damp forest mingling with the salty air. Thankfully, we were far enough from the village to escape the smell of fish up here. Tiny water droplets beaded on my arms from the dense forest, holding onto the moisture throughout the day. It wasn't much, but it was home. The only one I'd ever known, and we could always have it worse, I supposed.

Most of the village people lived in hovels like ours. The more successful fishermen took up larger log cabins closer to town. Those of us who managed meager means had our own little spots of land throughout the forested areas. We carved out a space of our own amongst the trees, providing their own form of privacy. It was more secluded out here, no one bothered us. I counted that as a small blessing.

Bracing myself, I took one last centering breath and pulled open the door. It stuck to the frame, having swelled from the moisture, and groaned against the strain. With another firm tug, it came loose and smacked me in the face.

"Ouch!" I exclaimed, muttering profanities under my breath, rubbing my nose. Thankfully, it wasn't bleeding. I walked in and looked up to see my father's stern gaze, his chest was already puffed—a telltale sign he was ready for an argument. I continued to hold my nose gingerly, the throbbing radiating through my face and looked toward the ground. "How was your day?"

"'Bout time you got here. Was wonderin' when you would show. Slept in this mornin' but mosey about till this late, eh?" His voice boomed through the house. I winced as it shook the windows.

"I'm sorry, Father, you didn't wake me. I made use of my time, though. I was out scouring the library while you were out to sea. "

I hated how whiney my voice came out. Hopefully, he would believe I was in the library all day. I couldn't very well mention that my mother was back and alive. Oh, by the way, she's a goddamn fish person. He raised a bushy brow at me, the question written plainly on his face.

"What were you looking fer this time, girl?" he gruffly demanded. My eyes darted to the corner of the house; I could feel my cheeks redden under his scrutiny. Begrudgingly, I held out the book I was still carrying from my chest.

"Sirens..." I mumbled, flashing him the cover. For only a moment, he froze, his mouth twisted slightly. Just as I was about to question him, his face went blank. His laughter echoed through the house, my blood rising, heating my cheeks further.

"You spent the day...researching legends? Myths, girl! I thought I taught ye better. How are you ever goin' to man a boat when you still believe in fairytales?" He stormed away, stomping up the stairs with his heavy boots. Our conversation instantly and promptly ended. This had happened more times than I cared to count over the years.

Tears of frustration welled in my eyes, burning as I rubbed them away. I hated that I was an angry crier. My shoulders shook with effort as I tried to hold my emotions back. The urge to flip him a finger was almost more potent than my reserve. I stalked into the kitchen, muttering under my breath, my eyes finding a huge bass half-eaten on a plate. I slapped the book down on the little two-seater table, the echo bouncing off the walls.

I grabbed a fork and started shoveling what was left into my gullet. Sobs overcame me as I breathed vocally around every bite, stuffing my face as the tears leaked onto the plate below.

So much for civil conversation. For a moment, I envisioned showing him the book I found and asking him about the mysterious handprint on the cover. Maybe he would have confessed to being interested in it. Hell, perhaps he had hoped Mother hadn't just died and held on to a hope that she could have come back. If only that would have been the conversation, I would have opened up and admitted to seeing her. I couldn't have hidden her from him if that were the case. Maybe, just maybe, we could have seen her together. We could have some messed up semblance of a family again. She would see she was wrong for staying away so long. Maybe I would have a caring father again. This could have been one thing we shared. Our little secret.

He could be so cruel, it got worse after Mother died. I thought about telling him she was alive anyway just out of spite, but he would never believe me. He thought the stories were tall tales for children, not for men. How could I blame him, though? I didn't fully believe it until I saw her for myself. A part of me hoped he would understand despite his always logical thinking. This whole, stupid town believed in them. Why was it such a crime that I am interested in finding out all I could?

These stories were below him, he believed in proof and science. Neither of which I was going to find to back up my statements. If only she would show herself to him.

When the fish was gone, I shoved the plate away, leaving it on the table for tomorrow and followed suit stomping up the stairs like an insolent child. I could hear his snoring from down the hall, to which I snarled my lip. Anger flared inside me once again as I shut the door to my room. I flopped in my bed and screamed my frustrations into my pillow. He would never understand. Weeping silently, I cried myself into a deep sleep.

Chapter 8

Being a Man

The days went on...Father and I did not speak much after our little fallout. We both had a bad habit of holding grudges and even the slightest disagreement could, and often would, snowball. Years ago, he managed to trade one of his prized possessions for one of the first copies of Dracula, one of the rare times a good merchant came to Greymouth. I recalled telling him it was boring, and he didn't speak to me for two weeks. We debated for months after that whether Dracula or Frankenstein was the superior literature. Of course, that was back when it was acceptable for me to read fantasy. We never spoke of the time I critiqued his favorite philosopher. That was a dark time.

I made sure to get up early every morning to avoid any more of his wrath. He made me start carrying big buckets of water to and from our village well in the mornings to build my strength. We had a well in our backyard, but he forbade me from trying to use it. I needed to be able to tie the ropes properly and bring up the nets without fail, or it could cost us food. For the first few days, even weeks, I struggled...it took all I had to get those buckets up the hill. Many times, I dropped the buckets and had to go back into town to fill them. I hated to see the discontent in my father's eyes when I failed. It happened a lot, but I was stubborn like a mule. I wasn't sure if I got that from my mother or father. I cursed the early morning bitter cold; as the weeks went on, it got progressively warmer. Soon enough, I no longer had to layer shirts for my trips.

Posthaste, I was tying the bowline, sheet bend, and clove knots as good as any seasoned fisherman. My father grunted his approval as he eyed them over. A withered smile spread across my cracked lips, causing them to bleed. I licked at them, tasting the iron on my tongue. My chest swelled at that little validation.

The long days under the sun had taken a toll on my body. My skin had turned dark after the initial burning subsided. Swollen bags under my eyes were the telltale sign of all my hard work and the little sleep I was getting. From the weeks of work towing the buckets, manning the ropes, and netting, my nimble figure was changing. My arms were now sculpted, noticeable biceps protruding, the curve well defined. My hands were hard with callouses from the weeks of trained labor.

I was now a fisherman; I could pull up a full net almost as swiftly as my father could. At least I filled out the sleeves of my male clothing. My waist was thinning and toning. I had a set of abs that I would secretly admire alone in my room. Six, I counted six, and I was damn proud of every one of them. I earned those. I may not have the typical stature of a man, but I was strong and lean. All wired with muscle, no longer thin and fragile. I was powerful.

Most of all, I loved the escape of getting to go out to sea. I loved seeing the dolphins dancing playfully through the water further out. I may have almost shit my pants the first time I saw a gray whale. It was massive, and our little boat was merely a fourth of its size. Father laughed at me when I cried out about there being a sea monster before I knew what it was. A sea lion jumped on our boat to avoid being eaten by an orca. *The Maiden of the Sea* groaned under its weight. My father tried to scare it off as the orca circled lazily in the water, stalking its prey. I begged him to leave it alone and let it remain with us until the beast left. There were times of quiet peace, even though my father and I worked long days, only to catch a few hours of sleep when we returned. Overall, we had a companionable partnership out on the boat.

Sleep for me was often restless. My mind still whirled with thoughts of the unknown Sirens. I devoured every last bit of that tome when I didn't collapse into bed once we returned. Unfortunately, there wasn't much more than a bunch of ramblings from a madman. At least, that's what Cross Blackwood seemed to be. I wouldn't be surprised if he had fallen victim to the Sirens' call and then wrote the book. By the end, it was nothing but senseless scattered thoughts. It was frustrating; I had hopes for this text. If only I could find those missing pages.

Much to the surprise of Mr. Ghostly bookkeeper, I returned the book and scoured the shelves once more to see if I could find anything else about Sirens. I wanted, no, needed to know more. It was quickly becoming an obsession. An endeavor I kept secret from my father. Ever since the night of our fight, I would not dare bring up any talk of the ladies of the sea. I hoped I would see one when we went out every day, but none ever appeared.

When Father was distracted, I would find one of the boisterous sailors and try to pry information out of them. They would talk for ages about their sightings of mermaids. One, in particular, had a grand story of his rescue from a capsized ship by one of them. His eyes glossed over as he spoke, as if he were in a far-off place, and a boyish smile was on his lips. His friend slapped him on the back to bring him out of it. He laughed off his fantasy.

No one else had a close encounter that they could re-call with one of the ladies of the sea. They sure did spin a pretty tale of spotting them sunbathing topless on a boulder or singing a lovely song. In fact, most of their stories involved the mermaids topless. Little did they know that mermaids couldn't sing above water; I grinned to myself with that insider information. Howev-er, no one uttered a damn word when it came to Sirens. They would spit on the ground and turn around three times whenever I brought it up, then ward me off with a few choice words that would make a seasoned sailor blush. It was disheartening, to say the least.

Sometimes, I would try to slip away unnoticed and go to the spot where the dense tree line opened to the sea. Usually, I went when Father was trying to sell our catch of the day. My mother somehow always knew when I would be there, and little time would pass before she would appear from under the surface. We would 'talk' for however long we could. It was always a tearful good-bye. She would speak in my mind about her new life and sisters under the sea.

She showed me the horrifying glimpses of the ship-wrecks she witnessed and how they would try to save as many lives as possible. The sight of those massive burn-ing ships was often featured in my nightmares. Only, in my mind, I was trapped on them. She showed me the trance-like state she and her sisters would put them in to lure them to safety. I was awestruck at the dedication they went through to try and save as many lives as they could. Maybe when my time comes, I would be a mer-maid just like her.

She showed me their homes, more beautiful than I could put words to. Their coral homes could rival At-lantia. I was fascinated by the towers they carved for themselves. The coral grows around the foundation. I had never seen vibrant colors, full of light pinks, sunset oranges, and bright yellows. As they were the guardians of the sea, all kinds of life surrounded them. Schools of fish, ones we didn't see on this coast.

Rockfish, different types of bass, kelp greenlings, sea turtles, and other species of dolphins that we didn't have around our bay. I had only read about fish like these before. She painted beautiful pictures in my mind of her new life; it made my heart ache and yearn to join her in the water. I wished for her to take me with her and show me herself. The images she flooded into my mind were simply not enough to quench my newfound thirst. I wanted so much more.

It crossed my mind; she was the one with the information I so desperately needed. My mind was set even as my heart thrummed nervously at the thought of asking her. The next time I could go see her, I would work up the courage. I needed to know more about the Sirens, and who better than to ask a mermaid. I paced my room quietly back and forth, working out my next moves.

"I will get my answers..." I muttered; my eyebrows knitted together in thought.

Chapter 9

Ask Your Questions

It had been weeks since I hatched my original plan to ask my questions and get some answers from my mother. However, trying to slip away from my father was almost impossible. Almost. He now relied on me to help with the boat; I got what I begged for. That came with zero days off. Long days under the sweltering summer heat were exhausting. By the time we got home most afternoons, I dragged myself up the stairs and went straight to bed. Bone tired didn't even begin to describe it. I was forced to feign being sick enough that he believed me—which involved complaining of stomach pains all day and spitting up some of my dinner.

When I awoke in the morning, the sky was a brilliant crimson, as if it were bleeding, throwing the red hues through my shudders. As I blinked away the sleep from my eyes, my stomach flipped uneasily. A tinge of some unknown emotion grabbed at my throat making it hard to swallow. Dry, my mouth was too dry. I grabbed my glass from my nightstand and downed the water in one swift gulp. My heart settled enough to stave off the growing feeling of dread. Throwing the covers off, I tiptoed out my door into the hallway. The house was silent.

A sigh of relief escaped me, my lips parting as I descended the steps, tugging on a tattered shirt; I missed a step and almost fell the rest of the way. I grasped the rail for dear life and corrected my footing. I yanked the shirt on the rest of the way and fumbled with my brown crop pants when I was on solid ground. I felt a dirty grim clinging to my skin in a thick layer. The waft of hard labor surrounded me, causing me to gag. My lip curled in distaste as I made my way into the kitchen.

The slop was cooking over the fire, and this time, I poured myself a bowl. Thankfully, the fish we had been catching lately had been high quality, so I slurped it down, chewing around the bones in chunks of meat. I groaned, the food settling happily in my gut; I only wished we had more spices to add some flavor. Once I shoveled the last drop into my mouth, I shuffled over to the sink and dropped the bowl in. Its clatter filled the empty room, sending a chill up my spine. Something did not feel right; I just couldn't put a finger on it. I slammed the door shut, and with it, the feelings of unease as I fled into the forest behind my house.

Following the trail I had come to know by heart, I made my way to the small creek within a few minutes. The chilled morning air lifted my hair from around my shoulders and tickled my neck. Thankfully, the humidity had yet to settle in for the day. Nothing was worse than the heavy, sticky air lingering on my skin like a bad smell. The sound of the water rippling over the rocks soothed what was left of my worry. I sighed deeply, breathing in the fresh forest air and letting my shoulders sag. One thing Father most certainly hated was lousy posture. Shoulders back, head up, chin out. That was forever ingrained in my brain. Over the treetops, red still peeked through as though the sky was bleeding; it was still early, but I would have thought it would have carried on to a blue by now. I shuddered against the breeze as it blew my hair from my face.

Stooping down at the creek's edge, I scooped the icy water to wash over my skin. Goose pimples rose from the surface as my body adjusted to the assault. I didn't feel like making the trip from the well and heating up a bath for myself. I was far too busy, and honestly tired of carrying buckets of water to and from. Even though there was a well much closer to our house, Father insisted I go to the one in town; something about building my stamina. It was a pain in my arse.

When Father used to tinker, he had connected the well by our house to the sink, running a pipe so we were able to wash dishes in there instead of bringing them to the creek. He had promised Mother he would hook something up so we could have running water to the tub, too, as our town lacked the modernization most of them had, so I've been told at least when I got to chatting with merchants from other areas. It was something that never came to fruition, much to my dismay.

I looked down at my reflection. It was wavy in the water below. The fair complexion I had just months ago was gone, replaced by dark sun crimsoned skin. My once slender arms now toiled with muscle. My eyes were the only thing that remained the same, a brilliant emerald green, that of a pirate's greatest treasure. Only now, they looked tired, so, so tired. I slapped the water, fed up with looking at my own reflection, and rose on the balls of my feet. My legs knew the way, heading toward the ocean before my brain could register its desired location.

Within a brief fifteen-minute walk, the thick forest parted, and I hopped down the little natural stone pathway. The sand greeted me. I removed my boots and set them aside so they wouldn't sink in; I relished the feeling of the grit between my toes. The large boulders that hid me from view were a welcome sight. I took a moment and leaned against the cool rock, trying to calm the racing pulse of my heart. I usually found peace here. A tiny part of the world was saved just for me, for us. However, my stomach was in knots. Looking out toward the sea, I waited, digging my toes in the cool sand underneath, until I saw the golden-brown locks rise from below. I licked my lips to bring moisture to my suddenly bone-dry mouth. A small smile tugged at the corners.

"Ah, young one, I was wondering when I would get to see you again." The intrusion was an odd feeling still,

hearing someone in my mind, almost like an itch I could not seem to scratch. I shuffled my feet, blush creeping over my cheeks.

"I'm sorry. I had to wait for Father to leave me for a day."

I could have sworn I saw a glimpse of worry in her eyes; it was gone before I could be sure.

"Tell me why you seem nervous." I could feel her hesitation as if it were my own. I bit my lip, forcing myself to inhale through my nose and exhale through my mouth.

"All the things you have shown me have opened my eyes to a whole new world. One I never knew existed. I have a glimpse of how your kind lives." I paused, cracking my knuckles, stalling. "I need to know more about …well…Sirens. We do not have much text about them in the village." My voice only came as a whisper, so much for the demanding confidence I was trying to channel. I watched as her face became grave. The glow around her seemed to dim before my eyes.

"Why do you want to know about these creatures?" I could hear the bitterness in her usually sweet melody. The look in her eyes made me flinch unconsciously.

"You know as well as I the rumors that haunt the village about them. I want to know more. There was only one tome in the library. You have to have more experience, after all this time you've lived in the sea," I pleaded as I tried to put reason behind my request.

She considered me, a graceful brow arched with distaste.

"They are not like us. We are the guardians of the sea, protecting life within and on it. Sirens are born of bloodshed and tragedy. They continue their lives that way. They dwell in the depths of the ocean caves. Until disaster strikes the sea again, that is when they surface to feast. When the storms are bad…"

She trailed off, a hiccup of a sob escaping her lips, *"They sing. Their song fills the hearts of unsuspecting men. It controls them…they must find the one producing the song. Once they are within reach, the pack swarms. Like sharks. They devour those souls lost to the sea."*

There was a moment of pause, tension palatable in the air around us.

"This is why we are the protectors of the sea; we try to reach them before the Sirens can swarm. Unfortunately, we are not always so lucky." Crystals formed in her tear ducts, gently rolling to the sea.

My heart ached. I didn't know if it was any better or worse now that she shared this information with me. She would not show me any images like she had with her life, claiming they were too horrific to show me. Even then, my curiosity had still peaked. There had to be more, more to the Siren than a simple monster. Monsters are created.

Tragic ends bring evil beginnings, after all. I refused to write them off as that and call it a day. I tried pulling more from her than I had gained from the text. Mother refused to talk about them anymore. Soon after, she left, and with a swift flip of her tail, she was gone. I watched as she faded into the distance, bitter cold seeping into my bones. Not from the weather. It was a chill I would not soon be rid of.

Chapter 10

The Storm

With only my thoughts to keep me company, I noticed how the winds had picked up. My hair billowed violently around me, and I cursed the fact I forgot my cap or a tie to bind it. I glanced up at the sky; by the sun's position, it was about two o'clock. Gusts blew angrily through the trees, even the biggest of them swaying viciously under her onslaught. I gazed out to the sea, curling my arms around my body for warmth. The waves were coming in short and abrupt. I tugged my shirt closer to my body, and worry crept back into my gut.

My feet carried me without thought, battling against the wind as I made a steady pace toward town. Worry churned like thick sludge as I made my way through the village. In the middle of town, fishermen were gathered in the market, spread across the tables throughout, ale in hand. It was too early for them to be back. They wouldn't have lost out on the precious hours of fishing. I swallowed thickly, my throat felt tight. Their voices carried loudly over the wind as they shouted to one another.

"Whoever 'tis out to sea, be a brave soul," I overheard one say. The sky above rumbled, dark gray clouds rolling in from the shore. It finally clicked, the feeling in my gut since I had awoken.

Red skies at morn, sailors warn.

I was running before my mind caught up. I sprinted to the shoreline; all but a few of the fishing boats were tied to the port, my father's nowhere to be seen. Panic started to rise in me like the current. With every thrash of a crashing wave, it was harder and harder to breathe. A lump formed in my throat. I tried to swallow, but my mouth was bone dry. Tears pricked at my eyes, blurring my vision. The wind whipped my hair about, making it difficult to see.

He is not stupid, but he is stubborn as a mule.

Guilt crept in waves, mixing with my panic, settling like a rock in my stomach.

If I had not pretended, I was sick...I could have convinced him to stay. This is my fault. I should be with him. I should be there.

Tears streamed down my face as I stared out into the sea. My eyes strained to see the slightest hint of my father's boat on the horizon. There were nothing but black clouds in the distance. The waves pulled the ships tied to the pier taught and snapped them back toward the dock. The smacking of wood against wood could be heard above the violent crash of the waves. Ships bobbed up and down wildly as the water crashed over the sides of the deck.

"Where are you?" I yelled into the wind, my voice cut short. "Come back home." My body was shaking violently with each sob heaving my shoulders.

"What are yew doin' girl? Get to yer shelter. 'Tis going to get worse." I turned to see a gruff, burly-looking man yelling my way. His black beard flew back into his face He gestured urgently to me, waving me to come back to the village, away from the shore.

"My father is out there!" I screamed back at him over the wind. Even with the gusts whipping my hair into my eyes, I saw his face drop and go pale.

"My prayers to you, girl." That was all he said. I took one last look at the sea, the sky fully engulfed in black, thick, imposing clouds rolling steadily to shore.

With a wretched sob, I forced my feet to move past the man and headed home. It was a challenging trek up the hill through the center of town, leading toward safety. The wind wanted to blow me back as I tried to ground myself with each step. The rain fell in heavy sheets, washing everything in a gray haze. It really took Greymouth to a whole new meaning. I could no longer tell the difference between my tears and the fat drops pelting my face. Either way, my vision was blurry, and I was a snotty wind-whipped mess. I stumbled in the mud, falling to my knees as I tried to grab ahold of something. My body wanted to collapse under the onslaught of the gusting wind. I let out a sob as tears flowed harder. I buried my hands in my hair and screamed, but no one heard me. No one cared; they were all safe in their homes. The only sound outside was the wind.

By the time my house was finally in sight, my legs burned from fighting against the onslaught. Every part of my body was battered and aching. My clothes were

sopping wet and clung to my skin in an icy layer. I noticed the gray shutters clanging against the walls forcefully, wincing; I fully expected for some of them to be
missing by the morning. In fact, I would not be surprised
if our little house would be blown away in the storm
completely. It almost seemed to sway along with the
gusts of wind, as if the house itself was breathing. Just
as laborious as I was. The front door burst open under
my grasp, and it took all the strength I had left to get it
closed.

Once inside, my ears filled with a dull ringing. No longer
under the onslaught of the gusting wind outside, the
silence was deafening. The wind howled its anguish
against the walls, causing them to moan back in protest.
By the time I regained some semblance of sound, I
heard the dripping, almost as if the sink was running.
My eyebrows knitted in confusion and I tramped into the
kitchen; the roof was leaking.

"Son of a pirate! This is just what I needed," I yelled,
spewing profanities under my breath. They didn't help,
but they sure made me feel better.

I grabbed what pots I could find and shoved them where
the water was streaming through. In my hurry, I dropped
some pots, and they clattered to the floor. I kicked
one over and water sloshed around me. Great, this is

just great. Once I managed to pull myself together just enough to sort out the pot to hole ratio, the house was filled with the mind-numbing pinging of water against metal. I took an old shirt and mopped up the floors, which did nothing but spread the water around.

Continuing as I might to soak up the water and muttering under my breath, my stomach flipped uneasily. Nausea rose and stuck in my throat like a lump, causing me to gag. I ran over to the sink just in time to dry heave until I managed to upchuck whatever was left in my stomach from this morning. I wiped my mouth as I tried to regain a steady breath, my body still convulsing. Snatching a glass from the counter I filled it with water, swallowing the cool liquid. It burned as it went down my raw throat.

Tears spilled from my eyes, my body tried desperately to rid me of anything else in my stomach. After dry heaving for another twenty minutes, I sank to the ground and sobbed into my arms. My lip quivered as each inhale shook my body. Tears and snot ran down my face. My vortex of thoughts consumed me, the image of my father out there alone haunting my vision even as I closed my eyes. Every breath was a chore. A cold sweat broke out over my body; I was hot. So hot. I stripped off my shirt, tossing it across the room.

This was all my fault.

That was my last thought as my mind went blank, my vision fading until it was nothing but black.

Chapter 11

Lyra POV- A Distant Memory

My heart was heavy as I left Naida. I tried not to let my worry show to my sweet once I learned Dunstan was out to sea. My beloved, my only. Tears fled my eyes, returning the salt to the water around me. My cries came in a melancholy melody, and my sisters joined in with my sorrowful tune. I could feel the weight of my sisters watching me, touching my tail gently with theirs in a comforting gesture as we swam back home. The current was growing more robust, the pull thumping against my body as we pierced the water, returning home.

Glimpses of my old life flashed before my eyes as we traveled. Giving birth to my young one. Holding her in my arms for the first time as Dunstan stood protectively around us. He was always so careful with her. His eyes, the color of the ocean, glistened when he held her. She was like a mouse in his burly arms, so delicate, so fragile. Watching him learn to take care of her was almost comical, how clumsy his movements were until he adjusted to her. He would read her stories of other worlds, other cultures seemingly planets apart. The way he spoke to her was always so soft, as if him speaking too loudly would break her. He was my knight in cotton armor. An outcast looking in, in this town of fishermen.

I let out a melancholy sound and it echoed in the water around me. I was his queen. Tears continued to slip out. I remembered how we would dance in the kitchen in the glow of the candlelight. He would run with Naida, chasing her around the grass leading to the forest. I remember it as if it was yesterday. He had her upon his broad shoulders. She giggled, carefree, her little hands buried in his black hair, and his gruff laughter echoed through the trees. I was silently watching ,a smile pulling my lips as I stared through the back doorway. Then, I fell. My strength left me; I was so weak. Dunstan pulled Naida into his arms and ran to me. He placed her down in a hurry and scooped me into his arms instead. The strain pulled at his eyes as he tried to conceal his concern.

Even then, I could feel his muscles rippling underneath me with tension.

"Everything will be fine my love." His voice soothed me as it always had.

After that, my health steadily declined. Even as he waited on me hand and foot, I could see he was suffering. The pain in his eyes as he shielded Naida from my grave condition. He knew our time was coming to an end—we both did. It was not long till my world became black. I was floating in a black sea of stars. For a moment, I no longer felt pain, no longer did I feel my body giving out on me. I was free. Free to swim in this endless floating bliss.

Then, I woke up. I opened my eyes, the sun glaring down on me. I looked around to find I was laying on the beach camouflaged by boulders. Dazed and in a dull pain again, panic set in as I took notice of my newly adorned fins and tail. A lack of legs.

My new family greeted me, and they showed me everything. They showed me things I never knew existed. A brand new life that, up until now, I believed could only be a fairytale. It took a while to adjust, months actually. I would sit in my room and sob. Sob for the life I had lost. The thought of my family tore at my heart every time they crossed my mind. Which was always. My sweet, sweet Naida. How I longed to hold her in my arms once again. I whispered in the water, guiding her, and watched Naida from afar. That was all I could do. Communicating to her as I was, was against the Elders' wishes. I did it in secret and only when she needed me. Her mother.

I wept harder then, at the thought of my beloved. The storm was approaching fast. A sickening feeling of loss hit me all over again. I would watch him go out to sea from below, helping guide fish into his nets to feed him and Naida. My heart ached as my fingers yearned to brush against his face once more. To feel his coarse facial hair on my fingertips. His face had become hard over the years. Toiled with stress and hard labor... loss. When he was alone, he would speak to the sea, he would mourn for me. My chest tightened painfully as I tasted his tears in the water. His soul was burdened.

Many times, I wanted to swim up to his boat and tell him I was still here, always watching. My sisters warned me against doing such a thing, the Elders had forbidden it. Still, it was hard to ignore what my heart called me to do. I yearned for him with every fiber of my being. They never approved of what distant relationship I held on to with my young one. How could I stay away from her? To deny feeling her pain through her tears as they swirled around me. I was her mother, after all. I would never abandon her, not again.

After some time, we approached home, at last. The bright oranges, yellows, and reds of the coral shining bright against the dark water. It was good to be home, some of the tension in my shoulders melted away. We would not stay long though, the storm was rolling in and we had much work to do to prepare. Yet, I feared that no matter how many preparations we got ready, it would not be enough.

The reef was buzzing with absolute chaos, mermaids swimming every which way gathering materials. We fell into our routine to prepare for what was coming. I grabbed my netted sack; stuffing long strands of seaweed wraps inside it. We used these to bind wounds, stopping the bleeding until we were able to get the sailors to shore. I tied lengths of seaweed onto broken chunks of coral to make a buoy of sorts, they helped us swim with the sailors gone overboard. Giant sea turtles gathered around us, waiting for their orders.

The current was growing stronger by the hour, it was taxing to stay in one place.

My stomach grew uneasy as the water darkened, almost black now. Soon, it would be a battle between life and death, fear pricked at the far reaches of my mind. It always did in times like these but now there was a superior price. Someone dear to me was at stake. I found my thoughts going back to Dunstan, quickly shaking off the impending doom that was sure to send me into a spiral. In times like these, I needed a clear head. We all did, we had an important job to do. I heard the thunder rumble from above.

May the waves be with us, help us to save what souls we could.

In a few moments, we were off, our tails propelling us with vast speed through the ocean. We echo that chant before every rescue mission...there have been many. The turtles followed close behind, always on standby for when we found someone. They took them to safety while we reached for others. An efficient system, for we could not afford a moment wasted. We spread out. I headed south of the main village, listening for interference in the water. Wooden planks floating above alerted me to a shipwreck before the bottom of the boat came into view.

With a swift flip of my tail, I was piercing through the water like a spear and broke the surface. A medium-sized fishing boat was set ablaze, most likely struck by lightning as the mast would indicate, which was split in two fracturing the top deck. I could hear the shouts piercing the air.

A man was caught under the mast, a curtain of flames separating him from the others. The other three men were panicking, trying to figure out how to get away. I called them the way I did to Naida with my voice through the water.

Jump! Save yourselves, and we will do the rest.

My melody cooed out as if talking to a newborn, they became entranced. Their shoulders slackened and they jumped off the deck. As soon as they hit the water, my sisters and I wrapped our coral and seaweed life preservers around their waists and guided them onto the turtles. Time was of the essence.

It would not be long until the Sirens hoarded, unleashing their wrath onto their prey. Once those in the water were safe, I flipped my tail, smacking it against the surface. It sent a wave overboard, extinguishing the flames around the trapped sailor.

I waited for the next large wave to come and rode on top of it, bringing me right to the ship. My sisters spoke into his mind as I crawled carefully over to the man. His eyes were glazed over, dazed. A look like the wonder of a child spread across his face. Shimmying my tail underneath the mast, I used it for leverage forcing it up off his legs. As soon as it was off, I cooed to him to crawl over to me. His legs looked broken; he would need immediate medical attention.

I reached into my sack, pulling out a roll of seaweed. I disassembled one of our buoy systems, attaching the coral to his leg and wrapping it in seaweed. I pulled him against my side, using my tail to wiggle off the ship. We plunged into the water as a wave surged up around us. My sisters came to my side, one on each of his arms leading him to the biggest turtle we had. I rushed to secure him, and they were off. As were we—onto the next wreckage.

With each shipwreck we came across, my heart thrummed louder in my ears. It was all I could hear above the blustering wind.

Inhaling deeply, I tried to center myself, pushing myself faster through the water. My body was exhausted, going full speed was taking its toll. That was when I saw it. My vision blurred as I let out a blood-curdling scream of anguish. My heart thrashed against my chest, airway tightening along with it. Dunstan's boat. I could spot that boat from anywhere. It was ripped in two pieces, bobbing against the waves and surrounded by a pack of Sirens.

The water seeping from the wreckage was red with blood. My cries filled the night.

Chapter 12

Morning After the Storm

I groaned, the sun shining its assault right into my eyes. I rolled over, my body stiff as I tried to blink away the sleep, wiping the crust from my eyes. I peeled myself off the couch; I did not remember going to sleep on it last night. Stumbling over to the windows, I opened the shutters. At least I managed to shut them. The position of the sun in the sky told me it was about noon.

Great, I must have blacked out.

I was still in yesterday's clothes. I glanced around the room; all the pots were full of water. They must have overflowed at some point in the night with the amount of water on the floor. I grabbed the mop out of the closet, grumbling to myself. I soaked up what I could of the water.

My head was throbbing as I bent to ring out the mop over the sink. I reached up, my fingers fluttering over a bump on my forehead; I must have knocked it when I blacked out. My head felt fuzzy, besides the throbbing in my temples. As my body adjusted to being awake, the pain crept in. I noticed my stomach cramping and my ribs were tender, mostly from vomiting, I assumed. The aches were coming in strong.

The events of yesterday came flooding back all at once. Speaking with Mom in the morning, the storm, my fath er...

"Dad!" I yelled as loud as I could, ignoring the flare-up in my abdomen and racing up the stairs two at a time to his bedroom.

I did not bother knocking and barged through the door. It was empty. My throat tightened as if someone were squeezing it, making my breaths shallow. I could feel my pulse quickening, thrumming through my chest and pulsing down my arms. Tears fell steadily, warming my cheeks. I licked the saltiness from my lips as I took off back downstairs. My head spun as I burst out of the front door, running as fast as possible through the village to the shoreline. My body was screaming at me, yet I felt numb. Completely numb. My footsteps faltered every now and then; I had to catch myself.

The dock was a mess; boards were broken, tree limbs lying about, and the water was eerily still for how bad the storm was last night. I wiped my eyes frantically, looking around for the *Maiden of the Sea*. It was nowhere to be found, neither were the other boats missing from the night before. My mind tried desperately to figure out a plan—racing, grasping for some solid thought.

I will steal a ship and go looking for him.

"That's it! I just need to steal a ship, set sail and go find him. Everything will be fine." I shook my head angrily, dragging a hand through my loose hair. "I can barely man a ship with my father. How will I do it on my own?"

A raging cry bubbled up from my throat, and I cursed and screamed into the ocean. I could feel eyes watching me. Another broad gone mad, they were probably thinking. I kicked at the sand, totally lost. I could overhear the townsfolk, the talk of the storm, of how the Sirens had a feast fit for the Kraken itself. Tears flooded down my face as I ran toward the only place I knew was safe—where I would be shielded from the world. I only hoped she would show up after everything that was said yesterday. It seemed so far away now. So trivial.

The boulders signaled I had arrived before my brain could register the familiar surroundings. I came to an abrupt halt. I placed my hands on my knees, gasping for any air I could suck in. The world spun for a moment, dizzy from all the exertion. I shook my head, trying to make the flashing lights in my vision stop as I made my way around the boulders.

"Mom?" I yelled out to the sea; my panic rising and my voice pitchy as it pierced the stillness.

Finally, I was able to breathe when I saw her head break the water. I was unaware I was holding it. But that moment of relief was short-lived as she came closer.

I am here, young one.

I had not heard her or seen her face so forlorn.

My breath caught in my throat once more. In her hands, she held the etching of the *Maiden of the Sea*.

At that moment, it was final.

I knew my father was not coming home. What was left of my strength abandoned me. My body crumpled, legs giving out; I fell into the water. For once, I did not feel the bone chilling cold, I felt nothing. I sputtered as I broke, trying to push myself up from the water. My arms wouldn't hold my weight. I choked on the salty water that filled my mouth as I gasped and heaved. Mother scooped me up in her arms; they felt like the only thing that could keep me from breaking completely. Her grip tightened, holding me together. I coughed up what was left of the water. She looked into my eyes, brushing the hair from my face. Seeing her own tears form brought mine back harder. We held onto each other for dear life and sobbed; it was the only thing we could do. Together, we sobbed into the sea.

Chapter 13

Numb

My body was numb, the goose-pimples covering my skin were the only sign of how cold I was. I could not feel anything except my heart shattering over and over. Mom continued to hold me until I could no longer cry and I did not have any tears left to spill.

After the heartbreak came regret, only regret. Regret for how our relationship had fallen to pieces over those last few months. Honestly, the previous eleven years. I wished we had the relationship a father and daughter should have had. One we were robbed of. Guilt over being selfish and putting my wants and needs above his when he did what he could to provide a life for us.

Lost...now, I had no one. I wanted to break down again, but my body had no energy to spare.

It seemed my mom could sense my body's needs before I could. She dipped under the water briefly and came back with a netted satchel. It flopped around as she held it out to me. I could see the fish peeking through the netting, wiggling about and trying to get free.

She smacked the satchel against the boulder beside us, and with two sickening thwacks, the fish inside stopped moving.

Take these, young one. You need your strength. Your father is always with you. She handed me the satchel, dropped it in my hands, and rubbed her thumb against my cheek. *It is time for me to leave you, for now. You know where to find me.*

I watched as she swam off, disappearing under the water. My stomach growled in earnest as I raised the pouch to eye level. She broke their backs; little droplets of blood fell into the ocean, turning the water around me pink.

It took every ounce of strength I had left to get up; my clothes clung to my shivering frame. It must have been a bodily instinct because I was unaware of the cold. I was numb to anything but the pangs of pain in my stomach.

Slowly, I made my way back toward home. Every step rattled my body with pain. I ached down to my bones.

After I walked through the threshold, I started a fire in the fireplace to begin drying out. I peeled off my garments as I went to try to warm myself. My feet carried me into the kitchen; I placed the fish on the counter while I hunted for my father's fileting knife. The sound of crunching bone echoed in my ears as the knife severed the heads. Usually, this would be my father's task; I did not care to filet the fish. Or any animal, for that matter. The knife ran seamlessly along the spine on both sides. When the pan was hot, I placed the fish in, and it sizzled as the aroma filled the room. Instantly, my mouth watered. I was ravenous.

All I needed was the meat cooked enough to be edible and I scarfed it down greedily. My taste buds tingled from the heat and the roof of my mouth was scorched. I did not care; I welcomed that pain over that which was in my stomach. What I could taste of it was delicious, before I burned my mouth to the point of not being able to taste it at all. Not knowing what he went through...Mom had spared me those details. I did not ask for them.

The house was so still. The sound of my plate hitting the sink echoed through the walls. Where would I go from here? I had food. She will help me with that. What about bills? How will I keep the house? The questions swirled in my head, threatening to take me down to Davy Jones's locker themselves.

"I'm on my own now," I whispered to the stale air.

A knock on the door startled me from my thoughts. I sniffed back tears, running my nose against my sleeve. Who would be here at this hour? It was almost dusk. I opened the door slowly, almost slamming it shut when I saw a wiry frame on the other side.

"I come in peace," the bookkeeper croaked, barely audible over the breeze.

"What on earth are you doing here? How did you know where I lived?" My questions flew out of me in a flurry; I brought a hand to my chest as if it would steady my racing heart.

"You haven't come in, in a few days; I heard about the storm. My condolences for your father. I was quite fond of that one."

I noted the bread and tome in his hand; wisps of grey hair blew across his face.

"I brought you bread, I supposed you don't have much with Dunstan gone. I know you are fond of mermaids, I found a tome you may have interest in."

My brows knitted in confusion as I took both items. "Thank you for this. I'm not sure I understand why you have come here."

A raspy scoffing noise comes out of him. "As I've said, I was fond of your father. And you have made my existence less dreary over the years. Even if you never put the tomes back in their correct space and leave crumbs where you sit. Don't think for a second I hadn't noticed you smuggling food into my sacred space."

"I wasn't aware of my father visiting the library," I muttered, staring at the loaf of bread like it held untold mysteries. "With all the dust littering the place, I didn't think you would mind." I quip back a smirk, tweaking my lips briefly.

"Yes well, that is none of your concern. I have other news for you." He paused, raising a brow at me expectantly. With a huff of frustration, I waved him on. "I don't see you staying in this village. Take this as you will. The pirates will be here in two months' time" I opened my mouth to question him, and he held up a withered hand. "Ask not how I know. Take your chance, or leave it. I care not either way"

"Thank you...I think," I said, running a hand behind my neck.

"Yes. Very well. I must return to my duties, as the light is disappearing," he murmured, turning away. "Ah one more thing, that Siren tome, it was one of your Father's favorites."

With that, he was gone like an apparition, here one moment and gone the next—leaving me with more questions than answers.

"What a weird night." I chomped down on the loaf of bread as I closed and locked the door.

My mind buzzed, but one thought was circling through it—an idea that had been a farfetched fantasy for a while. One that grew stronger every time I got on my father's boat. I did not know how to accomplish it, but my mind was set.

I need to make myself a believable fisherman, to fool those with the very sea in their blood.

It would not be an easy task. No, it would take dedication. One mistake could be my downfall. But I had nothing else to live for.

The pirates would come, as the Bookkeeper said, in two months. I had until then to learn their ways enough to fool them and get myself on the crew.

Two months. It took me two months of learning, watching, and gaining all the knowledge I could. I had the walk down: confident, tired, chest slightly puffed. Daring anyone to challenge me. I bartered some fish for a kohl stick from one of the village ladies; I used it to make small beard strokes on my face. It helped sharpen my softer features, filling out my delicately arched eyebrows.

I went to the extent of training my vocal cords to lower keys, making me sound gruff, not like a man, but a teenage boy. Thanks to the sun, my skin was golden brown. With the help of the kohl, I could define my collar bones, making them harsh and faking more hair on my arms than there.

I was content with my appearance. Still, there was plenty of work to be done. Making what repairs I could to the house helped me build more muscle. I was sculpted nicely, less feminine. My thighs were thick, and my biceps bulged at the slightest flex. Whenever I was ready to give up, thoughts of my father made me push myself harder. When I would go into the village, I would plop down with the sailors, letting my fist fall hard on the table as I sat. The men around me gave toothy grins and jeered, returning to whatever they were discussing.

Ale sloshed over the table as they talked, waving their steins in the air as they gestured.

"Seas be rough boys!" One fisherman bolstered.

"Aye!" They all retorted, bumping their steins to the table and spitting on the ground.

I had noticed spitting was a common practice, a disgusting one, but they did it whenever they talk about something unlucky.

Guess I will need to practice my spitting...

One of the men slid a tankard down the table to me. Ale spilled as it went. I grasped it in my palm and took a chug before them. It was warm and bitter; I had to keep the grimace from showing on my face, letting out a window-shattering belch instead.

They looked at each other, clanked the tankards together, and cheered. The conversation continued. It seemed I was fitting in.

"Tis' a shame, that storm a few months ago. Haven't seen somethin' quite like it in a while." My heart twinged painfully at the mention of it.

"We lost some great men." They raised their glasses.

"Those Sirens had quite a feast," one of them muttered, spitting on the ground.

My fist clenched as I resisted the urge to shove it in his mouth. I took another hard swing of ale, it burned as it went down.

The conversation drew on, but I had phased out following their actions robotically. I believed I had their lingo down enough to fool the pirates. I had been studying for weeks. Throwing myself entirely into my new character, my new self, was all I could do. I needed a way out. This was my only chance, with nothing tying me to the village anymore.

Ever since I was little, I only wanted to go to sea. The water all around me, the wind behind me. It was a fool's dream, since I was a woman. Something that could never happen...until now. I was confident I could do it. My wish would finally come true.

I overheard the fisherman speaking of the pirates; most were afraid of them or maybe just wistful of a life they could never lead—one of adventure and danger. It was rumored they would be here any day, and I would be ready.

In all this time, I barely got over to see Mom. It was hard. I told her of my plans, and she was not exactly thrilled. She knew the danger and the risk I was taking. She also knew there was nothing she could do to control the situation. Not only had she lost her husband, but her daughter was going out to sea with some of the most dangerous men there are. The worst part was, as much as I was nervous about it, I finally felt free. If I died, at least I would die happy.

Chapter 14

Sell Your Soul

Hushed whispers spread through the village...the pirates had arrived. There was a nervous energy buzzing through the small town. Fishermen made themselves busy, wives made themselves scarce and swept up the children to keep them inside where they were safe. The townspeople were superstitious to a fault; according to another local lore, pirates brought bad luck. They were dangerous and reckless, which did not sit well with this group.

You can do this. You have done all the preparations.

Nerves thrummed along my spine as I tried to convince myself to go through with my plans. It was easier when it was not right in front of me. It was daunting, like a mountain I had started to climb, and I vastly underestimated how steep it was.

They had docked last night, by this morning talk had spread through the town. The benefit of a small town: news spread like a wildfire. Using the kohl, I put all my practice to work, quick strokes along my jawline and cheeks filled in my beard, I deepened my furrowed brow, making them bolder and more caterpillar-like. I yanked on a stained white shirt and my brown knee-length pants. Haphazardly, I pulled on my boots, and I stumbled into the table, jamming my hip bone into the corner.

"Son of a pirate! Get yourself together! They are gonna see right through your lie otherwise!" I scolded myself under my breath. I try to steady my breathing—deep breaths in, short breaths out. My heartbeat raced under my skin. "Calm down, mate."

I felt foolish talking to myself. It had become a habit lately. I checked my appearance once more before I flew out the door, flinging myself from my safety, knowing I would have lost my nerve if I had not. My feet stumbled over the pathway I knew by heart—as if I had not traveled these cobbled paths my whole life. I probably looked like a drunk...fresh in the morning.

At least pirates loved their booze.

They came in a few times a year to gather supplies. Who am I kidding...they came to steal supplies while the townsfolk slept. Their only other task was gaining more foolish souls for their crew.

Here I was, throwing myself at them.

I made my way to the tavern; my feet felt as if they were made of lead the whole trip. After one deep breath to steady myself, I grasped the handle in a clammy hand and yanked the solid wooden door open. Only a few heads looked up as I made my entrance. Most were already too drunk to care about my insignificance.

My eyes roamed the dimly lit room, scouring for my mark. There was a table in the back of the tavern, and a few burly types stood around. I inhaled, pushed my shoulders back, my chest slightly puffed, and my feet led the way.

One man sat behind the table with a browning paper and an ink pen. Ink so dark it could have been crafted in the very pits of hell itself. I spotted only a few names on the list. My eyes darted back to his; his were hard, a steely gray. His head was adorned with a worn brown three-point hat and a gold earring in his right ear. He had a scar running over one eye, down to his cheek. It was swallowed up in his beard, black as night, which reached down to his barrel chest. All the air promptly left my lungs. I clenched my fist, fighting the urge to run and to keep my voice steady. Even as my knees threatened to buckle beneath me.

Was this a mistake?

"I am here to join yer crew." Surprisingly, my voice came steady and gruff, just like I had practiced.

The man sitting behind the table slowly raised his head to appraise me, then looked to the men to his left and right. They burst out laughing, their boisterous voices carrying through the tavern. I winced.

"How old are ye, lad?" His voice boomed. My fists balled up against my sides, pinching my flesh.

"I be eighteen, sir," I responded, my gaze locked hard onto his. He glanced at his fellow mates standing beside him.

"What do ye know 'bout sailin'?" He inquired; his brow arched in a doubting fashion, which only grated my nerves more.

"Been crewing the boat with me father, for 'bout a year. I know my way around the ropes." I allowed my chest to swell as I spoke, alluding to a confidence I no longer had under his steel gaze.

"What happened to yer old man?" He questioned. My heart thumped heavily in my chest.

"Lost at sea." The words tumbled out, feeling foreign to my ears.

He looked to his mates again as an unnerving grin spread across his face, revealing the yellowed teeth behind his thin lips.

"Aye, welcome to *The Shadow*, Lad. Ye be leavin' with us in the mornin'." He held out the ink pen to me.

I took it in my grasp and signed my life away with one scratch of the pen. I was Demi Godfrey, and my old life was gone.

Chapter 15

Bittersweet Goodbyes

It was a strange feeling to pack up my life in a matter of minutes. Thirty, to be exact.

Once the door shut to the Tavern, the air deflated from my lungs. My feigned courage left me entirely as I made the trek home. Opening that door felt like the last time I would set foot in this house again—my house. Home. Where I spent seventeen years of my life, where my mother left us, and where my father grew as harsh as our winters. It was not much, but it was the only home I had known. The exterior falling to shambles proved how drastically our lives have changed over the years.

My fingers trailed against the walls, the peeling paint rough beneath my fingertips as memories flooded my vision. My eyes grew heavy with tears, dropping to the floor as I solemnly walked to my room. I grabbed my bag, the one I would take on longer fishing trips, and started packing my life away: what few clothes I had, my kohl stick, binding wrap, a few books...

That was it. All I had to my name. There was a strange comfort in knowing I was not leaving much, if anything, behind. I looked out the window, the shutter coming off the hinge. It was dusty with neglect. There was far too much to fix with this house. I tried to leave it better for whoever would take it after I was gone. Would they take better care of it? Would a happy family once again fill its halls with laughter and joy? Something that had been missing for far too long. My chest ached.

My mind wandered as I stared out the tiny window, studying the village. My village. Here, I was safe, kept in my little corner of the world. Not excelling, simply surviving. If one could call it that, surviving wasn't living. I would either say goodbye to the life I was building, start looking for "woman's" work, and be forced to find myself a husband. Or I would continue the life of a fisherman, maybe saving enough money for my own boat. I would barely scrape by either path I chose. I could not—no, would not—accept that fate. Not when a life of adventure awaited me. Being in and a part of the sea is what my heart longed for, no matter the risk. What is a life worth living without risk? Turning from the window, I scooped my bag off the bed and closed the door behind me. I pressed my back against it and took a deep breath to ground my torrent of emotions.

A tug in my chest pulled my eyes down the hall to Father's room. The door loomed over me like the growing black pit in my chest since his death. My feet moved of their own accord. Before I could convince myself to stop, I turned the doorknob. The hinges creaked in protest, echoing the weight of the world around me.

Dingy light streamed in from the windows, casting the room in a golden glow. My throat tightened as I noticed some of my mother's items where she had left them. Her hairbrush was on a small vanity and a pearl necklace, and her pillow was still on the bed. Very few possessions belonged to my father as I gazed around the room. A stack of dusty books on his nightstand. I wandered over to them, tracing my fingers over the spines: *Mysteries of the Sea, The Deep, The Compleat Angler,* and at the very bottom, the book I had borrowed from the library. Both shock and fury washed over me, making my clothes seem too tight and this room too small. After our fight, the book had gone missing; I apologized to the book-keeper endlessly for my carelessness. An image of the handprint on the book flashed before me.

"It was him!" I smacked the stack of books off the night-stand; pages fluttered around the room, ripped from the worn spines.

I cursed and kicked the nightstand, cursing harder at the pain radiating from my foot, my boot too worn to protect it from impact. The nightstand wobbled and tipped over, opening a hidden compartment under-neath. A black journal poked out; I bent to pick it up, opening the first page. The familiar scrawl of my father's chicken scratch. It wasn't just a journal. It was *his* jour-nal. I swallowed over the lump in my throat, unsure how to process the emotions bombarding me. Cursing again, I shoved it in my bag; a nagging feeling told me I shouldn't, yet the yearning to know my father's secrets prevailed. Time was of the essence, and I had much left to do. Without another breath, I rushed out of the room like my life depended on it.

Thoughts of my mother came to mind as I made my way downstairs with the bag of my life on my shoulder. I dropped it at the door with a thud. I knew I needed to say goodbye, the day's most challenging task. I worried my lip, thinking about what I would say. She could never truly be a part of my life, not in the way I needed her to be, yetI wasn't ready to say goodbye or to let go of her like I was letting go of everything else familiar to me; I'd only just gotten her back.

My stomach growled angrily; I had forgotten to eat in all the commotion. Quickly, I shoved a bowl of whatever the slop in the cauldron consisted of into my stomach. I eyed it suspiciously as I took my bites, a slight wave of nausea passing over me. A loud belch carried through-out the house as I finished my meal. I wiped my mouth on my sleeve as I left to say goodbye.

My steps were leadened as I trudged through the woods. The dense trees felt like they were closing in on me, and my chest tightened painfully. This felt like a forever kind of goodbye. Tears slid down my face, silently falling to the path below me. I lumbered along the trail, scuffing my boots on overgrown roots, a tremor taking over my body as I made my way down to the clearing. Looming boulders came into view after what felt like an eternity, and the sense of the forest closing in eased from my shoulders. Mother was already there waiting for me, as if she knew. Of course, she did. Her face was melancholy as I approached her. My reserve faded, and I trembled as I dashed into her arms.

"I am leaving in the morning," I whispered into her cold shoulder. She gripped onto me tightly, her fingers digging into my skin. *Be safe, young one. Let the seas guide you.* Her melody was soft in my mind, a gentle caress. I could feel the sorrow it held.

"Will I see you again?" I shoved out of her arms just enough, placing my hands on her shoulders so I could look into her eyes, pleading.

I will always be with you, young one. As long as the sea is in your heart, I will not be far away.

I latched onto her again as if she was a lifeline I desperately needed to keep myself afloat. Her response was unclear, but who could say if and when we would meet again. I was setting sail to a new life; I just hoped, deep down, that it still had room for her.

We said our goodbyes with more tears and hugs. She brushed her thumb over my cheek, and I nuzzled my face into her palm.

"I love you," I called after her as she turned to swim away. She looked back at me and smiled, but it did not reach her eyes.

May we find each other again. I love you, Naida.

Then, she was gone, possibly out of my life for good.

Chapter 16

The Shadow

I awoke with the sun shining in my eyes, quickly wiping the drool from my mouth. I rushed out of bed, stumbling over my blanket. It was a restless night. The purple bags under my eyes showed it. I hurriedly went through my routine, dawning on my man "makeup." Beard. Check. Eyebrows. Check. Arm-hair. Check. Baggy clothing...always. One last-minute decision: I grabbed one of our bone carving knives downstairs. Heavy-footed, I dashed back upstairs to look in the mirror in my room. I breathed deeply—in, out, in—and swiftly, I gathered my hair and chopped it off at chin length. I stared down at the handful of my locks, tossing them in the waste bucket. I left enough to gather into a small ponytail, covering it with my cap. All that was left was to grab my bag, and I was out the door.

I turned for one last bitter look at my house; who knew if I would ever see it again.

Walking through the village, I took in the smells and the sounds. Children's laughter as they played tag. The fisherman talked boisterously as they readied their boats. Woman gossiped. The smell of fresh fish, the salty ocean on the breeze. Freshly baked bread. I took an apple as I walked past one of the stands, tossing a coin toward the owner. It crunched under my teeth, the juice flowing down my mouth. I grunted and carefully wiped my mouth on my sleeve to avoid disturbing my drawn-on beard.

The pirate ship was hard to miss. It was big enough to hold an entire army. Its mass loomed over the other boats still on the dock. Black sails, a black mast, black ship...the only color brought to it were the gold metal accents adorning the sides. I could spot the crew walking around on the deck as I stood below it. They seemed intimidating, even from where I was. Musk wafted toward me with a hint of rum carried on the breeze. My nose scrunched slightly in disgust.

That will take some getting used to. Here we go...

One last breath through the nose and out the mouth to calm my nerves. They were buzzing, like lightning racing through my veins. My boots clomped up the wood planks as I went. Breathe in and breathe out.

At the top, I was met with a broad man, standing about six feet five inches and two men wide. All built muscle and chiseled jaw dawned with scruff; his blue eyes icy enough to turn my blood cold. The sun glinted off his light brown skin, picking up his golden undertones. He looked like a god of old. The golden hoop in his lobe shone bright. The intensity rolling off him was overwhelming, and I gulped slightly.

"Who be you?" His voice boomed loud enough for the surrounding crewmates to stop and look over. I puffed up my chest, even though I wanted to run back down that plank faster than a mouse caught stealing cheese.

"Demi, reportin' for duty, sir!" I kept my hands at my side, and my eyes locked on his gaze. He crossed his arms over his broad chest and tilted his head slightly, assessing me.

"Aye, ye be a fresh one, alright. Porter, show the lad to the berth."

At his call, a thin man hurried over to his side. He looked like a dwarf mouse compared to the man beside him. His sandy brown hair was tousled and greasy.

"Right this way," he chirped sheepishly; his voice was nasally. Once we were safe from the brooding one, I spoke up.

"Who is he?" I tossed my head slightly in his direction. Porter looked at me with a tinge of fear in his eyes.

"He be the captain's first mate. Youngest first mate we've ever had, be sure not to cross em. Casper ain't the friendliest guy you'll meet. He is called the ghost of the sea, cause you'll never see em comin'." His voice came out in little squeaks. I looked over my shoulder at Casper again before we went below deck.

"So... we each be gettin' our owns quarters?" I questioned. Porter cracked a smile and laughed at my expense.

"Ye really are crazy if ye think that. What ye get be a hammock, we all share the space below deck. Only ones with private quarters be the captain 'n the first mate."

I just nodded, not sure why I was suddenly hopeful to have my own space. This may make my charade more difficult. The thought of having to go to the bathroom suddenly flashed through my mind and I had to choke down the panic. Porter raised an eyebrow as he observed my mini meltdown. I quickly regained composure of my face, focusing my attention on my walk and trying to exude confidence. He could see through the charade. He had played his own for quite some time before becoming this little mouse.

"Here we be, a queen size cot fit fer a princess." I laughed a little nervously at his joke. At least he had some personality, besides the brooding, possible murderers I had encountered. "I didn't catch ye name before."

"Demi." I stuck out my hand for him to shake. Instead, he shook his head and clapped my shoulder with his own.

"Welcome aboard, mate."

It was dark below deck; the only light was lanterns hanging on hooks or placed on barrels. I scrunch my nose at the musty smell: stale seawater, and a lot of B.O.

The hammocks hung three high, one above the other. I was thankful to get the bottom one; it would have been a hell of a time climbing to the top. There were three small chests placed accordingly by each tower of hammocks. I opened mine, it was coated in cobwebs. Using my bag to swipe at them, I cleared my trunk of the webbing. At the bottom, there was a dull key; it looked like, at one time, it would have been gold.

At least I can lock my things up.

The thought eased some of my tension as I shoved my bag inside it. I closed the lid, making sure the lock worked. Once that was done, I took another sweep of the room. On the other end, I could faintly make out the shape of... cages? I swallowed hard as I crept slowly over to that side. It was not lit over here. All the cells were thankfully empty of anything living. However, I made out the shape of some bones in the one, by the looks of it, they were human. A wave of terror and nausea swept over me.

What am I getting myself into?

It was much too late to turn back now. I was committed, my name and soul were now theirs. I heard boots stomping down the stairs and almost jumped out of my skin. I swiftly moved to the other side of the ship, trying to look like I was not snooping. Thankfully, it was just Porter.

"Aye, better get used to that, lad. Thar be no privacy here. Best to keep to yer owns business. Know yer surroundings. Ye never know who be listenin'." He spoke low, as if to emphasize his point.

I nodded slowly, trying not to let my worry show. Meanwhile, my heart raced in my chest and panic rose in my throat.

"What are those cages fer?" I whispered, tossing my head in that direction. He glanced over at the cages, a grimace contorting his features, and shuffled closer to me.

"Captives. Traitor pirates. Sometimes, we need ta loot a ship for a reward." His breath was hot against my ear. I felt pinneedles all over my arms.

"Aye," was my only response. He clapped me again on the shoulder, and I grunted.

"Aye, Demi. 'Tis time to meet the crew."

I gulped inaudibly, trying to find my strength again. I lifted my head and drew my shoulders back, puffing my chest slightly. He grinned and I noted his missing front tooth before following him up to the main deck. Once we got on deck, Porter guided me to three other men.

"Stand together, straight as an arrow, lads," Porter called. That was the loudest I had yet to hear him speak.

I followed the order and joined the others; we made the line as straight as possible. Casper walked over to us, his hands behind his back as he paced back and forth in front of our line.

"Alright, crew!" He shouted. "These be our newest crimps. Lads call out yer name 'n age." I looked down the line at the first lad. He looked to be about nineteen and had broad shoulders and a head full of golden hair.

"Adrian, 19," he called out. I smirked slightly as my guess was on point.

"Bran, 20." The next boy—or should I say, man—announced, chest puffed proudly. My god, he was a giant. He had to be at least 6' 11" easily, with long brown hair tied back in a slacked ponytail.

"Braxon, 25." He was barely standing at Bran's chest. He had wavy jet-black hair, and icy blue eyes much like the others in my village.

My turn was last, and my heart sped up a little with all the eyes on me. Blood pounded loudly in my ears. I followed suit, puffing my chest slightly.

"Demi, 18," I stated, my voice held more command than I thought it would have.

Casper looked over each of us, his hands clasped behind his back. His thick brow judging us as he went. It took all my will not to cower under his scrutiny.

"Aye, my name be Casper. I am the first mate. Heed me word the first time, or it may be yer last. I give the orders 'round here." His voice carried over us all. The ship was so quiet I might've heard the mice chewing the wood.

"Let's not forget who be the captain o' this ship!"

A loud voice boomed from the top deck. All our heads snapped to attention. My eyes landed on the same man in the tavern when I signed up.

"Aye!" All the crewmates jeered wearily. The look on Casper's face was anything but pleasant.

"Aye, this be Marduke's ship," Casper continued, as if that was his intent all along.

The captain tipped his hat and went back to his quarters. "When yer not doin' chores, ye will be training with the crew. Need to keep strong while at sea. There is a nightly watch rotation. If I find other uses fer ye, I will assign 'em. Let's teach these pups the ropes, lads!"

At Casper's call, the crew exploded in cheers. They swarmed around us like a pack of hungry dogs. Soon enough, there was a burlap sack over my head. Everything was dark. We were swept away by a sea of hands.

Chapter 17

Part of the Crew

We were jolted along the deck, down some stairs, and forcefully shoved onto what I assumed was a bench. I reached up and snatched the sack covering my head once they let my hands go. My gaze swiveled around the room as my eyes adjusted to the lighting. It looked like we were in the dining quarters.

The crew surrounded our small group as tankards slid down the table behind us. Each of us reached out to grab one as they went by.

"Aye, lads, welcome to the crew!" One of the men shouted. The rest followed, cheering loudly.

"Aye!" They replied, raising their tankards.

We did the same and took a hard swing of the caramel liquid in the cup.

I quickly realized this was not ale, but rum. My eyes bulged as I gagged, trying not to spew the rum all over the crew standing around us—causing a riot of laughter.

"Whelps! Seems we got ourselves a sprog," another man chimed in. He seemed to be missing an eye, and I noted his gold tooth. "Can nah handle the taste o' the rum, lad? Better get used to it; that be our water 'ere."

The mates laughed along with him, and I could feel my cheeks grow warm, as well as my belly, as I mustered another swing. This time, I tried hard not to make a reaction. It burned going down, like drinking fire, and I did not like it at all. The taste was...well, exactly as it smelled, harsh. I swallowed the rest of my cup in one glug—literal hellfire. The mates seemed impressed though as I felt hands clap on my shoulder; the other new recruits looked at me as though I was the scum beneath their boots.

I shrugged casually, trying to keep a straight face. The last thing I would do was show weakness before any of them.

"Ye had yer liquid courage, now lads, it be time to swab the poop deck!" The voice belonged to an older fellow in the back.

He looked like he had seen better days; his face was wrinkled and marred with scars. His gray hair fell around his shoulders haphazardly. He held some command with the crew, even though he may not be ranked.

"Gangway fer the ghost!" Another man chimed in, waving his hand in a woo-woo motion. The older man looked at him, the corner of his mouth twitching only for a second.

"Aye," he responded eerily, looking over at us. "Be the ghost o' Marie. The tale goes she once boarded our vessel. Once the Captain found out, he tossed her to the fish. She be told to haunt *The Shadow* ever since."

His words sent chills down my spine, and suddenly, my new liquid courage did nothing to help my panic. Not in the way he assumed, though.

"Be wary lads. Don't shite too loud, or she'll grab ye an take ye to Davy Jones' locker!"

The crew broke out in howls of laughter, and the boys and I looked at one another, grinning. It didn't do much to settle my nerves, but I plastered a grin on my face nonetheless. I wondered silently if there ever was a Marie, or if she was just a bad joke. They led us back on deck once the howls died out and the rum drained to the last drop. Unfortunately, he was serious about the swabbing. Now, from the top of the ship, I could see we had long set sail, the sky bleeding reds and yellows as the sun began its descent. We each were handed a mop and a bucket of murky water.

"Be sure to get her shinin', or else ye fate be with the captain," the old sailor warned, then simply turned his back and left us.

The boards below me were blackened from age; the ship has undoubtedly seen its history. If it was not from the weathered boards, it was from the patches in the wood where chunks were blown off at one point or another. I kept to myself, mopping along the ship's edge, catching glances at the dark waters below me. My village was no longer in sight, and my heart panged painfully. As I mopped, my mind began to travel with the repetition. Would I ever see my mother again? Is she right below me now? My feet ached to be back in the icy water with her arms wrapped around me. I could bear the thought no more, turning my back to the sea.

Adrian, Bran, and Braxon were chatting amongst themselves. I could hear their laughter every now and then. When any of them caught my gaze, they sneered and continued talking. I straightened my posture, shoulders back, chest puffed, a deep inhale to center myself, and started striding toward them.

"Listen here, lads, we may be the only mates we shall have on board. Best be lookin' out fer each other than against."

They raised their eyebrows at me, passing looks between each other, and a bout of laughter ensued.

"Aye, mates, we've got ourselves a live one, eh?" Adrian barked, his voice carrying as he elbowed Bran's arm. "Hardly looks like you can wrangle the ropes. I bet you won't last two months at sea." His boisterous laughter rubbed me the wrong way, bringing memories of the village kids of my youth. Memories I would much rather forget and ones I thought I'd left behind.

"I don't know what I've done to you, but trust I can handle meself just fine. You wouldn't want to find out either way," I retorted with a low voice in warning.

Of course, I had no backing for the threat, but the bullies back home weren't much for confrontation. It seemed to shut them up and take them off guard, though.

"Who are you exactly?" Braxon stated challengingly.

"I can be your worst nightmare or your greatest friend. Who I am, be up to you," I replied coldly; I would no longer stand for their whisperings against me. I refused to be as weak as I once was. I would prove my worth to them and myself. It grew quiet after that, and we swabbed the rest of the deck silently.

Chapter 18

Rough Seas Ahead

I would be lying if I said the first weeks on board were anything but rough. Adjusting to this new life was not as simple as I envisioned. Recruits had to earn their keep. We got the shit end of the stick, the jobs no one else wanted, the earlier shifts for work, and were the last ones for food. Tensions were high between the four of us, and I kept a wary eye on Braun and Braxon the most. They despised me and made sure to ostracize me at any given opportunity.

Deep down, I feared they knew my secret and were awaiting their moment to out me when it was most convenient. Thankfully, they had made no moves yet. Braxon was clearly from my village; I wracked my brain, trying to determine if we had ever crossed paths. I couldn't recall his face, with much of my childhood kept behind locked doors in my memory. Hopefully, the years of burying my head in books kept us apart.

Trying to keep my actual gender a secret had been troublesome. There were eyes and ears everywhere, like rats under the floorboards. Tricky. Yeah, that was one way to put it. I worried about how much medical gauze could go missing before it was questioned. I made sure to toss the red rags overboard at night under the cover of the stars, thankful my trousers were made of a dark material.

My body ached from the daily training; I vastly underestimated what Casper meant by that. The training was code for sparring for two or more hours daily. I cursed him worse on the days he woke us up before dawn to take laps around the deck, then fall into sparring. I was lousy, to say the least. Did I build muscle over the months at my village? Yes. Had I ever fought a day in my life? Only if I considered fighting the dragons in the books I loved. Otherwise, no.

Casper initially paired me with Adrian, much to my dismay. My respect for him grew slightly when he didn't beat the ever-loving shit out of me at every opportunity.

After the first week, Casper took me under his wing, saying I needed much improvement if I was to live at sea. I dreamed of punching him in the face. In reality, I had yet to land a blow on him. Meanwhile, my body was littered with nasty bruises.

"Keep yer face protected! Balance on the balls of yer feet," Casper barked, sweat poured down my back, and I debated diving head-first into the depths below.

Drowning would surely be better than this hell. At least on nights when I fell into my hammock, I could escape into my own world. My weary mind cooked up all sorts of ways of taking Casper out. That brightened my mood, and come morning, it darkened all over again, so the cycle repeated.

Porter had been my one true friend, more so a lifeline keeping me afloat. He would lend an ear on days I could have given up and offering advice on the days I thought I would. He made the isolation more bearable. We were both alone, surrounded by bodies on this ship. I told him some doctored memories of my past. He was from a small town himself, a merchant port, in fact. I found joy in his company after a long day of work. He did not speak much about his past but his life on the ship. It seemed to me he was not seen nor heard unless Casper or the Captain needed him for anything. He was just as lonely as I was.

He spun the most fantastical tales; I told him he was a natural storyteller and that he should write them down. I bet he would make a fortune off his stories. He told me once they had been out to sea for nearly a year, their supplies had almost run dry, and in their luck, they came across another ship. The crew was practically feral with starvation. They closed in under the cover of the stars and boarded the ship while the crew slept. They slit their throats and stole their goods right out from under their captain's nose. As he spoke, his eyes held the glossy twinkle of a child. Meanwhile, my stomach grew unsettled, and I chased it with a gulp of rum.

When the days seemed endless, the crew would break out into shanties to pass the time. Some of them I re-membered hearing in my village, and some seemed original. I enjoyed listening and watching the men as they sang and danced about. I even joined in on occasion. Porter was quite good at the Squeezebox. I found myself laughing as the days went on.

It had been a month since we left. Rumors were we headed north to gather supplies for our voyage to some unknown land. The story goes that it was what is now known as the Lost Sea. Once revered as the conqueror of ships and the souls on board, the sea dried up, leaving nothing but the wreckage behind. Yet, no one had been able to find its location, since it was forever lost to humanity. Marduke had come across a rumored location of a map that would guide us to this supposed sea. Maybe it was my father's voice in my mind, but I did not believe such a thing could exist. The captain, however, had other plans.

Often, long after the crew was still, sleep evaded me. Occasionally, I would find myself on the top deck at night. I swore I could see a fin breach the water, glinting in the moonlight. Such a night like tonight. I reveled in the taste of the salty spray on my lips, the breeze fluttering through my blouse and caressing my skin. The gentle rock of the ship through the water soothed me as I ached for home. I held my father's diary to my chest; I had yet to read it, afraid of what I would find. I fingered the leather binding, took a steadying breath, and finally opened it.

Aug 21st, 1888

Lyra,

I don't know how to do this without you. My soul is a gaping wound where you used to be. How am I to raise Naida by myself? Our world is dark without you, and I'm afraid. I'm so scared to fail her as I failed you. Looking into her eyes, your eyes, is too painful. Forgoing my passions, I have thrown myself into fishing; by providing for her, I can feel the distance grow between us. My sweet Naida. Lyra, I need your guidance.

A tear trailed down my cheek. He never spoke of my mother or the earlier years. I flipped the page as curiosity took over.

May 16th, 1892

Lyra,

I am seeing more and more of you in Naida. While I tend to the ship, I leave her, sometimes for days. It pains me to leave our ten-year-old alone. Most days she spends in the library, my pride swells seeing her take to tomes as I have. She is insistent on coming out with me. I am terrified. I am frightened to lose her. I have convinced her my hesitance is due to the town's superstitions. While that is true, we both know the truth. Her love for the sea outgrows yours by the day.

My inhale was shaky. A tear fell and stained the page, smudging his writing. I wish he would have shared himself with me. Maybe our past would have been different. Soft strumming brought me out of my thoughts. The tune was poetry spoken to the night sky above, a lover's caress. I huffed and closed the dairy, tucking it against my side. A smile spread across my lips; I leaned over the railing, trying to spy on who the melody came from. Much to my surprise, I spotted Casper as he sat on a crate across the ship.

His shoulder-length hair ruffled in midnight ringlets fell around his face as he bent over what looked like a guitar. I had only seen one on board; we did not have them around where I grew up. Casper's gaze swept across the ship lazily as his disposition relaxed. He started to hum softly, and the sound moved through me, bringing goosebumps to my flesh. His broad shoulders glimmered with the light of the moon; he was not so terrifying, at least not when he was like this.

A part of me that wanted to ring him around the neck softened. Our weeks of training had tinged my view of him red with my undying rage. Most of the crew avoided him at all costs; his temper quick as his cat of nine tails. After all, his ferocity gained him the rank of first mate at the young age of twenty. I realized then that he fought like he strummed his guitar—a fluid dance. I heard the passion he held while in battle in the notes he played.

I verbally sighed, forgetting where I was, still slowly taking in his broad figure. At the sound, his head snapped up. I reeled back, my cheeks blazing, and fell on my back end. Stunned and flaming with embarrassment, I continued to sit there with my hand on my face, praying to whatever sea god was listening that he would not come over. My luck ran short.

"Demi, ye alright, mate?" I flinched back against my better judgment as Casper appeared before me. "Kraken got ye tongue?" He stood there impatiently, waiting for a response.

I coughed nervously and brushed myself off. "Aye, I be fine." I deepened my voice to make up for some of the embarrassment.

He reached out his hand to help me up; I took it as it almost wrapped entirely around my own. I had to turn away so my cheeks would not set fire again. I straightened, feeling his eyes bore into me, refusing to meet his stare.

"Pirate's dream, a night like this." His voice was softer as he looked off to the side at the sea.

"Aye, it is indeed." I swallowed in response. Nervously, I followed him over to the side of the ship.

We looked at the ocean; the stars glinted off the water, making the ripples sparkle below. I glanced at Casper out of the corner of my eye. A small smile tugged on his lips as he looked out. I wondered what he was thinking about, what brought him out of his—I was sure—cozy bed. Anything must be more relaxing than the hammocks we were stuck in below deck.

"What brings ye up here at this hour?" His voice was as smooth as afternoon tide, yet still held its toe-curling husk. I shrugged my shoulders nonchalantly.

"It may be silly, but I like to come up here when I miss home. The sea has always been my... friend." My voice carried on the breeze. He looked at me sideways and nodded slowly.

"It has been mine too. Know the feelin' all too well. It's been four years since the sea has been my home. She's a cold mistress indeed." His voice was solemn and sent chills down my spine. My father said much of the same. I've never had that experience; the sea always brought me warmth and a feeling of belonging.

"Aye. You must miss the company of a woman," I spoke without thinking and stunned myself as the words slipped out on their own accord. I could have slapped myself.

Now you've done it!

I mentally scolded myself. He scoffed and slapped the railing lightly with his hand as he turned to me, leaning against it.

"Lad, I can get whatever strumpet I please. 'Tis the life of a pirate. A companion, though? Now, that is not the pirate's life. Gold 'n loot, all the plunder you wish, but it is a lonely life." His words caught me off guard, and my heart leaped in my chest.

That was a dangerous reaction. I knew this would lead to no good outcome for me. Yet my heart ached, and I found myself yearning to touch Casper's face and feel his skin in my palm. I mentally shook myself, reminding myself of all the times he laid me out on my ass. The fire in my belly returned, and I welcomed the feeling.

"A pirate's life indeed," I muttered my response, shoving my irrational feelings deep down inside me. He nodded in response.

"I saw you staring at me earlier," he stated smoothly.

For the love of a Kraken.

"Well, best be off to bed. Night!" I said quickly and brushed past him, hurrying below deck. My heart raced as I tramped down the stairs; I swore I heard him chuckling softly from above.

Chapter 19

Scrub Ye Scallywag

The mood on board had brightened as we drew near our destination. I had been looking forward to seeing a new town; I wondered if it would be anything like my old home. The wind was cooler against my face, the water below growing murky the farther north we went. My own nerves were a live wire the closer we got.

"Land Ho!" The lookout called, his voice carrying from the Crow's nest above.

I leaned over the rail, trying to spot land in the distance; I could see a faint tree line over the horizon. There were shouts from around the deck as other crewmates spotted it, too. A hand shoved my shoulder and roughed up my hair. I set my face in a scowl as I saw Porter had joined me.

"Watch the hair, mate!"

He laughed and nudged me harder, "Stop being a priss. No pirate fusses 'bout their hair."

"Not all of us keep it in a greasy mop," I retorted. For that one, I got a swift punch in the arm and whined as I rubbed it. "Ye can't argue. It is true."

Porter rolled his eyes, looking back out to the horizon. "Are you excited?"

"To get some fresh air? Yes. Ye all smell like a bunch of dirty pirates."

"Ye be included in that." Porter snorted, and I elbowed him in the side as he waved his hand before his nose.

"I am looking forward to being on solid ground again. I have never been outside of my village before. Have you been to this one?"

"Aye," he said, "But we do not visit this one often. It's not the most favorable port to be around. Watch yer loot here. There are pickpockets all around."

"Great. Just great," I muttered. I did not have any coin to spare, only what I came on board with, and I desperately needed a few new tops. Honestly, I could use a few new of, well, everything. "How long do ye think we'll be here for?"

Porter shrugged, side-eyeing me. "Hard to say. Only as long as Marduke takes to find this map."

"Do you believe the map exists?" I kept my voice low. Hopefully, no wandering ears could hear me.

"Best bite yer tongue. Questioning the captain will get you nothing but a lashing."

"Does that happen often?" I asked, arching a brow in his direction. He huffed out a laugh.

"Do ye want the honest answer?" I nodded. "It happens more often than I wish it would. Casper deals out those punishments."

Our conversation died shortly after, and we busied ourselves preparing to dock. The crew was chaotic, finish-
ing up the duties for the morning. I made a last-minute
decision and went below deck to grab the journal; I
stuffed it in my satchel as I grabbed what little coin I had
in my chest. I locked it up tight, making my way back up
deck. Soon enough, we were there. This town was much
larger than I expected. Where my own was a crescent,
this port covered the entire coast. Brick houses in varying colors of blues, tans, and reds were directly behind
the docks. Casper guided the ship perfectly to the port;
my father would have commended him. I laughed at the
sad thought of my father praising Casper when I strived
for years for the same thing, yet it was unattainable.

Before I would allow my mood to sour, I went to search
for Porter. It was no use when the plank was laid. The
crew was in a mad rush of bodies to get off the ship.
I found myself pushed and shoved till I made my way
down the dock, my head swiveling left and right, trying
to spot that mop of hair. Music traveled from beyond the
buildings—something one could dance to as the fiddle
played reverently, my foot tapping of its own accord to
the beat. There wasn't much music back home. I chuckled to myself at the thought of my father catching me
dancing. I could only imagine how wide my eyes were
as I tried to take everything in.

"Outta the way!" I was shoved as a sailor passed me with a flour sack on his shoulder. I grumbled back and was pushed to my left by another. "Get off the port if ye are goin' to stand there and stare."

I felt stern hands on my shoulders, guiding me out of the flow of sailors. Once out of the swarm, I felt like I could breathe again.

"Thank ye," I murmured, turning around to see who saved me. To my surprise, Casper stood in front of me.

"Ye may want to blend in, lad. You can see all over yer face how out of place you are." Casper's voice was rough.

I could not help the scowl that settled my features. "I can handle myself on my own."

"Oh please, ye looked like you were having a panic attack," he scoffed. "But next time, I won't help you."

"Good, I did not ask for your help," I stated, puffing my chest up a little, and turned away from him, heading toward the buildings.

"You are going the wrong way if you are heading toward the market." He called after me.

I stopped, turning on my heel to face him.

"It's this way." He jammed his thumb over his shoulder.

"Of course, it is. Why don't ye lead the way."

He chuckled lowly, which only helped to set my temper aflame. He had some nerve, acting like I needed his help with anything. I huffed and mumbled to myself as we walked over the cobblestone path. I admired the brickwork as we passed, brushing my fingers against its rough texture as we went. Casper led us down a path between two tall buildings that opened into the market.

"Try not to get lost or lose yer coin. Keep it close and haggle the prices. They expect it and ask too much for their wares." A few words of advice and Casper was gone, lost in a swarm of bodies.

I gulped, the lump of panic growing in my throat. The thought of being alone in unknown territory was utterly unnerving. I reviewed the list of things I needed, a rhythm of repetition to calm me.

Shirts. Trousers. Soap. Boots. Shirts. Trousers. Soap. Boots

I reached into my pocket, patting the few coins I had. Not enough for all of it. I clenched my fist around them, heading deeper into the market. The music was louder here. I saw the fiddler in the middle dancing around as he strummed his tune. We caught glances, and I smiled in his direction; he nodded slightly and continued his dance. The stands were set up around the middle in a circle, each a little wooden hut with glowing lanterns. I took one lazy lap around to see what each of them carried: fine leather-bound books, some bladesmiths, one blowing glass like I had never seen before. There was a fair share of cloth sellers, leather crafters, and soap makers to go around. I looked down at my boots, the leather sole peeling off enough to wiggle a toe out of the side. I sighed heavily; that would be most of my coin.

I approached an older woman, her auburn hair tied up in a neat bun, and streaks of gray hair fell loose around her face. Her little stand was cozy, lanterns propped all around, and she was huddled in the back against the cold breeze. I looked over her leather assortment: belts, wallets, pouches, boots, even a few...cuffs? My gaze lingered on those longer than the rest until I felt heat blossom on my face.

"See anything you like?" Her voice was scratchy from overuse. I nodded, grabbing a pair of boots that looked my size. "Go on, try them out."

She pointed toward a stool, and I plopped down, making haste to take mine off. I slipped the new ones on; they fit like a glove. Nice and warm, about shin height.

"How much for these?"

"Four doubloons," she quipped. "They are the finest leather in town."

"How about two doubloons?" I countered, raising a brow at her expectantly.

"Why don't you rob me while you're at it, eh? I will take three."

"Two, I won't go higher."

She appraised me, raking her eyes slowly up and down. I was almost sure she would deny my offer.

"You are lucky it is late in my day, and I feel generous. Two doubloons it is."

I smiled, holding back the ear-to-ear grin that wanted to come out. "Thank you, me lady." I tossed her the coin and left; my feet were thankful for the new leather. I managed to bargain with the seamstress for four tops and two pairs of trousers for my remaining two doubloons. All I had after that were a few copper pieces to my name. I looked longingly at the soap, the bars calling to me. The delightful scent of fresh florals, honey, and mint was heaven to my senses.

"You look worse fer wear, sailor." The young lady spoke behind her stall, her brown eyes twinkling.

"Aye, you can say that again. I apologize fer the stench." I looked down at myself, cheeks hot with embarrassment.

"No need, tis what I am 'ere fer." Her voice was bubbly, a welcomed change from how most were around here. "What scents do ye like?"

"They all smell wonderful, but I'm afraid I don't have enough for any of them." I frowned, counting the four coppers in my hand. She smiled knowingly at me.

"Your journey has been rough?" I nodded; she bent down behind her counter and rustled with something. "Ah, here ye are." She nudged me to open my hand and dropped a pile of soap ends into it. "It isn't much, but it is better than nothing."

"How much do I owe ye?" I fumbled with the coppers with the soap in my other hand. She held up her hand and shook her head.

"Don't bother. Ye need those more than I."

I smiled warmly. "You do not have to do that, but I thank and appreciate you."

She waved me off as I left, shoving the soap scraps in my pocket.

I spied Porter amongst the crowd; he was flirting with a young lady who seemed to still be in her teenage years.

"Lass, you are better off avoiding this one." I put on a beaming grin as I threw an arm around his shoulder.

Her bright green eyes shone with amusement as Porter shoved me away.

"Go find yer own mate," he groaned, and I ruffled his hair.

"What? Afraid she will choose me instead?" I teased back. He tried stifling his smile, but I saw the corner of his mouth tug. "I need yer help finding somewhere to wash this stench off, mate."

"Can't this wait?" He said, looking pointedly between me and the girl.

"Nah, I think you have had enough trouble brewing. Looks like she's found herself another anyway." I nodded. Porter turned to see she was off talking to a finely dressed gentleman.

"Damn you," he cursed me. "I was this close to some fun before ye showed up." He jutted his thumb and pointer finger in my face.

"The only thing you were close to be a room with the jailer, my friend," I muttered, guiding him away. He threw a string of curses bold enough to make a sailor blush at me under his breath. "So, where can I wash up?"

He glared at me and took a left, heading toward another row of buildings outside the market. "There be a bathhouse over this way."

I looked at him questioningly, brow raised. "A bathhouse?"

"Aye, with big Roman-style tubs." He nodded, and my eyebrows shot into my hairline.

"Group baths?" I squeaked, quickly coughing to cover it up, and deepened my voice again. "Are there private bathing chambers?"

He side-eyed me. "Yes, there be private rooms. Afraid of a big room full of men, eh?"

"I've seen enough naked men; I would rather not subject myself to more. That sounds like a cesspool of germs." I wrinkled my nose thinking about it.

"'Tis yer preference."

We made our way to a larger building than the rest along its row. The brick was painted a bold navy blue, chipping away from years of weather wear. *Cornelia's Bathhouse* in a fading gray was scrolled across the double-door entrance. Porter pulled the door open for me; I crossed the threshold and was immediately assaulted by air more humid than a pirate's swamp ass. Something I've grown uncomfortably familiar with over my time aboard. I swiped a hand across my brow as sweat started to bead.

"Welcome to Cornelia's! How can I be of assistance?"

"Aye lass, we need two bathing passes fer me friend and I," Porter stated softly, taking on his shy tendencies.

A smirk tugged the corner of my mouth. I was glad Porter felt comfortable enough around me to shed those. The bath keep nodded to us both and tossed two tokens on the counter.

"That'll be four doubloons." She smiled, crossing her arms over her chest, which was out proudly from her low-cut blouse.

"What be it with this town and four doubloons?" I muttered, looking at Porter apologetically. "I'm tapped, mate."

He sighed heavily, rubbing his forehead, and reached into his trouser pockets, tossing the coin on the desk and swiping up the tokens. I smiled broadly as he shoved one in my hand.

"Thank ye."

"To gain access to a room, whether private or one of the Roman rooms, you need to put the token into the token slot beside the door, and it will open. Toss your clothes in the bin, which will be laundered while you soak. Enjoy, gentlemen," she chimed sweetly.

I followed Porter to the back, where doors lined the hallway. "Here be the private rooms, yer majesty." He teased me.

I knocked my shoulder into his and slid my token into the slot. The door pulled open easily under my hand, and I sighed in relief. Soon, I could catch a whiff of myself without gagging. In the middle of the room sat a giant clawfoot tub. My eyes bulged; I had never seen one that big. The tub seemed to be drawn already, bubbles spilling over the top. I squealed, practically giddy, and quickly stripped out of my clothes, tossing them in the bin. The warm air caressed my bare skin. I was thankful the tiles seemed to be heated, and I giggled like a little girl. I pulled my hair out of my hair tie and sank into the tub.

The water scorched my skin for a moment, and I resisted the urge to get out until my skin adjusted and my muscles relaxed. A guttural moan left me. A little table to the side of the tub was filled with different soaps, washing rags, and little refreshments. I plucked through the soaps eagerly till I found one that smelled like sea mist and honeysuckle. I took my time scrubbing every inch of my body, enjoying how the silky lather slid across it. I scoured the kohl off my face and arms, enjoying the feel of being completely naked. I filled up my palm with an excessive amount of shampoo, lathering my locks as I massaged my scalp thoroughly. I washed the suds out, trading the shampoo for conditioner.

After a thorough scrub, I grabbed my towel to dry off my hands; I gripped the journal and sank more into the bubbles as I cracked it open.

July 8th, 1898

Lyra,

I cannot dissuade her any longer. She wants to join me out at sea. She begs me daily. I have grown weary. My only hope is to work her to the bone. Maybe she will finally drop this fascination. Our relationship has dwindled in the years since you've been gone. I know you would be saddened. My sweet Naida doesn't understand I am doing this to protect her. I am trying to save her from herself, Lyra. I will not fail her.

July 20th, 1898

Lyra,

You would be so proud. She has your determination and does her damnedest to prove me wrong. Every challenge I have thrown her way, she has taken on the chin. It wears on me constantly, tearing down her work. She is growing, but I fear the distance between us is unrepairable. Lyra, what can I do?

The tears streamed down my face, falling into the bubbles below. I had no idea. All this time, I swore he was ashamed of me. I could never compare to the pedestal he expected of me. I could feel the regret in his words, how I wish we could go back, go back and fix what we had broken. A sob escaped me as my shoulders shook.

I heard a soft clink, not registering what it was until the door opened and in strode Casper. I squeaked, and our eyes met. I tried to shield as much as I could with the bubbles.

"Get out!" I shouted at him, throwing the journal at the door.

"Sorry, sorry, I didn't know you were in here." He made haste, turning and leaving.

My heart was pounding erratically; I swore it would break through my chest.

Oh, my gods. Oh my GODS!

Did he see anything? Did he make out my bare face through the steam? Was my chest covered by the bubbles? I started heaving; it was all too much. Suddenly, the haze I was relishing a second ago was now choking me. It was hot, too hot. I scrambled out of the tub, grabbing my towel off the floor. I raked my fingers through my hair, ripping out some as I caught knots. My heart raged in my chest as I looked up at the door.

Fuck me! Fuck!

I spotted the golden latch across the room, where I had forgotten in my glee to lock the door.

Chapter 20

Lyra POV- Silently Watching

It is against our usual ways to travel from our group, but I couldn't help it. The thought of being without Naida was too painful to bear after the final loss of Dunstan. I would not lose my daughter, too. For that reason alone, I traveled away from my sisters, following her silently through the waters. I watched from below, only daring to breach the water at night when the crew was asleep.

I rose out of the water, gripping the sides of the ship. Through the portholes, I could make out her figure; however, it was more masculine than she used to look. A somber melody left my lips and an aching fear tugged at my heart—maybe because I was her mother and would always worry. Part of me thought her time was limited. It was the pirate way: easy disposal. I watched as her chest rose and fell with each breath. It was peaceful and managed to calm my worried heart.

My fingers ached to touch her cheek and brush the hair back from her face, even now as it was tucked away in her cap. Memories came back from when she was a babe, and I would sing her into slumber. Without thought, my lips parted and out came a low melody. It was not a song but a fluid motion of sound. Mermaids do not sing; only our other counterparts do, and that brings death. My tune was melancholy, one of loss and love, reunion...

Sometimes, I thought she saw me in the waters below. I had tried to be careful staying out of sight, but my feelings for her got the best of me. I wonder what she thought, how she was feeling. Did she miss me? Like I missed her...

The thought brought tears to my eyes, rolling down my face. I wish I could speak to her, but that would be dangerous. I was already in territory I needed to familiarize myself with; I had hoped to run into another group of mermaids by now, but they do not usually venture this far out in the sea.

"Oh, my young one," I whispered into the wind. "Why did you have to go?"

I felt vulnerable out here, alone, in the open. In the territory of the Sirens. They move as a pack like animals, hunting for their next meal. I prayed to Neptune that the waters remained calm and kept my young one safe. Food was scarce out here. With the energy I had been expelling and constant swimming, I would have to go out for food sooner or later.

A few days ago, I overheard the captain announce they were headed to the lost sea. There are rumors the land is cursed. I could only hope those are false, and maybe there is a group of sisters out that way. Then, I could hunt and regain my lost energy; we worked as a group always and fed off each other. Our strength weakens when we are alone, and I needed to remain strong to watch over my young one.

The sun started to crest over the horizon, and I sighed. Letting go of the ship, I returned to the waters below. I would repeat my routine once the moon rose to the highest point in the sky.

"Until then, my young one." My melody carried softly into the morning breeze.

Chapter 21

Lost Treasure

W e had been sailing for weeks. The crew was getting impatient, and it had been days since anyone had seen the captain. After he acquired the map, he holed away in his quarters during the day and mapped the stars at night. He ensured we had yet to see the map; not even Casper was trusted with it. There was no sign of land in sight, and I was starting to wonder if there actually was a lost sea to be found. Echoes of my father's voice carried in my mind, laughing at us all for believing in another so-called fairytale.

During the downtime, Casper picked up the training on board. His life would indeed be hell if any of my curses to his name stuck. Much to my dismay, he paired me with Braxon, the likes of whom I kept a solid distance from most of the time. We moved around each other, determining the opponents' next move. Braxon was slow, which helped; I had been getting better at fighting but was still no match for Casper.

"Ye going to avoid me all day er fight?" Braxon mocked as he took a wide swing at my head. I dodged just in time, feeling the wind sweep past my cheek.

"I was 'bout to ask the same. Seems yer body lags as much as yer brain."

I took a jab at his side, which he evaded, and I took the moment to sweep out his feet. He landed with an oof.

"Ay, what do ye mean by that?" He brushed off his arse as he regained his footing.

"Ah, knew you would catch up eventually." I grinned, and we continued our verbal and physical jabs until the sun grew warm on my shoulders. By the time we were done, I was dripping in sweat, my body sore from various assaults given oh so courteously by Braxon.

Meanwhile, I did my best to keep myself far away from Casper. After the bathhouse, I waited for the hammer to drop, but it never did. I was not bound to the mast or tied to the front of the ship. I counted my blessings for that. Whenever I did catch his eye, my cheeks blazed with eternal fire, and I was sure it was visible even through my kohl beard. I could not help but wonder if he genuinely had no ill intent or if maybe he saw nothing at all. I was abruptly drawn from my thoughts as I tried to catch my breath.

"Aye, Demi!" Porter greeted me with a clap on my shoulder. I flashed a beaming smile his way and chuckled.

"I was wonderin' where you were, mate.'' My response was cheery. "Thought you were gonna sleep till the tides changed." I tousled his mousey brown hair.

He scrunched his nose as he smoothed down his shaggy locks, then proceeded to yawn. My bellowing laughter carried over the sea breeze a little too loud.

"Keep talkin' like that. I outta feed ya to Marie." He followed his threat with an 'Ooooo' ghost noise, and we lost it again. The alleged ghost of the ship had become our little inside joke.

In my peripheral vision, I spotted Casper coming out of his quarters, my body stiffening.

"Let's get some grub, eh'," I said, steering Porter away with a guiding hand. He looked over his shoulder, noting who I was trying to avoid.

"Still stayin' clear of Casper, huh?" Porter replied with a smirk.

"Ye would too if he was constantly handing you yer arse. He paired me with Braxon today." I glowered, and he elbowed my side.

"'Tis all fun and games mate."

I hadn't dared speak a word of the bathhouse to anyone, let alone Porter. He was observant enough to pick up that something was amiss. Not that any crew went out of their way to be around Casper as it was. He was terrifying. The other day, he gave the old guy—I didn't care to learn his name—three lashes with the Cat-O-Nine tails for slacking on his duties. I grunted in response, and we headed to the dining hall below deck.

The eating quarters were long enough to hold at least forty people at a time, more than we currently had on board. Dimly lit with glass lanterns on the walls and two candelabras on each extended table. Little else decorated the space, but it was becoming my favorite part of the ship anyway. A smaller room adjoined to the right held the kitchen, where the cook was busy most of the day.

"What is the gruel you have for us today?" I asked the cook. He raised an unruly brow, his immense belly almost tearing the fabric of his shirt, which was heavily stained in lord knows what, a heavy scowl plastered across his face.

"It will be you if ye ever call me food gruel again." His voice rumbled. I audibly gulped in response and muttered an apology. He made a hmph noise. "We be havin' flyin' fish stew."

I thanked him, and he slapped the bowl in front of me, sloshing the stew over the side. Porter and I exchanged a sideways glance as we found a place to sit.

"Ye sure know how to piss off Bill, don't ye?" Porter scoffed, elbowing my side, which proceeded to slosh the stew again and burn my fingers. I sucked the side of my finger to relieve the burn, glowering at him. "You know he has tossed crew overboard for less than insulting his food. You should count yourself lucky."

Great, just my luck to piss off the guy who feeds me.

"Hopefully, he doesn't take to spittin' in it now," I grumbled.

As soon as we started chowing down, another crewman came stomping down the stairs so loud I thought he had fallen down them.

"Land Ho!" He bellowed, swiftly turning to dash back up the stairs.

We all stared silently for a few beats, and then a wave of jeering erupted. I pouted over my food that would now go forgotten as Porter yanked me to my feet. A wave of bodies swept over the hall and rushed up the stairs; it was almost comical how we bounced off each other. Everyone rushed to the ship's sides. Far in the distance, I could just make out the spot of land. Porter and I grinned and side-hugged each other. I fantasized about feeling the solid ground below my feet. The thought of sand squishing between my toes was enough to quicken the pace of my heart.

"What are ye doin', lads? Prepare the ship. Land Ho!" The captain boomed.

We all went our separate ways to ready the masts. My heart was beating fast like a hummingbird's wings as I grabbed hold of the ropes and tugged them into place, falling into the patterns my father had conditioned into my brain. My mind was going a thousand miles a minute at the thought of what we could find. Could this be the lost sea? This would go down in history if a soul ever found out about it. I recalled reading a tome years ago about the Lost City of Atlantis and thought about how it would feel to find such a thing lost to time. This was precisely how I imagined it would feel; hope dared to spark in my chest.

What if we actually find the treasure? God, I wish I could find some fresh coconuts, at least.

I shook my head to clear my thoughts, my mouth watering on its own accord. A pirate's life indeed; maybe it will all be worth it.

Chapter 22

The Lost Sea

The sun had risen to its highest point in the sky when our ship jerked to a stop. The anchors lowered to hold it in place. The rafts were lowered one by one as we clambered inside, dropping them into the steady waters below. I took my oars, and moving as a team, we began rowing to shore. The turquoise water begged me to dip my hands in it.

The journey to the bank took an eternity for the ball of energy in my chest. The shore seemed endless, even if it was only one hundred yards to the line of dense jungle. Vegetation was thick enough that I could not see through it beyond the border. I got my wish. I spotted palm trees ripe with coconuts. My mouth salivated, even as my feet ached for land and my arms tired from rowing. Tiered waterfalls were all I could see in the distance from higher elevations. There were no signs of human life or shipwrecks from what I could see in the raft. This meant we would have to slice our way into the jungle, and I groaned internally at the thought.

Our boat collided with a sandy bank, and we scrambled to pull it onto the shore. Once it was a comfortable distance from the tide, we dropped the sides and stared at the land before us. My sea legs wobbled against the sand as it gave way beneath my feet. Plumeria flowers were in full bloom, the vibrant orange-pink hues like the sun-kissed morning sky. Brilliant hibiscus dotted the tree line that hid the jungle beyond. I wanted to giggle and take off running; it took all my self-control not to. I was sure only my widened eyes told of my inner excitement, even as I burst at the seams and grinned like a madman.

"I can't believe it was real," Porter muttered in disbelief. I nodded in agreement and elbowed his ribs.

"Come on, I need your help gettin' some coconuts," I spoke low enough for only him to hear.

Following his lead, we scrambled over to the closest tree, and he climbed it like a damned spider monkey. It was eerie how agile he was, practically a blur as he shimmied up the thing. In less than five minutes, two coconuts fell to my feet. I sliced into one with my cutlass, tilting it into my mouth so I could taste the sweet water inside. My stomach gurgled angrily in response.

"I think my gut is pure rum by now, mate." I laughed as Porter dropped light-footed from the tree, grabbing the coconut I offered him.

The captain called for us to come to him, and we begrudgingly dropped our little treasures, dashing over to him as sand sprayed around us.

"Lads! Take all ye can carry and leave nothin' behind!"

We took off running in one wave at his order to the jungle line. The enthusiasm was short-lived as we spent hours cutting through the dense vines; it seemed neverending. My skin was littered with hundreds of red, itchy welts from insects. I tried not to stare at any one thing for too long, afraid I would see one of those eight-legged freaks of nature I was petrified of. A few times, too many, Porter saved me from the fangs of a snake I mistook for a vine. Unfortunately for the snake, that often resulted in a beheading. The birds' call was deafening; thousands had to call this island home. Croaking from the treefrogs married with the sound of their winged friends for an orchestra that made my head pound.

I started to doubt that there was anything of a treasure to be found. Mutterings of the crew around me told me they were thinking the same. My arms felt like jelly; every chop of my cutlass was laced with lightning coursing through my muscles. Who were we to believe we had found something lost for hundreds of years? Fools. We all were. The thought of turning back made my body ache down to my bones. The sun was about to set when the dense jungle broke into a clearing. It was utterly barren of anything but thick grass. We all stared in disbelief, looking at one another.

The captain pushed through us as the crew's voices grew louder and angrier. He started walking out into the clearing, muttering to himself too quietly for any of us to hear. Then, in the blink of an eye, he was gone, his shout of surprise carried across the clearing. We rushed over to where he disappeared, cautiously peering into the small hole he fell through. It was black. My stomach dropped, staring into the abyss. A flicker of flame came to life, then another spark, and another, until a steady flame held.

"What are you waiting for, lads? Get down here," Marduke bellowed from below.

Casper was the first to jump down, not hesitating for a moment. Before he jumped, he looked me square in the eyes, a glimpse of something shimmering in them before he disappeared. One by one, we jumped like obedient dogs—down into our possible doom. A five-foot drop caused butterflies to swoop in my gut and I tried not to cry out. As torches sprung to life, the canal around us glowed. We were in a tunnel of sorts, almost as if this was under sea level at one point. The stone walls were slick from erosion, and moss grew through cracks in the ceiling, dripping water from above. We followed Casper's lead, as the captain was already long gone. Our footsteps echoed around us. Eventually, the tunnel led to another opening, more significant than the one before. My stomach dropped at the sight before us, and a few shocked gasps sounded around me. There it was: a ship graveyard that would impress even Davy Jones. With the amount of wreckage in this clearing, hundreds, if not thousands, of lives had been lost. A haunting feeling crept along my skin, leaving me covered in goose pimples.

"We've made it, lads. Now make yourself useful and go pillage and plunder me booty!" The captain called from one of the ships ahead.

We searched the wreckage for the treasures she had held secret for all these years. Porter and I got separated in the mass of men running and yelling like children on Christmas day. I wove through the broken ships, going as far back as possible to avoid the others. I needed a moment of peace while I tried to contain all my emotions trying to break free. My eyes stung, threatening to set loose the flood. Flashes of my father's broken sign popped into my mind, and I tried to shove them into a dark recess to be locked away forever. That day still haunted me every single day. I stumbled over a broken cargo box, narrowly avoiding hitting my shins on a cannon, and came upon a ship almost as grand as the Black Pearl itself. Moving carefully around the side, I entered the massive vessel through a giant hole in its side, most likely caused by a cannonball. It smelled of mold and decay. Years in this damp environment had rotted the wood. This was a beautiful ship long ago, the inside layout wide open.

I admired the craftsmanship that went into this magnificent vessel, running my fingers along its walls littered with golden adornments and crown molding. If only my father could see this, he would go into one of his long-winded speeches about their history. What year it was made, the last voyage it had been on when it was lost to the sea. I hated those at one time; what I would give to just hear one more. Even if I did listen to it a hundred times, the way it would light up his face would be worth it. I glanced around; it seemed I was in what was once the dining hall; the plates and silverware were crafted of real silver. I itched to strip the room bare. The cutlery alone could have fed us through the harsh winter months. Goose pimples raised on my flesh as I rubbed my arm in memory of the times we barely scraped by. I never did find out how Father kept us alive through them.

If I were to find any real treasure, I needed to head up to the captain's quarters. I strode determinedly up the steps with caution as they moaned under my weight. The ship's main deck was littered with holes and missing boards, blackened with mold growth. I picked my way around, skirting the holes and putting pressure on the boards, avoiding those that bent too much under-foot. The last thing I needed was to fall through and break a leg.

The heavy wooden door to the captain's quarters was ajar. I gripped the handle, and the knob almost ripped out of the door in my hand. A flustered sigh left me. I grabbed the wood and pushed it open, the door creak-ing open slowly. This room dwarfed our entire sleeping chambers on our ship. Shabby crimson velvet curtains graced the window leading out the back of the ship. They once would have deemed this the greatest ship on the sea. A massive four-poster bed sat on one side with an ornate cast-iron headboard. Golden accents decorat-ed the room. The other side of the room was where the captain's big wooden desk was, and behind that sat the captain's skeleton. This was the first time I saw a dead body. My stomach lurched as I took in the dust-covered bones. His jaw hung open haphazardly. Suddenly, I felt much too hot and tugged at the collar of my blouse.

Do not throw up. Do not throw up.

My heart was going a thousand beats per minute; my vision was spinning.

"She's a beaut, isn't she?" Casper's voice made me jump as he materialized from the shadows.

A yelp escaped me, and I gripped my hands on my knees, trying to regain my breath. I felt his hand grab my shoulder as he tugged me up.

"Are you alright?"

I forced myself to look at him, hoping to the sea gods I wouldn't be sick as I saw double. His midnight ringlets were tussled around his face, catching in the light from the window. My cheeks betrayed me; I could feel them burning, my heart pounding a vicious rhythm in my chest.

"Ye scared me," I muttered disdainfully as I regained my breath. He laughed low, just once.

"And ye have been avoiding me," he responded, swiftly closing the remaining distance between us in a few strides.

I tried to rein myself in as glimpses of emotion passed in his eyes in a matter of seconds. My brows knitted in confusion. I tried to think of something to say as his eyes bore into mine. All I could think of was that damn moment in the bathhouse and the skeleton currently boring holes into my back. Casper's breath was hot on my face as he towered over me. I felt like nothing more than a mouse as he dwarfed me by more than a foot.

His lips pressed to mine before I could tell up from down or my brain could make any sense of the situation. I was so shocked I didn't move for a few beats. His lips pressed deep and needy, the passion flowing out between us. Then, my brain caught up to speed, and I jerked away, slapping his cheek violently. He did not flinch at all. He merely brought his hand to his cheek and rubbed it lightly, a grin tugging his lips. I glared at him.

"What are you doin'?" I shout-whispered hoarsely, trying to compose my entire being. My body was shaking with leftover panic and rage at the situation. Yet, my mind betrayed me; I did not understand why I desperately wanted his lips on mine again. "I thought ye liked women?"

I coughed, trying to deepen my voice again, even as it was stricken with shock. A slow smile spread across his face.

"Aye, but you be a woman." He stepped closer and removed my cap, pulling my hair from my tie.

My golden-brown locks fell around my shoulders in a heap, and I was completely frozen.

Chapter 23

Secrets

My blood ran cold, and my heart raced as quickly as the storm winds blew. I wanted to scream and cry, but all motor functions had abandoned me entirely in my state of fear. Ice ran through my veins, laced with fury. The realization of my imminent death numbed my body to its very core. How had I been so careless? Did any of the others know? One question alone rang through my mind.

"How did you know?" It escaped my lips as faint as a ghost's whisper.

My eyes flicked up to stare into his icy blue ones, the same ones that would lead me to my watery grave.

"I've been training with ye fer weeks. I don' know what wrappings you use, but there be no hiding your breasts up close and personal. Then, after our run-in that night a few weeks ago, I kept pondering what ye said and started watching ye more closely. I had suspicions but wasn't sure until I walked in on ye in the bathhouse," Casper responded, boring into my emerald eyes, even as they brimmed with tears. I gasped, wrapping an arm around my chest, and slapped him again. He grasped my hand in his, holding it tight against his face.

"What happens now?" My voice quivered, choking back tears as they threatened to flow freely. I was scared shit-less, and gods be damned, I was a rage crier as well.

He stepped closer, running his hand behind my neck to pull me closer, and his lips were on mine again. Fear kept me immobilized until the warmth of his hard-ened body pressed into mine melted me. My lips parted against his and moved on their own accord. I could feel my pulse thudding desperately in my throat. He tasted of rum and the sea. My fingers threaded through his locks; they were as soft as I had imagined, although they were currently greasy and unkempt. His hand was rough as it trailed down my neck to my shoulders, his callouses scraping along my skin. It was over as soon as it began. He released me from his grip, and the slap of the damp cavern air tussled my hair slightly. I ached for the contact of his lips on mine again. It made no sense; I should be fearing for my life. I knew what Casper could do on a good day, much less when my fate lay in his hands.

"As I said before, the pirates' life is lonely. The key has been right in front of me. Didn't know it held emeralds, though," Casper said softly. His breath brushed my cheeks as they betrayed me, turning red. I bristled at the comment.

"And you think you can just have me?" I questioned, a brow arched in warning. Why was I poking a dog with a stick? Who knows, but to just assume he could kiss me? The ice in my veins was being chased by the fire building within me.

"I can have whomever I want." I scoffed at his bold proclamation. "But I was hoping, in this case, you would want me too."

"So, you aren't going to tell anyone?"

I was afraid to vocalize that simple question that held my life on the line. What if I denied him? Would he tell everyone, then? Instead, he softly touched my cheek, running his thumb over my skin.

"It is our secret."

He granted me peace in those words, and hope ran through me again. I drew a deep breath as my shoulders sagged in relief; I hadn't realized I was holding my breath. I was not ready for my journey to end. It had only begun. Hell, this was my first godsdamned plunder!

"So, will you have me?" His vulnerability shocked me; all I could see in his gaze was sincerity.

Damnit, why do I believe him?

Maybe it was the desperate need for connection—for someone who knew the true me, someone I did not have to lie to, day in and day out. I knew the monster he held inside, yet I had always seen something more. When I would catch him alone at night strumming his guitar, singing softly to himself. The way he would irritate and tease me. Maybe I could get to know the man behind the mask.

"Yes." My answer left my lips before I realized I had agreed.

He kissed me once more. It was soft, almost a plea or a promise, which shocked me coming from a man like

Casper. I stepped back slightly to look over his features, seeing his scars up close just two shades darker than his skin tone. They went over his hands and up to his arms, some peeking out of the top of his shirt. One was rough and jagged; it looked like it went further down his chest—an almost fatal wound. His chin was sharp, black stubble covered his chiseled jawline; the depths of his eyes seemed endless. His golden earring glinted in the light. With his guard down, I could see some of his still-boyish features, which felt like I had found the lost city of Atlantis.

"We must be careful," Casper whispered, gripping my arm softly. "For your sake, we need to keep this a secret. No one can find out."

"Aye," I replied simply, swallowing the lump that threatened to choke me. Already, I yearned to know him, to read him as if he were the map to a great treasure. I had wanted to from day one, but now I fear that need would take root deep inside and never leave me.

Voices carried from beyond the door; they were getting closer, and we distanced ourselves. I tied my hair back and straightened my cap. We both rummaged on either side of the room, looking for items worth anything. I managed to get the captain's coin purse out from underneath his belt loop. I almost gagged again over the dusty skeleton and damn near jumped out of my skin when a spider crawled out of his eye socket. Casper moved a fallen beam that would have taken two men to carry, revealing a chest underneath. He was about to move it when Bran and Braxon barreled through the door. They both straightened when they saw Casper and side-eyed me.

"Just in time, lads, carry this out," Casper ordered, pointing to the chest. They both grumbled and glared at me.

"Why can't Demi take..." Braxon did not get to finish as Casper swept him up by the collar in his burly hand.

"I said yer takin' it, now go!" Even I recoiled a bit at Casper's tone; they did not say another word as they picked up the chest and left.

Once they were gone, Casper flashed me a half-smile, and we finished raiding the room before rejoining the crew.

Chapter 24

Booty

C asper helped me ensure everything was in order with my appearance before we rejoined the others. One last brief brush of our lips, and we grabbed our loot. It was bulky and heavy; my arms ached like I was carrying the buckets of water through town again. My pockets bulged from the coin stuffed in them. I felt guilty; I did not want to part with what I had found. I put in the work. Why should I share what I earned? Casper looked at me occasionally as we returned to the others, only to chuckle at my struggle. I glared at him, but it was half-hearted. It was not much longer till I heard the voices of the crew carrying loudly, bolstering the treasures they had found.

Once we came into sight of the crew, my eyes bulged at the small mountain of treasure heaped in the center of the crew. We dropped ours in the mound, my heart breaking as I emptied my pockets. There was enough gold and jewels to feed and house my entire village for years. I glanced up to find Porter staring at me oddly across the pile. I grinned and joined him, clasping my hand over his shoulder. He looked at me with one brow raised as I tousled his mop of hair; he swatted at me, mumbling his discontent.

"You seem in a good mood, friend," he squeaked, elbowing my side as he looked over at Casper. "You aren't avoiding him anymore?"

"We settled our differences. Good mood? How could I not be? Look at all the treasure we found!" I laughed and he smiled along, practically radiating beside me. The gold lust of a true pirate was evident in his eyes.

I was grateful he wasn't the most curious man I had encountered; it could prove hard to make up a story to appease him otherwise. I peered over my shoulder, spotting Bran and Braxon glaring at me intensely. I raised one brow in a challenge and turned my back to them in dismissal. My gaze caught Casper glancing between us, and I instinctively cracked my knuckles. A loud bang of a sword hit a stone, and everyone's attention turned to

Marduke. He stood on top of a large boulder, pointing the sword at the mountain of treasure.

"Lads! Ye have gathered quite a bit from your plunder. Tonight, we shall feast like kings!" His voice roared through the cavern, and we erupted with screams of joy, raising our swords in the air in celebration.

"Aye!" We cheered together. He raised his sword and pointed it at us.

"Now, take me booty to the ship!"

At his call, Casper raised his arm and pointed at the treasure before us in a motion to get a move on. We hustled over, loading up what we could carry, and started our trek back through the cavern. It became pretty evident no one thought about how we were getting out of the hole we fell through—or back to the blasted ship, for that matter. I groaned internally, dreading the journey back more and more. We gathered silently, looking at one another and then back at the gaping hole a few feet above us. Casper pushed his way to the front of the crowd.

"Porter!" He barked, and Porter came scrambling up to him after sending me a look of 'help me.' I bit my lip and shrugged in response.

"Yes, sir?" Porter squeaked, brushing the hair from his face. Casper clasped his hands together and bent down in front of Porter.

"Steady yourself on my shoulder, step into my palm and I'll hoist ye up," Casper instructed. Porter followed orders like a good little mutt.

Porter made it out of the hole in a wild monkey boy display, and I breathed a sigh of relief. I knew Porter. Strength was not one of his best qualities. How on earth would he hoist the treasure and the rest of the men up. Casper then turned and looked at me, to which I audibly gulped.

"Demi, ye be next," He motioned me to come over; he leaned down for me as I stepped up. "Easy goes it," he whispered to me.

I could feel his warmth through the thin cloth as my hand rested on his shoulder. My nerves were getting the best of me; I never did like being lifted. As he rose, I gripped Porter's extended hand; with all my upper arm strength, I pulled myself up once I could grasp the side of the hole. For once, I was glad for the water bucket training. Carrying those through the village was the only way I managed to pull myself up. We pulled the others up one by one, and the treasure followed suit. My arms burned with the fury of a woman scorned. Once the Captain was up, all that was left was Casper. I got on my belly and extended my hand to him; after giving me an 'are you kidding look,' he crouched and leaped up, grasping my forearm, his hand clasped firm. Grunting, I pulled him up to the ledge with all my might.

"Stronger than ye look, lad," Casper muttered into my ear.

"Aye," I chuckled at my response.

Chapter 25

Yo Ho, a Pirates' Life for Me

The sun was just breaking the horizon when we returned to the ship. Brilliant oranges and pinks bloomed across the sky like ink spilled in water. Exhaustion riddled my body from the treacherous journey; it reminded me of this constantly, greeting me with shooting pains following every step I took. Weariness settled in bone-deep, stifling most of the loot's giddiness.

My arms were so weary I feared I could not climb the rope ladder back onto the ship. If that were the case, the men could just tie the raft to the boat and drag me along, for all I cared. I finally breathed a sigh of relief once the last bit of treasure was on the ship. Porter looked at me, and we clasped shoulders in joyous and complete exhaustion. He was the only reason I could muster my remaining strength to hoist myself up the ladder. I hissed a curse at every rung as I jostled my body up and over the ship's side. I splayed out on the deck in a heap. Porter kicked my boot, hunched over as he tried to catch his breath, and he had the nerve to laugh at me.

"You aren't fairing much better, friend," I grumbled, wincing at the pain that shot through my leg.

"I don't look like a fish outta water." He smirked, reaching out a hand to pull me up. I accepted it begrudgingly and groaned as he hoisted me right-side up.

It took a few moments for everyone else to catch their breath before the bellow of jeers erupted. Porter and I were swept up in the rush of men to the dining quarters below. Tankards of rum sloshed their way down the tables, each of the crew grabbing one. The captain stomped three times to get everyone's attention.

"To us, lads! Drink and eat till ye bellies burst. Tonight, we dine like kings." His voice boomed in the enclosed space; the following roars were deafening.

The kitchen door slammed open, and soon, a few roasted pigs were presented on the tables, along with fresh fruits from the island. It looked like Bill was busy while we were scouring for the treasure. My mouth watered at the thought of fresh pineapple; it was a delicacy in my town, not something the traders brought in too often. When they did, it was too expensive for my father to buy. Honestly, I rarely ate anything besides fish; I was unsure if my stomach knew how to digest anything else. In front of me sat a pig. I could only admire its skin's glistening brown briefly before men ripped at the meat with their bare hands. I stabbed someone's hand with my fork to claim a chunk for myself.

You would think these men—myself included—had never seen fresh fruit and meat before with how we acted, devouring every morsel. Who could blame us? We had been out for over a day collecting the treasure. I sliced a chunk of pineapple with my dagger and bit into it without haste. The sweet juices ran down the sides of my face. It was good enough to cause my eyes to roll into the back of my head.

"Oh, yes." I practically moaned. Porter eyed me, and we both laughed.

"Aye, mate. Never had pineapple before, eh?" Porter laughed around a mouthful of pork. I raised my eyebrows in response, taking a swing of rum, and we clanked our tankards together.

Across the room, I spotted Casper looking at me, and I blushed suddenly, all too aware of the animal I was just behaving like. Promptly, I wiped my face and re-membered my drawn-on beard, which probably looked hellish after the island. I covered my chin in the crook of my elbow and started fake coughing to excuse myself from the dining hall. I hurried out and waved for Porter to stay and eat.

Once out, I quickly went to the sleeping chambers and over to my chest. I looked around to see if anyone fol-lowed me; I opened my chest and pulled out my kohl stick. We had one little mirror on the back wall that I used to draw on my beard while everyone was away.

I hastily stroked my face with the stick, fixing the smudges as I went. Heavy footsteps approached the sleeping quarters, and I shoved my kohl stick up my sleeve and spun on my heel to see who was coming into the chambers. The sound of the boots against the wooden floorboards grew louder as Casper appeared through the doorway. An audible sigh passed through my lips as my heart calmed its racing. He smiled as he approached me.

"Ye alright, Demi?" He asked softly as he brushed my face. "Ye left in a hurry."

I stepped away just enough to check my work in the mirror, nodding to him in the meantime.

"I be fine. Just had to fix something," I said, motioning to my face.

"Ah," he replied in a soft chuckle. "Ye were going at the pork like ya never seen it before."

Liquid fire spread through my cheeks. "Pork wasn't common in my village." Honestly, what was? Fish, grumpy sailors, a forgotten library, and overwhelming sadness.

"Aye... I was thinking you should come to my quarters tonight." Casper leaned in to whisper into my ear. The fire spread from my cheeks to my entire body. Well, he sure cut to the chase. If my mouth wasn't instantly dry, I would have spluttered, and that would have been a whole other show.

Ah, Davy Jones. A Kraken might as well swallow me whole.

The most I'd ever done with a boy was flirt. Father forbade me from having a boyfriend, much less knowing one intimately. Casper had been my first kiss, for Neptune's sake. Was that what Casper wanted? My head spun, my worry threatening to consume me. I knew down to my core this was a bad idea, but I would be careful and go only when everyone was asleep, even the mice. Panic gripped me in its icy clutches. I swallowed desperately, trying to moisten my mouth, which was bone dry. I was sure my heart was about to burst out of my chest at any moment; all I could do was nod in agreement. I was the master of my fate. He smiled as if I had just offered him our load of treasure and kissed my cheek.

"See ya tonight then...lass." It was but a whisper, but it set my heart racing faster than it ever had before.

As Casper left, I managed to make my feet move in the direction of my hammock and promptly flopped into it. I put my kohl stick back before my eyes fluttered closed, and I was swallowed in the intoxicating caress of darkness.

Chapter 26

The Witching Hour

I awoke with a start, fearing that I had slept through the night. Heavy snoring filled the room, and my bunkmate flopped over and farted loudly. I scrunched my nose in repulsion, batting his meaty hand away from my face as I tucked and rolled out. I cursed the stars that I was stuck below the crewmate nicknamed 'Flatus Jim Mattis.' His nightly routine made me nauseous in my sleep. A smirk pulled my lips as I recalled kicking him many of those nights. He thought Marie was out to get him. I hesitated momentarily, making sure no one stirred, and made my way silently through the sleeping chambers and up the stairs as quickly as a mouse. The moon was glowing bright; by the look of it, the witching hour was upon us.

I stood on the upper deck momentarily, relishing in the white glow shining on my skin. It did not do my complexion justice as my tan took on a sickly gray tone. My heart felt like it would pound right out of my chest and jump overboard. Maybe I should have listened to it and turned back—pretended I slept through the night by accident. It was perfectly believable. I briefly turned my gaze to the water, hoping it would calm my growing nerves as it always had. My throat constricted, and I worked to swallow the lump growing in it. A part of me hoped to see the flash of a tail below, but none were to be seen. I rubbed my palms on my trousers, cracking my knuckles, a nervous habit of mine.

Before I allowed myself to change my mind, I walked swiftly to Casper's quarters. My eyes kept darting around, looking toward the crow's nest to ensure I wasn't seen. I couldn't see the lookout; maybe it was just my luck. They had fallen asleep. Just in case, I slunk into the shadows, using them as cover. I stood in front of the door, still as the dead for at least five minutes, listening to my shallow breaths as I gulped nervously. The hair on my arm raised, gooseflesh littering my skin.

My fist paused, ready to knock. I begged internally for it to cooperate with me.

"You can do this," I muttered, shaking my arms and shuffling from one foot to the other. "Put your brave face on and just knock." I squeezed my eyes shut tight.

Two quick raps on the door took all the courage I could muster. All was silent for a few painstaking breaths as my heart almost stopped beating. Then, I heard shuffling around from the other side of the door. It opened under Casper's hand; he was ruffling his tangled, messy locks as he yawned broadly. He then seemed to notice it was me standing in front of the door and grabbed my wrist, quickly drawing me in.

He pulled me in with such urgency it caused me to misstep, almost sending me crashing to the floor. Unlike my feet, Casper's grip did not falter, and he pulled me into his chest. The warmth of him spread under my hand. His gaze caught me off guard as he bore into my own, almost reaching the very depths of my soul. Chills skittered down my spine, even as my chest brushed against his with every breath. A smile quirked his lips, revealing a dimple on his left cheek I had not noticed before.

"I was afraid you had forgotten, or changed your mind," he whispered. It was all he needed to do to make me blush; I'm sure he thought I had some strange skin condition by now.

"Well, here I am..." My heart was beating fast, blood rushing in my ears enough to make me dizzy.

I took in his room, wide-eyed; it was extravagant compared to our communal sleeping quarters. It sure paid to be the first mate. The amber glow from lanterns around the room cast the walls in a deep maroon color. He had a giant bed bolted to the floor to keep it from moving around at sea. Red curtains draped from the top posts. A heavy wooden desk sat on the opposite side of us, various maps sprawled about its surface.

"You sure don't want for much, do you," I murmured lowly as I looked around, spotting his guitar beside his bed.

His brows furrowed as he glanced behind me. "Aye, I pay my price for all this."

I grunted my response, not sure what to make of that.

His hand cupped my cheek as his thumb ran over my bottom lip. He tugged it down gently as he bit his own. I was nervous; there was no doubt about that. Fear threatened to drown me, even as I tried to force it down.

His brows pinched as he looked at me with concern, such a foreign emotion on his usually stone-cold face.

"Are ya ok, lass? You look green as seaweed," he questioned softly, rubbing my cheek in soothing circles with his thumb. It was rough against my skin.

I nodded, not wanting to speak for fear of my voice betraying me. He grabbed my hand, guiding me to his bed. The lantern's flames flickered, throwing dancing shadows across the panels behind it. Casper's room was decently decorated. I glanced around at the maroon walls; he had some paintings I couldn't see in the dim light. Piles of fur blankets on his four-poster, queen-sized bed made it look comfortable enough that I never wanted to part from it. I stroked my hand along the fur absentmindedly, my heart fluttering. I felt my palms getting clammy again. He gripped my waist in his firm hands, pulling me closer as he brushed his full lips against mine. The warmth was intoxicating, or maybe it was the leftover rum on his lips. Either way, I didn't want to pull away, even if my thoughts threatened to consume me.

"I will keep you safe," he murmured against my mouth.

My heart and body melted under his words and touch. I knew he couldn't make a promise like that, but I didn't care. It was nice to feel protected. Stable. It was a word I had not known since I left home, and a year had passed since then. My heart ached at the thought. The moments of all-consuming homesickness had long since ended, yet the tug on my heart for a home remained.

Casper's hands were rough against my skin, but mine were the same. However, his lips were soft as silk; I was not sure how he managed that with days under the sun. Mine were chapped; some days, so bad I could taste the iron on them. He continued kissing me, my lips parting with his feverishly. He gripped my waist roughly, pulling me to him as his tongue slipped between my lips. Rum ...and ecstasy. I swore my body exploded with his mere touch. I had never been touched like that, but I missed genuine human interaction, and my body craved it with every fiber of my being. I would have done it sooner if I knew simply kissing another human being could bring this much pleasure. Casper was sin, and I was ready to dive headfirst—my soul be damned.

We both longed to feel wanted, to have someone we could be fully open with. Or maybe that is what I hoped he longed for as well. Even with my friendship with Porter, I could not tell him who I was. It pained me every day to lie to my best friend. My only companion. Casper was the only one with that knowledge, and it formed a bond between us like no other simply because he held my life in his hands. I hoped he would let me see the so-called skeletons in his closet.

He was an expanse of sea I yearned to learn the depths of, wading myself slowly into the waters as our lips touched heatedly. I pushed my fears aside as his hands traced down to the small of my back, his muscles rippling and tense as I traced his bicep. I reeled at the feel of his flesh under my hand, his skin was so warm it was as if the sun shone within it. He reached up and took off my cap, letting my hair fall gently around my shoulders. A small smile played on his lips.

"I want to know you, Casper," I whispered. He looked up at me, his blue eyes crystal clear.

"Aye, ye will lass." He spoke softly in return as he leaned over and blew out the light.

Chapter 27

Risky Business

I groaned as the bright sunlight rested right over my eye, turning over and snuggling deeper under the blanket. A warm presence beside me...I bolted upright as the sleepy haze faded from my mind. It all came crashing back. I was still in Casper's quarters, in his bed.

Oh no, no, this is not good.

He groaned beside me, throwing an arm around my waist and pulling me against his body—his deliciously ripped body. It dawned on him then that I was still there, his eyes opening, a scowl on his face. Once he recognized me, the scowl softened, and a small smile graced his plump lips. He eyed me as I pulled the blanket around my chest, my cheeks reddening. I was all too aware I was as naked as the day I was born. The heat of his gaze had my body flaring within seconds; I rubbed my hand over my arm to distract me from the feeling.

"Morning." His voice was raspy with lingering sleep. My mind skipped what happened last night, and my blush deepened as I bit my lip. Reveling in the faint ache throughout my muscles.

"Good morning." I smiled at him, gazing into those glacial blue orbs, sighing as I ruffled my fingers through my knotty hair. "I hate to ruin the moment, but how will I get out of here?"

His smile vanished, his lips tightened, and his eyes looked serious. Already, I ached for the tenderness he showed me last night. The way he worked my body over, knowing all the places to touch. I suspected the rumors were true. It's no secret how Casper enjoyed a woman's body. A tug of jealousy ran through me, but I had no doubt they were not privy to the caring or passionate side he showed me last night. I only hoped I was up to par. My lack of knowledge was certainly demonstrated by my awkward movements.

I vaguely remembered slapping him by accident during one of his many position changes. He was the great unknown, and I had something those other women did not, I was a companion forbidden on the sea. I, however, had not meant to fall asleep again, yet I did not regret spending the night in an actual bed. The warmth from him and his many furs was an added benefit.

Casper got up from the bed, the blanket falling off him, and I bit my lip as my eyes met his perfectly rounded bottom. I averted my gaze quickly but couldn't help the urge to sneak another peek before he pulled on his trousers. The golden brown of his skin was absolute perfection, and that peach was begging me to take a bite. His gaze turned back to me, and my skin warmed over, being caught staring.

"Get dressed." His voice was calm, and I scurried quickly off the bed to the pile of my clothes.

I could feel his eyes on me as I got dressed, and my stomach was swarming with butterflies under his scrutiny. I pulled on my trousers and shirt as quickly as possible, slipping into my boots. There was a mirror on his wall, and I checked it to ensure my makeup was intact. My heart lurched as I looked at the smears, looking like soot on my face. I would have to sneak out of here and return to the sleeping chambers without anyone seeing me. I took a mental note to bring my kohl stick next time.

Will there be a next time?

My heart fluttered in my chest thinking about it. I hoped there would be a next time, even though I knew it was dangerous. There was so much more I wanted to discover about Casper. I caught myself staring at him, drinking in the way the sun made the golden tones of his skin stand out in the light. His dark hair, a mop of black curls on top of his head from not being brushed through. My fingers twitched, wanting to brush it out of his face. He peeked out from behind the curtain covering his window, looking at the deck. The light glinting off his sharp jawline made me inhale quickly as my heart sped up.

"I will go out first. Watch for my signal to follow." He glanced my way, motioning me over before he opened the door; I grabbed his hand, pulling him toward me. Our lips touched briefly, and it set my heart a blaze.

He pushed me behind him out of view and stepped through the door. I watched him through the window, my heart beating rapidly as I cracked my knuckles, my nervous habit getting the best of me. He looked around the deck and gave a quick "ok" symbol behind his back. I drew in a shaky breath, quickly rushing out the door.

Darting past him, I made my way below deck to the sleeping quarters, keeping my head down the whole time. Thankfully, it sounded like most of the crew were in the dining hall for breakfast.

I made my way to my chest, opened it quickly, and looking for the stick, I made hasty markings on my face in the mirror, fixing the smudges as I went. Soon, I could feel my heart unclench as my makeup was in place. I redid my eyebrows, thickening them as well as my arm hair. The kohl felt sticky on my skin from the buildup. Honestly, I could not wait for the next chance of a shower to wash off all the grime. Maybe I could track down a bowl of water and some of my soap scraps for a pirate bath. I thought I was going nose blind to the smell until a gust of wind gave me a good whiff of myself. My nose wrinkled as I recalled sending a silent thank you that Casper had not noted it last night. I made my way quietly to the dining hall.

I threw Bill a quick smile as I made my way to grab some food. He returned my smile with a grunt and slapped my tray in front of me.

Okay, noted he holds a grudge.

I grabbed my tray, eyeing it wearily; it looked like some type of fish filets, surprise, surprise. Looking around, I spotted Porter and shuffled my way through the tables of grumbling sailors over to him. Sighing as I sat down, I smiled at him as he raised his eyebrow at me in question.

"I was wonderin' where you've been, mate," he said over a mouth full of food. "You weren't in the hammock all night or this mornin'."

"Aye, got up in the middle of the night. Couldn't sleep. Ended up passin' out with the goats below deck," I muttered, shoving a forkful of fish in my gullet. He looked at me with speculation written all over his face. I frowned, drawing my attention back to my food.

"Have you been havin' troubles?" He inquired, playing with his food. I let out a forced yawn.

"Off n on, mate," I responded, glancing up. My eyes caught Casper walking into the hall, and a smile tugged my lips before I squashed it. "I think it's just a bit of homesickness." It was honest, at least; I did miss home. I missed her.

Porter glanced at me, licking his fingers. "Aye, mate. It gets us all."

We finished eating with idle chatter and went about our chores on deck. The sun was bright, not a cloud in the sky. Sweat beaded my brow within minutes of getting to work. I yanked my cap to shield my face from the brunt of its force. The captain was nowhere in sight, no doubt fondling his newfound booty. Envy rolled through me like a green viper, ready to strike at the thought. Hopefully, we would see a portion of our bounty at some point. Porter had promised me we would get our fair cut and not to worry about it. I fought against the saying that burned into my mind since childhood. Never trust a pirate.

"Sail Ho! Sail Ho!"

The call came from the crows-nest and, with it, a feeling of dread. Everyone clambered onto the main deck, peering into the distance. There was indistinct murmuring from the crew as we awaited orders. I saw Casper pushing his way through.

"Make way, lads!" He called, grabbing his spyglass from his hip. "Sails are black mates, afraid we are in for a chase. All hands on deck and ready for anythin'."

We took up positions around the deck. When I joined, I was given a cutlass and never had a chance to use it. My body thrummed with adrenaline and anxiety. I searched the crowd for Porter as I went below deck. I'd never had to use the damn thing, so I never kept it on me. Pushing through the chaos of bodies, I reached the sleeping quarters, digging into my pocket for my key. The chest banged open as I fumbled with it, reaching in a panic for my cutlass. The scabbard holder fell out of my clammy fingers.

"Fer fuck's sake! Pull it together, mate," I muttered to myself, bent down to get the sheath. I secured it roughly around my belt and thrust my cutlass into it. No one was left in here to witness the ordeal—thank any of the gods, at this point.

My heart thundered in my chest as I made it to Top Deck again, peering around for Porter. I couldn't spot his mousy head anywhere, and godsdamnit, I needed some reassurance. By the time I regained my position, the ship was within eyesight. Indeed, another pirate ship and a large one at that; she had speed that our own didn't have. They must have followed us from the lost sea; we hadn't seen any ships since we left port. I didn't see any other explanation. I yelped as a firm hand grasped my upper arm, tugging me away; I looked up, startled to see Casper's grim face.

"Ready yerself. This is going to be a fight."

I yanked myself from him, "How can ye be so certain? Maybe they need assistance."

"Assistance?" Casper chuckled darkly. " Surely, you aren't that wet behind the ears. With their jolly rogers up and the speed, they be lookin' fer one thing. Loot."

I once again glanced around for Porter, gulping down the rush of fear.

"We don't back down. *The Shadow* does not lose ye hear me?" Casper lowered his voice, speaking into my ear. "Stay with me. I will keep ye safe."

There it was again—safe—and somehow I believe him.

The ship gained on us within twenty minutes, the mid-day sun beaming down our backs. I gripped my cutlass as if my life depended on it. Let us hope the months of training would aid me today. Marduke made his way on deck and bellowed to the other ship.

"Best turn yer ship around. Nothin' ere fer ye!"

Laughter could be heard from the other ship amongst the shouts.

"Run a shot across the bow, lads!" Casper shouted.

I braced myself as a warning canon was shot off, the ball blowing through the railing, sending the crew shouting. The next moments were chaos; the ship hit us broadside, and pirates swung over to us by ropes, cutlasses at the ready. I hardly had time to register what was happening, feeling my heartbeat in my throat when a sword was being swung at my head. I dodged, raising my own; the sound of metal hitting metal set my nerves on end. My footing was sloppy, keeping me, unfortunately, on the defense. I tried using my body weight to throw them off, but he was pure, stocky muscle. I yelled and swiped my sword at the back of his knees; he landed hard, crumpling to the deck. I tried looking for Casper but couldn't spot him amongst the bodies. It looked more like a tavern brawl on deck; it was hard to tell who was on who's side. Shots were being fired from the other ship, drowning out the shouting.

Panic threatened to take hold of me if I didn't do something. I kicked out another pirate's knee and swung my cutlass, gliding the blade across his throat. A spray of blood coated my shirt. The air hung heavy with iron already. I was about to dash to another when my legs were kicked out, and I went sprawling to the deck, busting my chin in the process. Readying my sword, I shoved myself up to see Bran above me. Did he seriously fucking trip me?

"Ye Bilge-Sucking asshole. Now is nigh the time for yer bullshit," I yelled, spitting blood on the deck and elbowing him in the face.

I pushed my way further in the crowd, trying to catch sight of Casper and losing Bran in the process. I took an elbow to the nose and dodged a swipe to my side, raising my cutlass in time to ward off another sword aimed at my shoulder. A strong hand landed on my shoulder, and I reeled my elbow back, connecting with flesh. There was a loud grunt as I turned to see my attacker, Casper, before me. I felt pale; I just hit the first mate.

"I would be pissed if I weren't impressed. Nice shot, lad." Casper nodded to me, a smirk lifting the corner of his mouth, "Stay to me back."

I nodded, and we continued our fight, metal clashing ringing through my ears. It set off my equilibrium, and I stumbled as someone kicked my knee, sending me to the deck. I raised my cutlass and stabbed them in the thigh with a dagger I found on deck, launching myself up to strike at them with my cutlass in a follow-through. The way Casper moved behind me was a dance, his blade singing off the others. I chanced a look at him; he was magnetic in how he twisted and sliced. I paid for that mistake as I took an elbow to the cheek, feeling a slice across my side. White hot pain spread through me as I yelled in pain. I slipped in something, my knees crashing to the deck, the vibration running up my legs. A shadow approached, and I knew I didn't have time to deflect the oncoming blow. I sent a quick prayer up—or down, I should have said—to Neptune below.

Before metal could meet my neck, it was met with a cutlass; I looked up to see Casper hovering over me. He moved so fast the blade flew out of the opponent's hand, and Casper caught it mid-air, slicing his way down their torso as he went. I was awed as the sun haloed him, and he appeared as if he was a god before me.

"Get up, lad! Ye need to move." He hauled me to my feet with one swift jerk of my elbow. "Get back into position."

I yelped, and his gaze flickered to my side. He cursed, seeing the blood quickly soaking my tunic. He looked around, surveying his options.

"There be too many of them. We have to fight, Demi. Fight. With all ye got."

We fought. I gave it everything I had til my sight grew fuzzy, and I saw double. Casper was half holding me up as he continued cutting down pirates.

Why couldn't they have men like this in my village?

I lost time as my sight darkened; faintly, I heard cheers. The other crew abandoned the ship as they grew out-numbered.

"We did it," Casper whispered in my ear as I finally gave in to the blackness.

I woke up a day later in the med bay, shooting up in a panic and almost passing out as pain seared down my side. Everything hurt, and my mouth tasted like I was sucking on coppers. A gentle hand gripped my shoulder.

"At ease, lad."

I glanced over to see Casper in a chair in the corner.

"What are ye doing here?" I hissed under my breath.

He snorts, "So much, thanks fer saving yer life." He leaned closer. "Don't worry, I was just checking on ye. I saw to yer stitches meself, so no one saw anything."

His breath tickled the shell of my ear. A warmth spread through my chest.

"Do ye happen to have any rum?" I coughed as I strained to sit up, moving the pillow behind my back. A grin spread over his face as he handed me a skin. "Thank Neptune," I praised, raising my eyes to the ceiling as I took a swig. The rum burned going down in the best way, reminding me I was still breathing. I was alive, and I owed that to Casper.

Another day of rest was all I was granted, and then I was ordered back to swabbing duty. As ol' Crusty stated, "if I can swab with one leg, ye can swab with two." Crusty was now his nickname. I cursed him to Davey Jones' locker with every pull of a stitch.

I found myself sneaking peeks at Casper throughout the day, blocking out the pain by relishing the phantom feelings of his lips running down my body. The stiffness running through my body was stretching uncomfortably as I mopped. Recovery was going slower than I hoped. But at least I survived my first ship attack. I counted myself lucky; Porter told me how many pirates he tossed to the sharks. As for the other night with Casper...did I regret any of it? Not a single moment. There were moments of pain and moments of pleasure that took my breath away. My cheeks grew warm, and a smile played on my lips as I continued mopping, the repetitive thwack of the mop slapping the deck filled my ears.

A shadow loomed over me, and I looked up just in time to see Braxon kick my bucket over, sending water all over the deck. He towered over me in an intimidating stance with a smirk. I noticed he didn't look as worse for wear as I did.

"Oops, didn't see ya there." His voice boomed as he shoulder-checked me with enough force to send me tumbling. Falling directly into the freshly spilled water, I could feel it seeping through my trousers. Sharp pain laced up the side of me as my stitches pulled.

Fury raced through my veins in a roaring rage, my fists clenched at my sides tight enough I could feel the blood pulsing through them. Braxon's low laugh rang through my ears as I picked myself up. Bran right by his side, as always.

"What in fuck's sake was that for?" I was boiling mad, spittle leaving my lips as I spoke.

"Aye mate, Casper's pet speaks for himself after all."
Bran elbowed Braxon's side laughing. I stormed over to
Bran, shoving him back, getting up close and personal
in his face. All pain was forgotten in that moment.

"I'm nobody's pet, mate," I growled lowly as I swung at
his jaw.

A satisfying crunch sounded as my fist connected, sending him reeling back. The satisfaction was short-lived
as I saw Braxon striding toward me angrily. I gulped as
panic shot through my system, only slightly suppressed
by the adrenaline racing through my veins. Braxon towered over me by a good foot and a half, but I puffed my
chest, standing my ground. I saw his right hook coming
and dodged it, but I missed the uppercut to follow, led
by enough force to snap my head back, sending me
flying.

Stars dotted my vision briefly as I fought the wave of
dizziness, stumbling as I got back to my feet. Bran had
regained his composure, and both men were stalking
over to me. I gulped loudly, waiting for the end. Panic
rushed over me again, and the adrenaline seemingly
fled my system. They would pummel me to a bloody
pulp and toss me overboard for the sharks. Father may
never have taught me to fight, but he certainly taught
me not to cower.

How was I going to get them both?

Just as I regained my footing, a blip of a shadow crossed my vision, and Braxon flew back, landing hard, and smashing through some cargo boxes. I looked over to see Casper, the most terrifying I had ever seen him. My blood ran cold as I took in the rage that twisted his features into that of a monster. Now I knew why they called him the *Ghost of the Sea*.

Chapter 28

Brawl

I was terrified and completely turned on by the fuming ball of a man beside me, flashing back to the fight only a few days ago when we worked together. Adrenaline was back, coursing through my veins. Casper stalked over to Bran, but I put a hand on his chest; he faltered, looking at me as fury flashed in his eyes.

"He is mine," I growled, nodding to him with a slight smirk.

I cracked my knuckles and got into a fighting stance as I faced Bran, wincing as I crouched. Braxon was already back on his feet, though I couldn't help but notice the slight sway as he steadied himself. Bran lunged a quick jab in my direction; luckily, I dodged it faster, following with a right hook. He licked his teeth, spitting blood out on the deck, fury glinting dangerously in his eyes. His foot collided with my shin, causing me to bend, and at the same time, his fist came up in a nasty uppercut. Again, I felt myself reeling; it was not as powerful as Braxon's, but I still saw stars.

Holy Neptune, these guys know how to throw a punch.

"Nah, much o' a fighter, even with the training, huh?" He muttered through a bloody grin. I steadied myself and flashed one right back.

"Ye call this a fight?" I scoffed.

His smile turned tight, and he took another jab at me; I didn't move as fast, and he caught my shoulder. I leaned into him, striking him in the kidney, and he buckled, groaning. I took a moment to look at Casper, who had just thrown Braxon against the mast. The taste of iron filled my mouth, and I spit out the blood as Bran had earlier. My body was alive with the need to continue fighting; I may not have been good, but gods be damned if I wasn't going to give it one hell of a go. They had awakened a thirst in me I wanted to quench. I jumped out of my skin as Casper placed a sturdy hand on my shoulder.

"Let's go," he murmured low into my ear.

I gazed at Bran and Braxon, who had not moved to get up again. Deciding against my need to pummel Bran's face into something unrecognizable, I let Casper guide me away. The pain started setting in once more as the adrenaline left me, and I leaned my weight onto Casper. He led us back to his chambers to clean up. Once we were inside, I let out a ragged breath, groaning as I touched my jaw gently. His jaw flexed as he looked at me, his eyes almost white with rage. "Sit."

Under his intense gaze, I sat immediately on his bed, leaning into the soft fur blankets beneath me. He grabbed some things, turning to me with a bowl in his hand, sloshing as he approached me. A hiss rushed through my lips as he touched a rag to my jaw, cleaning the blood off my lip with a gentleness that shocked me. He lightly swiped at my face, rubbing the rag over it, and my fingers gripped his wrist.

"What are you doing?" I whispered harshly, "My beard..." He silenced me with a kiss that sent pain racing through my lip.

"Aye, I want to see your face," he responded, bringing his hand up to cradle the back of my neck. "You will stay here. Out of sight."

I opened my mouth to protest; staying would be too risky. Why would he put himself on the line for a lowly crewman? I was sure someone had to have seen us and were now thinking that exact question.

"Why didn't you just take me to the med bay? I'm sure they can handle a busted lip. After all, I just left the fucking place," I muttered, fisting the blankets.

"I shall not hear another word. You will be stayin' here." He looked at me, his eyes hard, still colored so lightly he looked as if he had no irises at all.

I gulped nervously and nodded, not wanting to speak. He resumed cleaning my wounds and rubbing an ointment on the cuts. I tried to be still as the cream stung my open wounds. Once he was finished, he tugged my shirt over my head.

"What are you doin'?" I asked, my voice coming out tight from the pain.

"You took a good blow to yer shoulder." His jaw flexed as he looked at my bare skin. Even though my breasts were wrapped, my hands covered them instinctively.

I tracked his flaring glaze down, spotting the deep purple that had bloomed over my shoulder. It looked worse against my pale skin, the parts of me that were not touched by days under the sun. A hiss escaped my lips as my eyes widened in surprise. He prodded my stitches with gentle fingers, making sure none had torn and nodded to himself once he was sure.

"Son of a pirate," I muttered angrily at the mark, bringing my fingertips to prod it gently. Casper smirked at me; it was so unexpected after seeing his rage. The tilt in his lips caused my heart to flutter.

"You always find ways to surprise me." He lifted his hand to brush the hair falling from my cap behind my ear. "One hell of a swing you got, too. Bout time, after all my work."

A sharp snort-laugh escaped me, and my cheeks turned fiery red. "Only because they talk more than work most of the days. Caught them off guard."

He side-eyed me, his lips lifting slightly at the corners, and he gently kissed my swollen cheek.

"If they touch you again, they will swim with the fish." His tone was serious as it could be, but a smile crept on my lips.

"You know better than to show favoritism," I scolded him as he raised a brow.

"I'm the first mate, I can do what I damn well please as long as I follow Marduke's command."

I liked this; I enjoyed being taken care of for once in my life. It was a relief not having to fend for myself for a moment. The simple act of him stepping in and helping me in that fight made butterflies swarm in my stomach, and my heart squeezed in my chest. His hand wrapped around my waist, pulling me over to him gently. I tried to snuggle into his side, feeling his warmth spread over me, wincing slightly as my shoulder throbbed. He chuckled softly; I felt him shift beside me.

"I cannot lie. It was hot watchin' ye fight." His lips were pressed against the shell of my ear. My cheeks blazed again as he stroked my cheek, slowly running his hand down my neck and back.

"I had to. They called me your pet," I spit, my eyes darkening at the word pet. He cupped my cheek in his hand, bringing my face to meet him.

"They won't be makin' that mistake again," he murmured. "You look like hell. Why don't you sleep fer a while? Get your rest, and I will be back. I'll make Bill cook a fresh batch of biscuits."

I scoffed at his remark, but I couldn't help the lack of energy that was catching up to me.

"He doesn't like me," I murmured.

Casper's eyes danced with amusement, then flicked behind me, his brows drawing together. I glanced back, seeing what caught his eye. There was blood higher up on the sheet where I was sleeping a few nights before.

"Is that from your wounds? I thought I cleaned it all before you got on the bed."

I felt my face come alive as his gaze flicked back to me. He searched my face, and his jaw slackened as he found his answer.

"Was I your first?" His voice was but a whisper.

I worried my lip, "Casper, I..." I looked into his eyes, seeing the emotions flicker through them. "I should have told you."

He shook his head slowly, grabbing my hand. He turned it over and bent, kissing the tender skin of my wrist. "I hope I did not hurt you."

I saw the vulnerability that crossed over his features and wanted to squeeze him tight. Who would have thought he would have been worried about a virgin's opinions?

I mulled it over briefly, thinking over that night, and answered him honestly. I tabled my insecurity at that moment.

"It was everything I could have wanted."

He smiled at me, honestly, and it took my breath away. The look that fell over his face, like I just told him the sun would never set again and all he wished for would be his. I had not seen a smile like that since before my mother had gotten sick. A well of emotions caught in my throat. He leaned down, gently kissing me. Once his lips met my own, butterflies sprung to life in my stomach. His eyes softened as he gazed into mine. He released me from his hold, and I scooched up the bed as carefully as possible. He tugged the blankets up around me and kissed my forehead before he parted. It was not long before my eyes were too heavy to keep open, and I was lulled into a deep sleep.

Chapter 29

Lashings

There was no denying the throbbing, sending piercing pain through me as I tried to adjust to the comforter that entangled me. I groaned, wincing as I tried to detangle myself, the after-effects of the fight in full swing. Everything was too hot. I needed to unbury myself from the mound of blankets. It was suffocating; I hated being bound.

My entire body was stiff, and my shoulder hurt more than I cared to admit, along with a searing pain in my jaw as I moved it around. Touching my fingertips gently to the area, a hiss of agony escaped me. I searched the room, slightly disappointed to find Casper had yet to return while I slept. Then, internally, I rolled my eyes at the ache in my chest over his absence.

The sun still glimmered in from behind the thick curtains; I sighed as I carefully eased my legs over the side of the bed. I had only been asleep for a few hours. I'm sure Casper had other duties besides staying with me.

So much for being wholly independent, Naida.

My body groaned in protest as I tried to stand, my muscles straining against their stiffness. The bowl of water still sat on his nightstand beside the bed, the liquid a pale pink from him tending my wounds; I grabbed it as I walked gingerly over to the mirror to see what damage was done. I inhaled a sharp gasp as I took in my image. He had removed all my makeup; my jaw was lined with deep purple bruises from the blows Bran and Braxon had dealt. My fingers flew to my jaw, touching it lightly.

"Son of a pirate," I hissed as I prodded the purple skin. My eyes flicked down to my shoulder, my skin tinted with varying shades of purple and green surrounding the deep purple center. I grimaced at the sight of it and rolled my shoulder slowly, trying to ease the rigor in my muscles.

They would pay for this.

A loud crack followed by a cry of anguish and jeering startled me from staring at my reflection. I moved as swiftly as my body would allow me to the window, peeping carefully behind the curtain. The sight before me was even more shocking than my reflection had been. Braxon and Bran were tied to the mast, shirtless, and their chests pressed firmly to the pole. A Cat O' Nine Tails dangled lazily at Casper's side, thick liquid dripping from its ends.

Blood.

My brain registered the thick red droplets, just as he brought it up again, a flash of the whip was all I saw as another blow landed across Bran's back. My stomach turned at the sight of his flesh turning to ribbons, blood seeping from the open wounds in rivers cascading down his flesh. Casper lashed the whip again, sending the tails across Braxon's back. His wails of pain were followed by jeers from the bloodthirsty group surrounding them. The look on Casper's face was bone-chilling, his eyes betraying how much he enjoyed this, if not more, than the pirates surrounding the scene.

Both men were slumped against the mast. The rise and fall of their chests were rapid. I licked my lips, unconsciously tasting the salt of tears I had unknowingly shed. Yes, I wanted them both to suffer for making life a living hell on this ship, but not like this. My stomach churned painfully as another blow landed across their backs; I stumbled over to the trashcan by the bed just in time to empty the contents of my gut in full. My breaths were ragged as I brought a quivering hand to my face, wiping the remaining bile from my lips.

The look on Casper's face haunted me just as much as the sight of flesh being flayed in front of me. My stomach gurgled again, but there was nothing more to upchuck. Porter was never shy in telling me how fearsome Casper was, but now I saw it firsthand. I could hear Casper's voice faintly through the door and pulled myself over to listen as I wiped away the remaining tears.

"Let this be a lesson to ye. Those who disobey will be lashed. Heed this warning, it will be the last." His voice boomed over the silent group. The shirt he wore was coated in sprays of blood. "We are all stuck on this blasted ship. We need ta work together. Anyone who feels different is free to walk the plank."

The remaining crowd was still silent as the grave. A few solemn "Ayes" were uttered in response.

"Now get back to work!" He boomed, and the crowd scattered like a startled flock of birds. He took out his cutlass, chopping the ropes that held them to the mast in one swift movement. If I would have blinked, I would have missed it. They slumped with heavy thuds to the deck. "I need two of ye to carry these arseholes to the infirmary."

Obediently, two men came over and grabbed Bran and Braxon, carrying them off to the medical room. Casper ran a hand ruggedly through his hair as he walked toward me. I gulped, my heart pounding erratically in my chest; I could feel the beats pulsing in my throat. My hands grew clammy as the panic rose; I didn't want him to know I was watching, but I couldn't hide the terror growing by the second either. I sat on the edge of the bed just as he walked through the door.

He grimaced as soon as it closed behind him. I could see the tension rolling through his body. The bitter scent of copper slapped me in the face. There was a thick spray that coated his shirt, as well as the open skin on his chest. Reddish-brown speckled over his face. Another wave of nausea coursed through me as I took in his appearance. Finally, his icy blue eyes landed on me briefly, and he froze.

"How much did you see?" His usually loud voice was but a whisper. I looked down at my hands as I cracked my knuckles.

"I saw enough." My voice was like a ghost; I was surprised he heard me. I usually made myself scarce during lashings, not caring for the bloodshed. Sometimes, I forgot this was his job.

"Don't think of me any less. I cannot have you thinking I'm nothing but a monster too." His voice was still low, but his gaze threw a thousand emotions my way. I gulped slowly, feeling like my throat was swelling, barely allowing air to pass through. My voice failed me; I could only shake my head slowly, feeling tears springing back into my eyes.

He removed himself from the door, heading toward the bowl of water. I observed him as he removed his shirt and cleaned the blood off him, the water turning a deep red. He was beautiful and terrifying, and I had an inner battle trying to decide how to view him. Once he dried himself with a towel, he sauntered over to me and knelt on the floor between my legs.

"Are you scared of me?" His voice was rough with emotion. I fought the urge to flinch as his hands rested on the tops of my thighs. I looked into his eyes and saw the waves of emotions flashing through them. I was not afraid of what he had done; it was the look on his face while he did it.

"No." My voice was soft although hoarse with my turmoil. I had gotten to know another side of him, the softer side he kept just for me. I couldn't just brush that off like it hadn't happened. His grip tightened on my thighs; I heard his sigh of relief.

My gaze met his again; I didn't think it was possible to be more bowled over after the lashings. The *Ghost of the Sea*, the most feared man of the seven seas. His cheeks were red and stained with tear tracks.

He knelt before me, crying.

Chapter 30

Naida

My jaw slackened with disbelief; I had never once witnessed a man cry besides my father when Mom died. Never in my wildest dreams had I thought I would see the most feared man on the seas cry. He still knelt between my legs, his shoulders slightly heaving from his silent sobs. I was frozen, unaware of what I should do; my heart lurched as I carefully wrapped my arms around him. He let me pull him into my torso and wrapped his burly arms around my waist, being careful of my stitches. The only sound was his erratic breathing and my heartbeat pounding dully in my ears.

"You will be ok." My voice was soothing. I tried to mimic what my mother had done for me. Flashes of the morning after the storm bombarded me, threatening to drown me in that sorrow all over again. I recalled how my mother held me for hours, letting me sob into her embrace. I would do the same for him.

His grip tightened around my waist slightly, and we continued like that for at least ten minutes while I tried to soothe him. Finally, he released his hold, rising to his feet slowly and clearing his throat. I looked up at him, worry plastered all over my face.

"No one sees this side of me. I'm not the cruel monster everyone thinks I am. I had to protect you," he murmured, looking at the ground. "I am to be feared, but I am just in my actions."

I gulped over the growing lump in my throat; I could feel my tears brimming for him. This was my fault, this fantasy of us having something on board this ship. Every day, my life was at risk, and now I'd brought him into my mess. It was selfish of me.

"This is my fault; I never should have let this go so far." I stared at my hands, cracking my knuckles nervously as I spoke. Casper grabbed my chin in his rough fingers and held me so I could see nothing but his eyes.

"You are all I have ever wanted." His voice was so sincere that it broke the barrier that kept the tears from flowing freely. He brought his thumb up to gingerly wipe away the tears on my cheeks as they fell.

I rose and wrapped my arms around his neck, ignoring the pain screaming back at me. Our lips molded together in a fevered desire, a raw need for a connection. My lips parted hungrily with his, our tongues mingled in a dance of dominance and need. He scooped me up by my bottom, encouraging my legs to wrap around his torso as he laid us on the bed. His body caged me against him. He kept his weight off me, but he was in complete control. I pulled his hips toward me with my legs still tightly wrapped around him. A low chuckle rumbled from his throat that I could feel reverberating in my chest as his lips pressed harder into mine. A heat spread through my body like a roaring inferno as he removed my shirt, being somewhat careful. I winced, and he pulled back, but I tugged him closer. No amount of pain was about to dampen the mood setting fire before us.

Thoughts of our last time together made the flame come alive; I felt the blood rising to my cheeks as my hands explored his body. His muscles were taught underneath my touch; feeling every inch as he moved against me.

Reflexively, my hands snaked under his shirt as I yanked it off. I felt l his length through his trousers as his hands skimmed down my body. A soft moan left my lips into his mouth as he groped my breast with an eagerness I was unprepared for. I knew then, this wouldn't be the slow, tender sex like last time. This would be raw. An almost animalistic need radiated between us. His rough thumb rubbed slow circles around the supple skin of my nipple, causing me to gasp in pleasure, my desire for him only deepening.

"Casper." The moan was but a whisper, leaving my lips before I could stop it. His blue eyes darkened with lust as he gazed down at me. Warmth blossomed from my stomach, encasing my body in a flame I was ready to set blazing.

"Demi, you are so beautiful." His voice was hoarse as his eyes skimmed my face.

My lips parted; a brief deliberation crossed my mind before I made a choice I could never take back.

"Naida, my name is Naida." I looked into his eyes; this was my most vulnerable. He knew my real name, my only lasting secret.

Casper only stilled for a moment above me before his lips claimed mine once again, roughly as he stroked my tongue with his own. I groaned helplessly against his onslaught; he broke apart just as I was gasping for a breath.

"Naida." The sound of my name on his lips was like a prayer. "Naida...Naida"

Hearing my name in his accent was enough to make my toes curl. My heart pounded heavily; I swore I found ecstasy in that moment alone. The way it played on his lips was a sweet caress, a song played for my heart alone. It captivated me, I was entranced by the sound like I had never been before. My bruised lips parted as I stared up at him; he captured me in his intense gaze.

"I don't believe I've heard a sweeter sound in my life." My voice was but a breath his proximity swallowed whole.

"What sound, lass?" He murmured, dropping closer so his lips brushed mine.

"The one with my name on your lips. My true name."

His gaze turned so full of lust it may have been feral, sending a wave of molten lava straight to my core.

"Nothing's sweeter than hearing mine come from yours."

He captured my mouth with his own, claiming me completely. His hands found my trouser buttons and removed them in seconds, which caught me off guard. I used my legs and a bit of surprise to flip us over, straddling him. He looked up at me, eyes wide in shock that I had bested him in that instant, claiming control.

"Never in me six years on the seven seas have I met someone like you. You astound me," he said softly, sending chills up my spine.

I never thought love would find me on board *The Shadow*.

Love? Was this love? Had I fallen for the Ghost of the Sea?

I stared down at him, incredulous with myself. It was irrefutably stupid of me to let myself fall in love. This was not how it was supposed to go. I had but one thing I loved, and that was the ocean in all her glory. My life aboard this ship was for nothing more than that. Yet, there he was beneath me, telling me things I never knew I longed for. To be entirely accepted for who I was? That was irreplaceable. I was not naive enough to think we had a life together. But a moment? That would have to be enough.

I bent down and captured him again with my lips, running my hand down his broad chest. Stroking my fingers through the puff of curls, I felt every muscle and his heartbeat under my palm. He gripped my bottom, digging his fingers lightly into my skin. With that, I let my thoughts die and surrendered to the passion we both longed for.

Yes, this was enough.

Chapter 31

Stale Seas

I listened to Casper's even breathing, watching his chest's gentle rise and fall. Almost reluctantly, I unwrapped myself from his burly arms, trying not to wake him. My stomach was aware of how long it had been since I had eaten, and it would no longer be ignored. I winced as the floor creaked under my weight while I hurriedly scooped up my clothes. Surprisingly, my shoulder didn't hurt as badly as it did earlier; I pulled my shirt on with only a little issue.

The way the sun shone into Casper's quarters told it was nearly dinner time. I looked in the mirror, almost forgetting Casper removed my makeup earlier. A stranger with emerald eyes peered back through the mirror. My long brown locks were tangled and greasy but hung down almost to my mid-back. It was an unfamiliar sight, seeing myself like this.

After a solid year of hiding everything feminine about me, taking in my bare face was almost too much, not to mention seeing my naked body, now sheathed comfortably under my baggy shirt. Reaching gingerly in my pant pockets for my kohl stick, I began to smudge on my facial hair once again. As soon as my freshly drawn beard adorned my face, I felt more comfortable. It was my security blanket—just as my wrapped chest was, my added layer of protection.

I allowed my eyes to drift briefly over Casper's naked chest as he slept, utterly unaware. My fingers twitched, wanting to comb through the tuft of black curls between his pectorals and trace over the long scar usually hidden by his shirt, the story of how it came to be still unknown. Pulling my attention back to the task at hand, I peered behind his curtains to ensure no one was watching as I made my swift exit. I kept my pace until I was a safe distance from his quarters. The sun was casting down unusually blistering rays for the time of day, not a cloud in the sky for as far as the eye could see.

At least that meant good weather. However, no wind pushing the sails was not ideal. We could be stagnant for days, depending on whether the wind picked up. That meant a bunch of hot, stinky, grumpy men...well, worse than usual, anyway. I sighed, wiping away the sweat already forming on my brow. My stomach reminded me of its hunger with a growl I am pretty sure the whole crew heard as I turned to the dining hall entrance.

The hall was not as boisterous as usual. Only murmurs and the clanking of metal and tankards were to be heard. The lashings earlier this morning had surely been the cause for the relative silence, putting a sour taste in everyone's mouths. I only hoped they did not know I was the cause. To top off the sour mood, Bill greeted me with his usual glower and grumbled as he slid me my tray of food. No matter the tension, my stomach growled again as the smell wafted to my nostrils.

Once I spotted Porter in the corner, only recognizable by his mop of hair, I approached him. His head was down as I approached, eating his food in silence.

"Aye, Mate." I broke the silence with a cheery smile.

He flinched slightly, startled. "Aye, Demi. You be too quiet."

I plopped my tray down, letting it clatter against the table. "Is that better?"

I started shoveling food into my gullet as fast as I could swallow it down. Porter looked up at me, a strange look on his face.

"Where have you been?" His voice was nearly a whisper.

My brow arched in question, "What do you mean?"

"I have been lookin' fer you all day. You were nowhere to be found," Porter murmured lowly, his eyes boring into my own.

"Aye, I have been lyin' low with all that was going on." I spoke around a mouth full of food, one brow arched at his question.

He eyed me thoughtfully but turned his attention back to his plate, seeming to accept my excuse. I couldn't help the nerves fluttering uneasily in my stomach. Letting my thoughts die once again, I smiled over at Porter, though he didn't see it.

"Do you want to play a game of Liar's Dice and chat?" I suggested, deeply missing the conversation with my friend over the recent days.

"I can nah. I was assigned duty in the med deck tonight. Another time?"

I was a little disheartened, but the work never ended on this ship. Porter got up to dump his trash, and I followed. After he emptied his tray, he turned around, colliding with my side. I muttered curses as he knocked into my shoulder. The ache flared up again.

"Aye sorry, Demi," he murmured as he passed me, leaving me in the mess hall alone.

The conversation left a sour taste in my mouth; I hoped Porter was not mad at me. Maybe he knew it was my fault for the lashing. The last thing I wanted was to alienate my only friend aboard this blasted ship. I would make it a personal mission for us to spend more time together. A little distance between Casper and me might be a good thing; I was feeling too open and vulnerable after yesterday. I couldn't help but wonder if I made a mistake in letting him know my name. It felt so damn good to get it off my chest, to let someone see me fully.

He opened up to me, and the walls I put around my heart burst open.

Who am I kidding? He had my heart from that first night.

I returned to the berth to safely deposit my kohl stick into my chest. Once I checked the room was clear, I felt around my pockets for my lock key, only to find empty pockets in return. I always kept my key on me.

"Strange, I must have left it with Casper," I whispered under my breath.

Chapter 32

Porter's POV- Quite as a Mouse

I left Demi in the mess hall. Once I was sure he was not behind me, I kept to the shadows and out of sight. My gut was unsettled; I knew I shouldn't have eaten much. Seeing Demi made it worse. It had been a few days since the last meeting, followed by days of watching from the background. Always watching, just out of sight. Bran and Braxon had their asses handed to them during the brawl; they were pretty much begging for the after-effects as well. I shuddered inwardly at the thought of the flesh hanging loosely from their backs. That sight would plague me for nights on end. I found sleep to be restless as it was.

No one paid that much attention to my whereabouts; I stood toward the back of the crowd, watching in silent horror as Casper repeatedly brought down the Cat O Nine tails. My body betrayed my repulsion in unintentional flinches with each heavy-handed crack. The sound was almost defended by the animalistic jeers of the crew.

"Bloodthirsty Blokes." I spit toward the deck.

Keep your head down, and your time onboard will be longer. That was my motto. Too often, I had watched in the background as prisoners were brought on board, and the fellow crew was punished under Casper's rule. I had hope for Demi, hope for a true friendship for once on this blasted ship. The worst mistake of my life in the guise of untold treasure...and women, I supposed. It was a fool's wish, the one thing I regretted from the first moments aboard. Once you sign your life away, there is no returning, no claiming it back. This life sounds so pretty on the lips of others.

They don't mention the spoils, the rotten food, the treatment of lesser crew on board, or the risk of crossing the first mate. Days upon days of hard work for what? A few specs of treasure now and then. Risking your life on the merciless sea day in and day out. I counted the lucky stars every night we avoided a storm.

A dirty bunch of thieving animals, the lot of them.

I knocked twice on the giant wooden doors before me, a burly voice answered from behind.

"Enter," it called.

I slipped through the doors like a ghost in the night, the room inside lit dimly with lanterns mounted on its walls. My feet led to the desk, where I plopped heavily in the chair before it.

"Do ye have news?"

I looked up slowly, my eyes meeting his steely gray ones. "Aye, Captain, it be true." My voice came out lazily as I held his gaze with my own, refusing to flinch.

I could see by the rise of his chest he was furious.

Good, we all should be.

"Aye, Porter. I shall not forget this. Seems we have a traitor on board." His voice, even controlled, still commanded the room.

I had been watching for months. Silent as the mouse I was. I had to be sure before I brought this to the captain. Only a brief thought crossed my mind whether I had done the right thing. The bond I had forged tugged desperately at my cold heart.

Right thing? Who am I kidding? Her neck now may save mine later.

"What comes next?" I tried to steel my nerves as I spoke, showing no weakness.

"Now, we wait. Just keep watching me, wee mouse. We need proof."

I glanced lazily at him as I fingered the key in my pocket, turning it methodically in my fingers. The cold bite of the metal seeped into my skin.

"I have just the thing."

He nodded in approval and waved his hand to dismiss me. I left as silent as I came. No eyes were watching me; why would they? After all, I was no one. At least not yet.

All I needed was one piece of proof.

Not much, if any, was usually needed, but because she had wiggled her way into Casper's protection, I needed something. Anything.

"It won't be long now," I whispered to myself.

I could feel a storm coming; one not everyone would survive.

Chapter 33

Close Encounters

I had unintentionally fallen asleep after dinner, only awakening the following day with the bustle of the crew. My back felt like one giant knot. Spending too much time in Casper's extremely comfortable bed had me spoiled. After all, these hammocks were not a queen-size bed fit for a princess. I stretched as I stood, my body making similar groaning noises to the ones I'd heard from the ship multiple times before. A longing for Casper's arms around me and his lips against my neck washed over me. I shoved the feeling back down. Distance would do me some good, indeed.

As I went to the dining hall, my stomach growled in protest against its empty state. A fog of sleep coated my brain as I stumbled down the aisle. The scent of breakfast wafting out of the archway made my stomach do a backflip, and my mouth watered immediately. I did not care what Mr. Grumpy was making; it was enough to put a perk in my step.

The hall was buzzing, as usual; the gruff voices and clank of tankards carried throughout the room. It was never too early for rum. The air already smelled thick of it with the telltale signs of belching from the crew. I shuffled over to grab my grub as my eyes wandered around the room, looking for Porter, but his mousy hair was nowhere to be seen. A tug of disappointment resonated in my chest.

I guess he is still sleeping...

I took my seat and examined today's meal closer: biscuits and some sort of dried beef with a thick gravy-like substance. My nose scrunched at the look of it; I was tired of the salted meals. Even if it did smell fantastic, I held a silent funeral for my tastebuds. *May they ever rest in peace.* I was sure they were forever tried between the salt and the rum. Looking around, Casper was nowhere to be seen either, and that pathetic ache I was coming to know was back. Our forbidden love—at least I hoped that's what it was—was a shared infatuation. Whether our fates were aligned in the stars or simply because our paths crossed would always be a mystery to me. I sent a thank you up to them regardless. I was grateful to have him in my life, either way.

My thoughts drifted off, taking me back to father and mother, and how they interacted with each other. There was not a single doubt in my mind that they loved each other deeply. Her passing, after all, was the death of my father's happiness. She was his passion, and without her flame, he was cold till his bitter end. I struggled, trying to grasp onto any of my memories from before she passed. They blinked in and out, I could feel them but never truly brought them to my mind's eye. I wished I had asked her about that time, and if she remembered anything in detail from her life before her transformation.

I never pictured myself living that way, with a stable home, a husband, and a family. Yet, there was a tug in my heart for a life that was never meant to be—a life that ended the instant I became Demi. It never bothered me before; all I cared about was having a life of my own and exploring the bounds of this seemingly endless sea. A life I chose for myself. This was my freedom. Nothing to be tethered to, no responsibilities to bind me to one place.

I couldn't help but imagine another world, where Casper and I would have met. One where I had stayed. Maybe he was a merchant who came to my village. We bumped into each other in the middle of the square, and he laughed as he picked up the books that had fallen from my arms. We fell in love, then fixed up my parent's house and made it our own. I would take our children, only knee height, to my secret place to meet their grandmother. She would teach them how to swim, and we could all learn together. We would watch them grow, and every night, Casper would come home and envelope me in his arms. He would speak softly of his day; we would reminisce about our journeys. I would tell him about the book I had dived into. He would chuckle as I was lost in another world. I could almost hear their laughter carrying on through the house. I watched over time as they ran through the house, every time they passed, they would be another head higher than before. I felt robbed of alife I never wanted in the first place.

I quickly wiped at a tear that had strayed down my cheek as I came back into reality. How foolish of me to fantasize about that life, even as I mourned it. I sniffed and cleared my throat, looking around the empty dining hall. Tossing what was left of my cold meal and my unraveled emotions, I headed out to the main deck to find Porter. Unfortunately, it was not him that greeted me up on deck.

It didn't take long for me to notice Bran and Braxon working their mops across the deck slowly. From their slowed movements, it was clear they were still recovering from Casper's lashings. Honestly, it shocked me that they were able to stand, let alone mop with the condition he left them in. No doubt they were forced to continue work as the rest of their punishment. It took all my will to repress a shudder when flashes of their flesh crossed my mind. I walked past them slowly, trying to remain unnoticed.

"Pet," Braxon muttered loud enough for me to hear. It was enough to cause a stutter in my footstep.

"Remember, dead men tell no tales," Bran followed.

My breath caught in my throat, but I refused to show weakness in front of them. If I did, I would soon feed the fish below.

"If ye have something to say, say it to my face. If not, shut yer mouth. I don't believe you could handle another lashin'," I challenged, puffing my chest and standing tall.

Why did I insist on poking the bear?

I could not handle another fight; I was still recovering from the last. I would be damned if I let them know that. After all, their backs are still scabbing over the ribbons of flesh left on it. I'm sure they wouldn't fare any better than I would.

"Mighty big words fer someone who has the first mate doing their bidding. Just wait till ye aren't under Casper's protection," Bran stated as he turned to face me.

"Who knows what could happen." Braxon followed as they looked between themselves, shrugging their shoulders.

"Is that a threat? I don't believe Casper would take kindly to his orders being disobeyed." I stood my ground, cracking my knuckles reflexively.

Forget poking the bear; at this point, I am setting a fire underneath it and watching it burn.

"Demi!" Porter called, just as I saw each of them take a step toward me. All attention landed on him. "I need yer assistance in the med unit."

I breathed a silent sigh of relief. "Gentlemen." I nodded my cap their way and headed swiftly toward Porter.

"Ye cannot stay out of trouble, can you?" Porter spoke in a hushed tone as we walked away. I glanced sideways at him as a smile tugged the corner of my mouth.

"Eh, they had it comin'. Though, I didn't reckon they would be ready to fight so soon." I grinned, even though I knew alone I would not have lasted long against both of them. My mind slipped for a second to Casper; I had not seen him around either. "How was yer shift in the Sickbay yesterday?"

"Me shift where? Oh, right there be some crew with cases of scurvy. Captain assigned me wound duty." Porter shrugged in response. "Of course, that means you will see less of me around."

My brow quirked in response. "Do you need me to help you out? I don't mind tending to the crew in need."

He stopped abruptly. I almost tripped over a loose rope, turning back to face him. His eyes glazed over for a moment before he snapped back to attention and continued forward as if nothing had happened.

"No, it is best to keep as many healthy bodies as possible out of the sickbay. No need to spread anything more."

My fists bunched at my sides, out of habit, I cracked my knuckles in my fist. Porter was behaving strangely; maybe he was simply overworked by the captain.

"Where are we headin'?" I was hoping for a subject change. We were on the way to the back of the ship.

"Anywhere to get ye away from them. I heard the captain nattering earlier about stopping at the port within a week or more's time," he muttered, looking at the deck ahead of us as we made our way up the steps two at a time.

"What for?"

"You know, restock supplies, fresh water, gathering more crew. We need more with the scurvy wiping some out. The lads enjoy their visits to this port, more so for the supply of strumpets." He paused briefly. "Casper enjoys them the most at this port."

My breath faltered, but I made sure to keep my pace moving. Instead, I plastered a shit-eating grin on my face, turning to look at him, even as my heart wanted to crumple at the thought of him with those women.

"Aye, it's been a long while since I've seen the flesh of a woman. Touched a breast or two. I am sure all the men will jump at the chance."

"Plenty of ale and rum to go around." He grinned back, and the tension between my shoulders melted away. Fresh air flooded my lungs. I elbowed him gently as we came to the back rail, looking over to the sea below.

The waters below lapped against the ship, as dark as the night sky, the sun glinting off it as if stars were glittering across the surface. My mind played evil tricks on me, spotting a fin out the side of my eye. I hadn't caught any sign of my mother being around in months, even though I knew full well she was not the only one of her kind. Even if I did see a fin, chances were it was someone else. The breeze caressed my face gently, sweeping some whips of hair as it went. I chuckled gleefully. I had been so wrapped up in the drama of this ship I had forgotten the whole point of my being here. This was my freedom.

Having the ocean below me, greeting me like a long-lost friend. I admired the clear sky, the sun hanging above, signaling midday. There was not a cloud to be seen and the water stretching endlessly around us. Not even a seagull to be spotted. Porter clapped a hand against my shoulder.

"I better head back to the sickbay to see if anyone needs tending to."

I nodded in his direction, turning my attention to the sea to stay a few moments longer, letting the salty air hit my tongue as I inhaled deeply. Maybe one day, we would sail to the end of the world. Would we be sucked over the edge? Like a giant waterfall? Or maybe we would just travel the expanse of the sea for the rest of time. Would I ever see my mother again?

A single tear strayed down my cheek as I swept it away. My wayward emotions weren't under wraps like I thought. What if Casper and I just disappeared once we reached the port? It's not like we had anything to be left behind. I knew it was a fool's dream, even as it crossed my mind. If we were caught, we would both get the noose if we were lucky. If not, I was sure we would be feeding the fish shortly after. I ran a hand over the back of my neck, squeezing it lightly.

Boom Boom Boom

I jumped at the sound of the captain's sword hitting the main deck and made haste heading back toward the main deck. The rest of the crew crowded around as I shuffled my way down the steps lightly. I kept a wary eye on Bran and Braxon, making sure there was plenty of distance between us.

"Listen up, ye scallywags. We be heading fer The Devil's Port!" Marduke's voice boomed, and the crew was in an instant uproar.

Chapter 34

Land Ho

"Land Ho!"

I rushed to the side of the ship along with everyone else on deck. The ship swayed under the uneven weight. I fought off the claustrophobia as the crew packed in around me like sardines. It had been two weeks since the captain had announced we were heading for *The Devil's Port*. The small dark mass was a sight for sore eyes; even the grog had been rationed for the past couple of days. The only thing keeping the crew from killing each other was the promise of women and ale to come. Even with my dulled sense of smell, the men—myself included—were quite ripe. I had started to notice the increased amount of fly carcasses in the berth.

The almost foreign sound of seagulls cawing was a welcomed call. A smile pulled the corner of my mouth, and I was practically jumping out of my boots giddy. Hopefully, my feet would not be too unsteady on solid ground. By the looks of it, we would make land by tomorrow. Just as I turned to search for Porter, I felt a firm hand grasp my shoulder, knocking me into the railing with a huff.

"Aye, Demi. It will be good to have solid ground under me boots. Fresh water in my stomach," Porter laughed as he snuck in beside me.

"Are ye even a pirate? I would have thought it was the rum you were worried about," I rumbled in reply, risking sticky hands to ruffle his hair.

"Anythin' to stop this gut rot," he spoke lowly, rubbing his stomach. "Honestly, I am looking forward to anythin' that ain't dry or salted to hell."

"Now that, I can agree to, just don't tell Bill," I whispered in fear that somehow he would hear me, to which Porter bellowed out a laugh and clapped me on the shoulder a few times.

One thing I was thankful for these past two weeks, though Porter was busy, we made time for each other. Between the dice games and joining in the crew singing in good spirits, I got him to open up more about his past. He had grown up in a small village like I had, family was in poverty. His mother was sickly, and his father was a mean drunk. As soon as he was eighteen, he left them for *The Shadow*. My heart felt for him. I knew the strained fatherly relationship. Thankfully, mine had not been a drunk, but for every night Porter's missed at the tavern, mine made up for his distancing from me. His town was landlocked. Porter had snuck out in the night to make it two towns over to where the pirates recruited. He said his father had caught him on his way out of town, and he ran for his life to lose his trail. I feared for my friend, even if it was in the past; heat rolled through my chest in anger for him. He wouldn't dwell on it; however, he did mention the beatings he had taken under his father's hand.

All the while, my key never showed up to my chest. I had made it a point to avoid Casper as much as possible, though I couldn't help the heartache in my chest. Thoughts of him with the strumpets from *The Devil's Port* plagued me nightly. Which grew more painful with every mile we came closer to the island. I had known I was not his first and most likely would not be his last; I was not dim. I was a convenience. In my heart, I had hoped the feelings growing within me were not one-sided. Even now, as my eyes swept over the crew, I could not see him in the crowd. Maybe he was avoiding *The Devil's Port* for as long as possible like I was.

"I dunno about you, but I am looking forward to the crew smelling' better." I forced my attention back to Porter.

"Aye, they better all take baths, or I will toss them off deck myself," Porter chuckled in response. I looked at him with one eyebrow raised in accusation."I doubt ye could toss anyone overboard."

Everyone had been too excited about land slowly approaching to do much of the work we were supposed to do. Most of the crew took over the dining hall, setting up gambling stations to win some more doubloons before we arrived. More doubloons, more women, and I was told there would be plenty to go around. Those that weren't held up in the hall were on board singing sea shanties to pass the time. I swept up the deck, feeling the buzz of rum Porter had hidden till now. We had polished off the bottle in celebration. He was still gambling away his earnings; his streak was not a lucky one. I heard guitar strumming as a new shanty started, the tune slower than they had been playing. I stumbled to the rail, spotting Casper perched on a crate in all his magnificent glory, the guitar in his hands.

Yeah, I've tapped that.

I chuckled to myself, hiccupping a belch and leaning against the rail to listen.

"*We sail for Port my plead goes unheard turn me home turn me home turn me home*

My Eyre is burning my girl I shall wed

turn me home turn me home turn me home

I grab for my sword, swing at that bastard's head

turn me home turn me home turn me home

Take me to the briq better take me there dead

turn me home turn me home turn me home

Turn us towards Nassau or I'll swim there meself

I'll give up my portion of all of this wealth

I'll leave here with nothing but me heart and me health

turn me home turn me home turn me home"

My heart swelled in my chest as his shanty plucked at its strings. His voice glided over me, making me sway slightly in appreciation. Once he was done with his first verse, the crew picked up the chorus of the next one.

"The stars now be shining high over my head

turn me home turn me home turn me home

The crew threw me over deep water I tread

turn me home turn me home turn me home

I may die for me crimes, I've succumbed to my fate

turn me home turn me home turn me home

But in heaven I promise my soul will await

turn me home turn me home turn me home

Turn us towards Nassau or I'll swim there meself I'll give up my portion of all of this wealth

I'll leave here with nothing but me heart and me health

turn me home turn me home turn me home"

His voice faded, and the crew jeered loudly before falling into the next shanty they knew. Casper's eyes met mine briefly, and my heart melted—hook, line, and sinker.

By nightfall, my stomach was uneasy; I untangled my limbs from the hammock and made my way to the upper deck. Flatus Jim Mattis had been at it again, the rum that warmed my belly threatened to make a reappearance. His noxious fumes mixing with the BO was too much for me to take. The moon was full above us, the stars glittering across the waters. I took a deep breath of the fresh salty air, gripping the rail, willing my stomach to settle.

"Mother, I don't know if you're out there, but I hope and wish you are. I miss you. Your guidance would come in handy right now," I laughed softly. "Not that I took it the last time."

The wind picked up, carrying wisps of loose hair across my neck. A soft sigh left my lips as I gazed into the water below. I hoped our paths would cross again, that our goodbye was not forever.

"Sea, if you are listening, hear my prayer that my mother and I will be together again someday," I whispered as the breeze swept away my words as I spoke them as if they were an offering.

"Demi," I heard Casper's gentle rumble behind me before I felt his burly arms around my waist.

I breathed him in, taking comfort in his warmth spreading across my back. I tried to turn to face him, but he held me in place.

"I've missed you." These three simple words melted me completely.

"You know where I've been. It hasn't been hard to find me," I murmured simply in response.

"You know as well as I do that you've been avoiding me. What be in that beautiful chaos of a mind?" He whispered as he turned me gently to face him.

An abrupt laugh bubbled up of its own accord, "If only ye knew." I glanced into his eyes. "I am afraid for what will come when we reach *Devil's Port*."

He nodded slowly in understanding as he brushed some hair behind my ears. "I know, I am as well, for once." He glanced away briefly. "I have no doubts you've heard the rumors of my past."

"Ye can say that." I puffed out, rubbing my arm, discomfort wrapping around me. I didn't want to care, didn't want it to matter to me.

"Listen, I have been avoiding *Devil's Port* as much as ye have. I am nah the same since you have come into my life, lass." He squeezed my shoulder; I wasn't sure if it was meant to calm me or reassure him. Either way, my stomach did a little flip.

"Well, 'twas from your lips that the sea be a lonely mistress," I muttered softly, envy snaking into my words and lacing them with venom.

Casper grazed my arm with his finger pads; such a little delicate motion caused a roaring fire to dance over my skin and settle in my abdomen. My lips parted as a soft puff of air left them. My eyes lingered from his fingertips slowly tracking up his arm, the sweep of his collarbone, to meet his blue eyes, the night hiding their light. He gazed back at me, his features softening even as a tick set in his jaw.

"What if we left?" His voice was so low I wasn't sure I heard him correctly.

Did I just hear that right?

My mind could not fathom those words coming out of his lips, the same ones I had secretly been thinking about.

"What?" I whispered, my eyes two giant orbs set on my face, my mouth set in shock.

"I mean it. What if we left? When we got to *Devil's Port*." He wrapped his arms, pulling me against his strong form.

I shook my head slowly, raking my hand—which was now visibly shaking—over my neck. I felt warmth under my chin as he tilted my head so he could look at me.

"Marduke would kill us both."

"Only if he found us," Casper murmured, his lips brushing against mine.

"Why?" I wanted to say so much more, but that was all I could think of.

"I would change the tides for you; I would pluck the stars from the sky and offer them to you if you asked me to. Nothing else matters to me anymore. I would fight Neptune himself if it would prove I was worthy of you."

His voice held so much earnestness; I knew down to my soul he meant every word he had said, and that scared the shit out of me because I would do the same for him. My freedom, my life, it revolved around him. I wouldn't admit it to myself, because once I did, it was real. Once it was real, it could be ripped away from me like everything else had been.

At that moment, my chest swelled, and my belly blossomed with warmth, enough to make my knees weak. He held me in place, only to have my body crashing against him seconds later. Worry of who was in the crow's nest fled my mind; there was nothing but him. The firm set of his mouth soon softened against mine. This was the fiercest kiss of my life—what little experience I had. None of that mattered. With those words, he had confirmed what I was feeling was not one-sided. That maybe, just maybe, he loved me too. I felt his rough hands slipping under my tunic as they glided their way up my back. I pressed myself against him, wanting him in that moment with every fiber of my being. By the time our mouths parted, we were both gasping for air.

"We shall take this to my quarters." His breath fanned over my face in warm waves.

I could only nod as I fought to regain the breath he had stolen. His hand found mine, and he practically dragged me to his chambers, making sure to scan the area for the crew before we slipped in. As soon as the door shut, his mouth was on mine again, however, his hands did not stop at my back. He wrapped my legs around his waist as he picked me up by my bottom and carried me to his bed. The scent of him surrounded me as he laid me down. Rum and the sea threatened to drown me. Our mouths feverishly devoured each other's tongues in a heated combat.

I heard fabric ripping before I felt the cool air against my abdomen; before it registered that he had just ripped my shirt off. He heard my groan of protest and chuckled against me.

"I will buy you a new one on the morrow," he murmured. He was more delicate with the wrap around my chest, his long fingers surprisingly nimble, undoing the bindings swiftly. I breathed a sigh of relief as the constriction I had become used to came undone.

I could not imagine having to wear a corset.

My hands wandered to his chest, my fingers scouring the planes of his pecs. There was a moment of hesitation before a wicked smile tugged at my lips. Casper caught my eyes a second before I returned the favor; this time, the sound of fabric ripping sent waves of tingles down my body, like lightning coursing through my skin. I could see he was about to make a similar protest to mine before I interrupted with a deepened kiss. His hand gripped my side as the other held his weight off me, it slowly tracked up my skin leaving gooseflesh in its wake, meeting at the hardened point of my nipple before he grazed his thumb over it in excruciatingly slow circles. A soft moan escaped me, and he had barely touched me.

Good gods, what is this man doing to me?

After tonight, I was ready to plead utter insanity, and I was perfectly okay with that. For once, it was not the sea that consumed my thoughts, it was Casper. He crashed in waves around my mind, filling my body with the joy I had only once known through her. The lantern flickered on the nightstand, casting the shadows of our joined bodies against the wall. His touch on my breast soon traveled beneath my navel, and I gasped softly in anticipation. Somehow, he managed to undo my breeches and take them off without moving me.

He hesitated for a moment and pulled away from me. My eyebrows knitted together in confusion as he made his way across the room. With his back turned, my eyes took their time devouring the rivets of muscles lining his back, traveling over the various scars that littered his flesh and down to the plump curves of his bottom, the kind that made me think of a sweet, rare summer fruit we would see occasionally in the village. Recalling the sweet nectar that always dribbled down my mouth as I bit into it, I licked my lips; I could take a bite out of that. Even as his trousers kept me from seeing it fully. He was entirely too clothed for my liking.

When he turned around, my gaze traveled from the v of muscles pointing to his waist up as he was wringing out a rag. He crossed to me slowly, watching me, devouring me as if he were the hunter and I the prey. My question died on my lips as he skimmed the cool rag over my body. The slight smell of honey reached my nose. He took his time going over my skin, the pits of my arms, and between my thighs.

Gods, a pirate with hygiene.

It could have been an embarrassing act; he was washing me, for god's sake. But he did it so sensually that I merely enjoyed the feel of his hand over the length of me. My body was the temple he intended to worship.

"Where did ye find clean water?" I murmured, my eyes fluttering closed as the sweet scent of honey enveloped me. I heard his chuckle rumble deep in his chest, and my toes almost curled at the sound.

"It isn't clean enough to drink, but it is swab enough to do the intended job. I figured ye would appreciate us nah, well, smellin' like pirates."

A smile blossomed over my face as he refreshed the rag. I took my turn skimming it over the ripples of his body, enjoying every moment of it. When I reached his trousers, I hesitated, and his eyes met mine, the expanse of the bluest ocean staring back at me. He tossed the rag to the floor and bent back down toward me. My body adjusted to his weight instantly. He dropped his head back down to my neck, his lips leaving a moist path.

His kisses lit small fires along my skin, trailing down the length of my body over my abs and below to the center of my thighs. A warmth pooled there, his tongue with the talent of a fine bladesmith and the precision of a pirate speared me to my core. My body moved of its own volition; the sounds that left me I was not aware one could make. This may be our last time on this ship, and I was going to savor every moment of it. He pinned my hands softly at my sides.

"Lass, I do nah plan on drowning at sea."

A surprised giggle bubbled up out of me, though it was short-lived before it turned to a deeper lustful sound. He grinned deviously up at me, as he stalked back up my body. His trousers were already unbuttoned and the gap protruding. A little smirk captured my lips as my eyes lingered; I already knew what awaited me there. Let us say this bladesmith had a mighty sword.

"Look at me, Naida. I want to see yer face."

Casper's voice was a low purr that reverberated in his chest and mine. I looked into his eyes, the blue was liquid metal with hunger and need, only a second before I gasped and my own fluttered closed. He filled me completely, and a storm took hold in my center. My body was moving against his, riding the waves of pleasure. The warmth spreading and taking hold of my being. I could feel his groans, even as I heard them mixing with my own. Our essence combines into one being. I was happy to succumb to it. To allow the pleasure to envelop me, to take over me. The waves were growing higher and stronger, crashing through me only to build again. The sensation was causing my head to spin. Until it was not. The storm broke, the waves breaking free. Tremors pulsed down my body, over and over again. I could no longer hear myself, though I am sure I was calling out to whatever gods I believed in or not.

I slowly came back down to earth after drowning happily in the waves of pleasure, only to hear Casper's groans intensifying and soon enough he had joined me. I watched what I just experienced take over him and a smile was plastered to my face. To see that I could bring him that release took over a vital part of me. He laid down beside me, his chest rising and falling as rapidly as mine was. We both tried to regain our breath. His hand found my own, and he laced our fingers together.

"I love you," I murmured. Shock overcame me as the words registered in my head.

Oh, for the love of a pirate.

"I love ye too."

My gaze whipped to his. My ears were ringing, I was sure my heart was trying to leap out of my chest and run away. Warmth blossomed over my face; I felt my cheeks growing red hot. He pulled me over to him and kissed my forehead softly. It was such a gentle gesture, one that meant the world to me.

"I love ye too," he repeated softly as if he needed to hear it too.

There we stayed, wrapped in each other's embrace, for the remainder of the night. It was the best night of sleep I'd had in a while.

Chapter 35

The Devil's Port

Streaks of sunlight are what I awoke to, my eyes fluttering open, blinking back sleep only to be blinded by the light. I groaned softly, rolling over. My hand gently padded the empty space beside me, and I frowned. Of course, Casper would not be here, we were soon to be reaching *Devil's Port*. I was sure Marduke had tasks for him. It was the first hand's responsibility to ready the crew and the ship for boarding.

I inhaled deeply, only to smell the lingering scent of honey on the linens. A small smile tugged at my lips, even as the weight of the events that happened last night took hold of my soul. Casper wanted to leave this life behind. The one he has known for years, the one I left everything to have. He wanted me, and while that thought brought warmth through my entire being, my heart tugged painfully. The emotions I felt were dangerous, uncharted territory I was terrified to explore the depths of.

"Can I do this?" I whispered aloud, not meaning to talk to myself.

I raked my hands over my face and tugged my hair as I rolled over, smothering my shouts in a pillow. I recognized my frustration. Could I leave what I have yearned for, for years behind? For Casper? Could I abandon Casper for the sea? Neither option sat well with me. Maybe we could find a ship of our own and start a new dream. The best of both worlds could be ours. Giving up this life didn't mean we were trading it for a stagnant one. The thought alone sent shivers down my spine.

He said he loved me.

My heart sang with joy, so much I was sure it would pop out of my chest. A moment later, it gave a crushing squeeze.

"I said I loved him..." I groaned and yelled into the pillow once more. "What's the matter with me?"

I was startled from my thoughts by shouts coming from the deck. I was about to dash out to see what the commotion was when I remembered I had no shirt. I groaned again, grabbing one of Casper's. I was going to look like a child dwarfed in the fabric, I rewrapped my chest and tugged it over my head. I stuffed it in my pants and checked my reflection in the mirror.

Good enough.

The door creaked open, but the sound was drowned out by the continued shouts from the sides of the ship. I looked around habitually for anyone looking this way; I saw my opportunity and slipped out. My eyes widened; it seemed every crew member was aboard ship on either side. I could tell they were joyous whoops, though I could not yet see the cause until I looked to my right and saw a mass of land. I rushed to the nets and started climbing. The mass of land came into view, making my little village seem like it was built for mice. My mouth dropped as one hand dangled from the net; there was no doubt in my mind this was a trading port. There were ships of all sizes as far as the eye could see along the port, I could count at least fifty.

Soon my cheers joined the others. We would be docking in less than a half hour. Less than a half hour... My arms started descending from the net before my brain registered. I needed to pack. Hurrying to the berth, my heartbeat quickened.

So little time. I got to my hammock and glanced down at my chest. I was a little shocked when I saw the key in its hole, the key I had lost weeks ago. I opened the chest and what I owned remained in there, a spare charcoal stick and some extra bandages for my chest, along with some books I had brought from home. On the top, my father's journal; without the key, I hadn't been able to read the final passages. I scooped up my cutlass, strapping it to my hip with nimble fingers.

There was no time for the sinking feeling threatening to take hold of my chest. I grabbed a leather satchel and stuffed what was left of my belongings in them; making sure to tuck the journal in the bottom. I slipped it over my neck and under the tunic of Casper's, thankfully it hid the satchel since it was four sizes too big. Once again, I was packing my life up in one bag; it brought me back to the day I left over a year ago. When I said goodbye to all I knew for one last time. The excitement, the nerves, and the anxiety all clawed at my insides, ripping them to ribbons and trying to burst out of me. It all felt familiar now.

I slammed the chest shut, locking it for whatever reason, and made my way back on deck. Falling in line, I helped the others finish readying the ropes, and lugged up our empty barrels until we arrived fully to land. A wild grin spread over my face when I heard a loud thud as a plank was placed from the dock to the ship so we could get everything to shore. I had a pile of empty flour sacks over one shoulder and a barrel in the other arm. Casper was at the side of the ship beside the plank, handing what looked to be little leather sacks to each crewmate.

"Yer earnings, lads." I heard him say to those ahead of me. When it came to my turn, our gaze latched on to the others.

"Demi, here be your earnings," he said, then lowered his head to mine. "Meet me at the edge of the dock after everything is unloaded."

I responded with a curt nod and made my way down the plank, a little unsteady. Hefting my sack of doubloons up and down a few times in my palm and feeling the weight of it brought a bout of butterflies to my chest. This was the most money I'd ever had in my possession, and I was damn giddy over it. I looped it carefully around one of my belt loops and tucked it into my pocket, patting the outside happily. It was not long till everything was off the ship that needed to be replaced. I waited as Casper had said to, helping the crew organize what was unloaded. Soon enough, I saw his midnight ringlets shining against the sun, his head above most in the crowd, and headed my way.

"Follow me," he said lowly, just as he was interrupted by a loud shriek that could wound eardrums forever.

We both turned, only for a pair of long arms to wrap around his neck. Ones that belonged to a sun-kissed woman, her thick mane fell in ringlets of ebony down her back. The dress she wore had a scarlet corset bodice, which her breasts were practically spilling out of, and layered skirts accentuating her curves. One side was tied to her bodice, revealing the entire length of her golden-skinned leg. I arched a brow, remaining in stunned silence.

"Casper, when they said you docked, I damn well didn't believe it. What has it been, three years?" She spoke in breathy gasps, continuing to press herself fully against him. I fought the urge to punch the wench. How dare she wrap herself around him like that?

He quickly captured her hips, giving her an arm's length distance between them. "Misty, aye, it be good to see ya."

"Shall I prepare your room?" Misty replied, dragging her finger down his chest, stopping just before his trousers. I rolled my eyes, practically seething with rage.

Yep, I was going to kill her.

He grabbed her hand and dropped it. "That would be wonderful." He took another step back.

She huffed, taking a fan out of I wasn't sure where; she flicked it open and fanned herself. "Shall I send up your usual as well?"

My gaze flew to him, my nostrils expanded slightly, though the rest of my face remained stoic. His eyes flashed to mine for a second and back to *Misty.*

"That won't be necessary." His voice was low but offered her a smile. I was thinking of the ways I wanted to stab her.

Looks like she has ample tender flesh I could skewer with my cutlass. If she flicks her hair one more time... just once, I swear.

Her gaze shifted to mine for the first time since she started yapping. "Aye, maybe your friend could use some company, then?"

My eyes widened slowly. "Or maybe nah."

Her eyes shifted down at me, assessing. "Doesn't look like he be of age anyway."

I cast my gaze anywhere else before I pulled my cutlass off my hip and stabbed her. Casper grasped her arm gently.

"Thank you for being so gracious, Misty. A cabin be all I will require."

She nodded to him and shot me an unfriendly look before she sauntered away, flouncing to the rest of the crewmates.

"Usual, huh?" I growled, keeping my eyes averted.

"Not here." He grabbed my arm, urging me to follow.

I kept my eyes on the cobblestone path so I wouldn't trip as I tried to keep up with his long strides. With quick stolen glances, I noted most buildings were two or three stories tall, which were larger than most of the buildings back in my town. There were hundreds of people in the streets, we had to bob and weave in between them. I was starting to lose sight of Casper when his large hand wrapped around my wrist and pulled me into a darkened alley. I gave a little squeak of surprise as he pulled me to his chest, which I proceeded to slap and scowl up at him.

"Why did you do that?" I gasped, trying to regain my breath and taking a measured step back from him.

"We needed some time alone; I didn't expect Misty to be there when we unloaded. I realize that doesn't look the best fer me." Casper's eyes were like glaciers, the set of his jaw firm.

"Oh? The fact that you have your own room at a gods-damn brothel?" I spit out, looking at the cobblestone below my feet as if it personally offended me.

He gripped my chin roughly, bringing my face to meet his. "You are going to judge me for a past you had no part in?"

"No," I muttered harshly, "but I still want to punch you nonetheless."

"That is exactly why I will choose you. Always." He cupped my face in his palm, the warmth from him spreading through my cheeks.

He kissed me; it was quick but made my heart flutter even still. This was our first kiss in public. The heat seeped from my face to my lower regions, which had no business happening. I was still pissed, even though I knew I had no reason to be.

"So where will our room be?" I asked, balling and un-balling my hands.

A grin cocked his lips to the right, bringing out his dimple. "*The Crowing Cock* be three blocks from here."

One of my eyebrows arched. "Why am I not surprised by the name?"

His chuckle was more of a low rumble in his chest as he grinned at me, flashing the whites of his teeth.

A pirate with good hygiene.

My heart fluttered about like a bird in my chest. We strolled through the marketplace, and I couldn't see one face I recognized. It was a relief. There were little shops built of gray slab rock instead of wood. Out front of most were wooden stands where their goods were put out for display. The lingering scent hit my nose from a bakery we passed, and my stomach flipped, rumbling its displeasures. My mouth salivated immediately. I glanced around in awe; draperies shielded us from the sun above, casting colors of purples, reds, and golds. Being surrounded by all these people was unsettling and extraordinarily overwhelming to my senses after being on the ship for so long. Those that passed us made a show of covering their noses and a flash of embarrassment flared through me.

"We are almost there," Casper spoke so only I would hear, as if he could read my mind.

A large sign came into view, *The Growing Cock.* Someone replaced the C of the sign above the brothel, and I couldn't help the ungodly laugh that escaped me—loud enough for those around to pause briefly to stare. My cheeks flamed hot again.

Casper's smile grew warm, a light to his eyes. "They tend to have issues with the town folk changing their sign."

He took my hand and led me inside. Once we passed the threshold, he dropped it again. I tried to stifle the frown that pulled the corners of my lips. If I thought outside was overwhelming, that was now a drastic understatement. It smelled of rum, cinnamon, and sex. My nose wrinkled from the assault. I wasn't sure if I preferred the smell of the ship or here. Both were...pungent.

What furniture brandished the establishment was a deep plum velvet. The large windows draped with thick black curtains blocked out the outside view. The walls were painted a scarlet red that matched the head mistress's dress from before. Those were minor details compared to the women of the brothel. I had never seen so many naked bodies in my life—not that I was experienced in the realm of naked people in any sense of the word. Unfortunately, my eyes had been forever branded with the sight of naked man flesh. So. Much. Hair.

I could feel my face blazing with heat as my eyes roamed. So many breasts. Skinny women, tall women, curvy women, fat women, older women, assorted skin tones. There was a lady for every taste one could hope for. All were adorned with little garments, some only necklaces of pearls, some stockings and garters, all were in heels at least five inches high. My jaw was practically on the floor. Some had their hair pinned up, some let it fall in cascading ringlets around their shoulders and lower.

It wasn't long until eyes fell on us—to be more correct, on Casper—and the urge to stab people was back making my fingers twitch. I heard a glee-filled squeal and turned my gaze as a tall strawberry-blonde woman brushed past others to get to Casper. Her perky tits were out and proud as she bounded over to him, her heels clicking loudly on the floor. I cracked my knuckles habitually.

"My oh my, when Misty said you returned, I didn't believe my ears." Her voice was filled with seduction as she trailed a neatly filed claw down his chest.

"It's true, we shall be here fer a few days," Casper responded with his voice of gravel. One brow raised at that tone as I assessed them together.

Ah, so she is his usual.

I tried to keep my face blank of expression even as my heart pumped rapidly.

"Are you in need of company?" She tossed her hair casually, revealing the curve of her gracefully long neck. I noted it had one or two love marks on it.

Classy.

"Nah this time, just my cabin, Veronica." His voice was smooth as chocolate. A deep frown set on her pretty little face. I smirked to myself.

Sorry, dove, looks like you will be getting your feathers ruffled by another tonight.

"I see, right this way, then."

She guided us up the stairs, past doors where sounds that made me blush quite harshly seeped out. To the back, the last door on the right. She produced a key out of a hidden pocket in the layers of her dress.

"Here you are," she said slowly. "If you change your mind, you know where to find me."

One finely plucked brow raised delicately as she glanced over at me before she left us to the room.

Once the door was closed firmly, I let my grumbles out. "Doesn't seem like I am very welcome here."

Casper's laugh was rich like honey. "Do ye want to be?" He raised a brow in my direction.

The thought crossed my mind briefly: sharing Casper with another. All those limbs, mouths. I could feel the heat take over me as I shook my head roughly in response. I knew my voice would betray me. I thought he did as well. Seeing all that flesh on display had twisted my stomach, but I was not ready to be compared to another yet.

I glanced around the room; it was scarce of most furnishings, except for a queen-sized bed, a nightstand, and a little breakfast table and chairs. I noticed an alcove leading into a smaller room when Casper handed me towels.

"There be a shower in there." His breath brushed my ear, sending tingles racing over my skin. I groaned deliciously as I thought of the water on my skin. I grabbed the towel and dashed into the room before he could say anything else.

Slamming the wooden door shut, I heard Casper's low chuckle from the other side. The sweet scent of honey and mint hit me, wrapping me in a warm hug. Stepping carefully out of my trousers and tossing the clothes aside, I stared at the contraption in front of me. It looked to be big enough to hold four or more people; a blush crept up my cheeks at the thought. This brothel must be making a decent profit to have a running shower, not many places had them in my village. I turned the handle, and water plumed out of the head. I played with the handle till I found the right temperature, which was just below scalding. Steam billowed from the head as water raced down the drain. A smile spread across my face as I lightly tapped my fingers in the water. I groaned in delight feeling it at last on my skin, like a dense rain against my flesh. I sighed heavily as I stepped into the steady assail of water droplets, succumbing to the stream as it pelted over my body. Practically feeling the layers of dirt built up over the last year peel off my skin. I noted the puddle of water—tinged brown.

Gross.

I lathered up the square bar of soap with a washcloth, marveling at the feel of the bubbles between my fingers. Energized with light of almost one thousand suns, I scrubbed every inch of my body three times before I was sated, washing my hair the same amount. I wanted to drown in the sudsy goodness. A sigh of relief left me as I finally turned off the water, my skin prickling at the sudden temperature change.

I snatched the towel from the ground, wrapping the slightly scratchy material around my body. Funny how a shower can make me feel like a completely new person. I swiped my palm across the mirror to be greeted by two bright emerald eyes.

"Hello, old friend," I murmured to my reflection where Naida stared back at me.

A version of myself I no longer recognized without drawn-on scruff and hardened eyebrows. I gingerly traced the scars cutting across my skin, a detailed map of my history in the past year. My thoughts drifted to Casper, and I slipped light-footed to the door, pressing my ear against the wood. There was no sound from the other side. My shoulders relaxed as a relieved sigh left me. I needed a few moments, time to simply breathe and think about my next move—our next moves, I sup-posed. Honestly, just some time to settle and drown in my thoughts alone.

I opened the bathroom door, the steam pluming out after me. There was an oil lantern lit on the night-stand and a plate heaped with food on the little table. My stomach made a ghastly noise at the sight. Fresh fruit, cheeses, smoked meats. Nothing looked salted. I thanked whoever may be listening for the sight.

Silently, I apologized to Casper as I scarfed nearly everything on that plate. It had been so long since we had fresh fruit or anything that had not been killed—even after death—with salt. My teeth were grateful for the soft options. The biscuits Bill had been making could put a hole in the ship if they were thrown hard enough—and they had been. Hardtack, he called them. I called them stone, they might as well have been. We could sail for years before they spoiled, I feared they would live in my gut forever.

Only after I had finished the plate of food did I realize I was still in a towel. The thought of sliding back into my grungy clothes made my nose wrinkle. I glanced at the bed to see there was a pile of cloth stacked neatly. Casper must have asked for the garments before he left. My heart thudded loudly in my chest.

Damn him for doing this to me.

I gingerly touched the fabric, the color of it was a blue I have only seen in the deepest parts of the sea. A light smile played on my lips as I fingered the delicate silk. I plucked it from the bed and gasped. It was a beautiful dress, the bust a simple corset with golden ribbon.

The bustles in front were tied up, coming to the tops of my knees, the back draping down to my ankles. It was gorgeous, not something I ever intended to wear in my life. Not even my old one. Underneath the dress was a pair of black leather leggings. I was ecstatic to still have some form of pants and pulled them on hurriedly. I stepped into the dress and shrugged it up over my hips, slipping the straps over my arms and noting the lack of sleeves. The last step was to tighten the ribbons in front. My breath was cut short not used to the constriction.

"Davy Jones, who the fuck thought this would be fashionable?" I muttered to no one in particular. "A man must have designed this torture device."

I stepped back, looking into the mirror that hung on the wall. The image before me was unsettling. I barely recognized myself, even as my fingertips brushed my hollowed cheeks. Weeks of rationing had eaten away at some of my muscle mass. My golden skin appeared darker in the depths of the fabric; I took the time to put my hair in a simple French twist at the nape of my neck. If only my father could see me now. A proper lady was all he ever wished me to be.

Well, youre little girl is all grown up now.

I strapped my brass knife into its holster on my thigh, hidden by the folds of my skirt. My cutlass would be hard to hide and harder to explain away. Weapons were not fit for ladies. I sneered at my reflection; I was not a lady. A soft knock on the door startled me out of my thoughts.

I crossed the room swiftly, trying not to trip on my skirts as my fingertips danced over my blade tucked safely at my side. One of the girls from downstairs stood on the other side as I cracked the door open.

"Fresh towels," she murmured, her eyes trailing over my face.

"Thank you." I opened the door wider as I took them from her. I went to place them on the bed and noticed she stepped inside the doorway.

"Are you finished with the food?" She nodded toward the little table, and I grabbed the empty plates.

"Yes, thank you for bringing it up."

"Anything Casper requests, he gets." Her voice remained unwavering, but I noticed a hard line set on her face as she took the plates. "He asked that you meet him down in the market."

"Thank you."

She gave a curt nod before she turned back down the hall. I waited till I could no longer hear the shuffle of fabric and made my way quickly out of the room. I hastened my pace past the rows of doors even as their sounds begged me to stay and listen. I could feel my cheeks growing warm. The stairs creaked under my weight; I kept my eyes on my leather boots, concentrating on not tripping. That would be all I needed, to make a fool of myself in a brothel full of naked people.

The scent of the brothel hit me again, musk, cinnamon, and sex. Alluring. My heart began fluttering wildly at the thought of Casper seeing me like this.

I would do unspeakable things for one of those personal fans Misty pulled out of her bodice earlier. The air was thick as it clung to my skin, glistening it with a sheen of sweat as I made my way to the market—at least I hoped I was headed the right way. I allowed my thoughts to unfocus, to lose myself in the noise of the people surrounding the streets and take in the scent of freshly baked bread.

Harmonicas and ukuleles harmonized, their tune floating lightly on the breeze. Children's laughter followed along as the view opened to the market below. The heels of my boots clicked along the cobblestone as I walked. Each of my senses was alive and alert as I made my way through the stands. The gold and purple tapestries shielded patrons from the sun.

Soon enough, the market opened into a large square, one I did not recall passing before. In the middle, all sorts of people gathered in the center. I watched from the outskirts as they danced. This was the source of the music. Fabrics of all colors and materials spun out before my eyes as women twirled and swayed, going from partner to partner. Their gleeful laughs were a song of their own, following the beat of the music. I felt the corners of my mouth pull up without command.

"May I have this here dance?" A figure bowed in front of me, lending me their hand. The voice tugged at my mind. I knew this voice.

I did not realize who stood in front of me until they glanced up. Bran. A grim line settled on my lips briefly before I managed a tight smile.

"Thank you, but I am waiting for someone," I said through gritted teeth, trying to muster a friendly tone.

"Awe come on; I'm sure they wouldn't mind just one little dance." A sly grin spread across his face.

I was shoved from behind before I was able to respond, and he pulled me into the swarm of flashing skirts. My heart thundered in my chest as he spun me around. I had never danced before, much less with someone I despised down to my core or one I worried would recognize me with every passing moment. My eyes darted around as he swung me in broad circles trying to spot an exit. There was nothing but a mass of bodies, and I was drowning in my panic. His arms are an unforgiving cage around me.

The tempo hastened and Bran responded seamlessly, as if he had danced most of his life instead of sailing the seas. I was starting to get lightheaded from the movement when we were interrupted.

"I believe it be time the lass had a different partner."

My back stiffened and relaxed as I saw Casper in front of Bran, whose composure changed completely. Gone was the friendly stranger, there was the cruel man I knew.

"The lass may beg to differ. Ye have no power here," he spit. "Where be your pet, anyway? I haven't spied him around."

"He is off with one of the strumpets, why don't you do the same?" Casper's tone was as harsh as my glower at the mention of the whores.

"I been plannin' on it, why do ye think I asked this here lass to dance?"

My face was hot with fury, almost as much as my right hook that caught him in the jaw. Bran's head snapped back. His howl of pain was lost to the sound of the rising music as I shook my hand out.

Damn, that felt good.

"I am no whore. Mark me, it will be the last time you call me that."

I could see the rage spread across his face, fury flashing in his wide eyes. Casper took hold of my arm and tucked me behind himself.

"You should know better than that, speaking to a proud beauty in that manner." Casper's voice held a warning as he took me away.

I could feel Bran's gaze boring into my back as he led me away. Once we could only hear the music softly, Casper's pace slowed and I was able to catch my breath.

"Curse this blessed corset, it's hard to breathe," I gasped out, holding my hand to my abdomen.

"It sure is pretty to look at though. You look gorgeous. The color suits ye."

That cursed blush was once again blossoming over my cheeks.

"Thank you for getting it for me."

"Eh, 'twas nothing, I promised you a new garment. Did I nah?"

I rolled my eyes. "I thought you meant a new shirt. Not something like this."

I looked down, playing with my skirts idly, my cheeks still warm. Casper slipped his hand under my chin, bringing my face to meet his.

"A gown suited fer a princess, my beauty."

He brought his lips to mine. Just a brush against my own. I stood on my tiptoes to press harder into him. His taste was intoxicating, with sweet promises and a hint of rum.

"I wanted that dance; he stole that from me," he murmured against my mouth.

"What is one dance, when we have the world?" I whispered, a smile playing on my lips as I gazed into his eyes.

"Aye. The world."

Chapter 36

New Beginnings

"**G**ood morning, my love."

Casper's fingers traced gently down the lines of my face and curled into his touch. I pulled the blanket higher around my neck, taking comfort in my personal heater beside me.

"Mmm, good morning. What time is it?" I mumbled, my eyes still closed in protest. My mind was groggy with sleep, and I wanted to succumb to its embrace.

"'Tis just passed dawn," he murmured, pressing his lips to my temple and leaving a warm wet mark.

"Then why, might I ask, are you bothering me?" I grumbled, tucking my knees closer to myself—as if that act alone would ward him off.

He chuckled. "Ye are grumpy when you wake up."

I snorted. "I am not a morning person. You would know that if you ever stayed till morning."

"I always stayed as long as I could, me love."

My eyes snapped open upon hearing the tight emotion in his voice. I pressed my palm against his scruffy cheek, capturing his eyes with my own. "I'm sorry. That wasn't fair of me to say. Nor does it matter now. We have every morning together from now on."

His gaze was steady as his fingers roamed the canvas of my side. My breathing hitched as his fingers trailed under the blanket, then tugged at the fabric of my nightgown before venturing underneath. His touch scorched every inch of flesh he brushed over, his thumb tracing little circles into my hip. My eyes fluttered closed as he bent toward me, his lips gliding down my jawline to my throat. A soft moan left me as his kiss deepened at my collarbone. His mouth was warm against my flesh as he laved his tongue over my sensitive skin. The next thing I knew, my nightgown was being discarded on the floor in a flutter of fabric and Casper hovered over me, caging me in with his body. His eyes roamed over me just as his fingers had as I lay bare beneath him at my most vulnerable. My soul bared to him and only him.

Maybe I hated that the most. Someone having this kind of trust over me.

My thoughts were quick to cease as soon as his lips grazed my skin once again, leaving a lingering fire everywhere they touched. A pool of warmth was already swelling in my core, filled with pure anticipation for that talented tongue of his. Precise and unforgiving. He rested between my legs, scooping my thighs up in his arms. They were iron locks that held me in place as he began his sweet torture. My hips bucked without my consent, yet he remained unfazed. I swore I saw stars. His sweet torture over the most sensitive part of me was enough to send me into a frenzy. I had heard women speaking of men who didn't like to please in my village, I felt bad for them. I got one of the lucky ones that lived for my pleasure. He pressed his mouth firmly against my core, his tongue running firm lines over my apex of nerves.

It was mere minutes before my world exploded in vivid color. Waves of ecstasy crashed into me. Casper groaned between my thighs, mixing with my moans of pleasure. My body shuddered around him, reeling in the throes of bliss. Once I could breathe again, he removed himself from between my legs.

"Ye taste sweet as ever." He looked at me with pure heat in his eyes as he ran his tongue slowly over his bottom lip.

The blush that settled over my cheeks was uncontrollable as I descended from the stars he tossed me into. Casper prowled up my body from between my thighs to capture my lips in a hungry kiss—one that was meant to devour my body, mind, soul. I did not know which, maybe all. My entire essence. It was his for the claiming. When our lips finally parted, I was gasping for air all over again.

Moments passed before he claimed me from the inside. Our bodies clashed in a thunderous storm of flesh. My legs wrapped around his waist, pinning him, guiding him against me. He was not the only one needing to devour. I needed him more than I needed air at that moment. Every moment, really, after he barreled into my life and changed my future forever. This moment, this was real. I was Naida, laid bare before him in more ways than my body. Here we were, simply existing, with no lies, no worries, just us enjoying each other.

I drank in every minute. The taste of him. The scent of him. I wanted his imprint on my soul to last past this lifetime into the next. I memorized every sharp angle of his face, the stubble lining his jaw and the way his eyes bore into mine until I could no longer focus on anything.

"Lift your hips for me, love," Casper murmured against my neck.

A thrilled raced through my veins as I did exactly as he ordered and he stroked me deeper.

"Right there lass, good girl," he praised, and I felt my core get wetter, liquifying for him and only him.

The storm brewing between us threatened to unleash and take me with it. My body relinquished its stronghold, only to be washed over with pure ecstasy, one he joined me in. Together, our worlds crashed and burned because, in that moment, it was just us. We collapsed in sweaty heaps beside each other, the air cool against our slicken skin.

Only after we had regained our breaths did we hop in the shower—which was not as spacious with a big hunk of man meat. Casper had to duck under the showerhead because he was so tall. We scrambled around each other trying to wash ourselves and find our respective items. It was not as sexy as I had envisioned but it was nice and normal. Wherever we went next, I hoped that there would be a shower. I could get used to the ease of this instead of filling a tub with boiling water. Oh, how I longed to never carry a water bucket again.

The realization of what came after this blissfully normal shower was threatening to be my undoing. Once we gathered supplies, that was it. We were walking away from the life we knew. Casper mentioned he had arranged a horse for us at the edge of town. It would take us to the other side of the island, where a smaller boat waited for us. One that was safe for me. They agreed to take us to their next port location as long as we worked while aboard. Apparently, women on board was not a superstition in their parts. I was thankful for that, not having to hide while on board would be a wonderful change.

My heart tugged painfully in my chest thinking about leaving Porter. My friend. Would I see him before we leave? Could I risk seeking him out? No, it would be too dangerous. I would never bring him into this. He was there for me when no one else was and I would be there for him. Leaving without his knowledge would protect him and us. I couldn't imagine he would understand, anyway. If he found out I had been lying all this time, he would feel betrayed, and I would forever mourn the loss of trust he had in me.

We made haste to get dressed. I found a dark tunic and a pair of trousers waiting for me. Casper could see the question on my face before I spoke.

"Ye have never ridden a horse, have ye?" His hand cupped my cheek, and I shook my head. "'Tis easier to ride in pants."

"Ah." I nodded my agreement and stepped into my pants. The tunic was soft as I tugged it over my head, a nice change from the scratchy material I was used to.

"We need enough supplies to last, but nah too much to bring notice. It would be best if we shop separately." He glanced over at me as he rummaged around the nightstand. "Take this."

He plopped a small coin bag into my hands. "Buy enough clothes to last, and a new pair of boots. Ones with good tread. Some grub that will not spoil fast. I dunno the conditions of the galleon we shall be takin'."

I nodded as I strapped the coin bag to my belt, tucking it into my pocket.

"On second thought, buy another dagger too. A sharp one."

"Why?" My eyebrows knitted in confusion as my stomach turned uneasily.

He shrugged as if the answer were simple. "Ye can never trust a pirate."

He kissed me quickly before we split to conquer our separate tasks at the market. My heart was pumping wildly in my chest, my palms grew clammy, and I wiped them on my pants. I had a cloth pouch strapped to my other hip with some of the things from our room. The only items I had taken from the ship when I left.

Before I could set foot out the door, I felt a tug of urgency to finish my father's journal. Grabbing it from within the satchel, I plopped on the edge of the bed. My pulse raced, facing the final moments of my father.

August 16th, 1898

Lyra,

Naida and I got into an argument. My soul burns with the words I spoke to her. She brought home the book on Sirens, one I have read many times. You knew my curiosity about these creatures. I should have burned that book, even if it was against everything my soul stood for. Fear overtook me when I saw the tome in her hands. Your death flashed before my eyes, yet I knelt on shaky knees, holding our daughter. I have never been more grateful for tearing those cursed pages from that tome. I burned the pages I feared our daughter finding the most. In a way, I suppose I knew she would seek it out, seek the answers I myself longed to find. In my bones, I can feel it. I have ruined our relationship for good. I fear a fate worse than death awaits our daughter. I often feel your presence while I am out to sea; please, Lyra, protect her when I cannot. I have failed.

I let the pain wash over me again, feeling the loss like it was yesterday. As tears ran down my cheeks I continued.

August 25th, 1898

Lyra,

We haven't spoken in weeks. Naida is training, building herself, and proving her worth every day. I wish I could tell her that. Still, I see the dark circles under her eyes and the hollow of her cheeks. She has changed as much as I have over these years without you. This morning, I have a harrowing feeling in my gut. The sky bleeds. We need food. I just hope I have done enough.

Naida,

If you find this, please understand. Everything I have done; everything has been for you. I'm sorry I couldn't be there for you as I once was. Fear made my heart cold. Be smart, my daughter. When I can no longer be with you, know I am so proud of you in your heart.

This was the first time he said he was proud of me. Reading these passages made me feel more connected to him than I did after years of living with him, even though he was now out of reach. I clutched the journal to my chest, allowing myself a few moments to feel the grief, to mourn the loss of something I never had. Once the tears dried, I sniffed and stood, placing the journal back into my satchel.

For you, Father, I will live.

The market was alive and bustling, even this early in the morning. Fresh-baked pastries wafted through the air, making my stomach grumble. I grabbed a golden croissant that flaked under my touch and tossed the vendor a coin. The buttery pastry melted in my mouth, causing a low moan to rumble in my throat. I smiled like a fool around the mouthful of flakey goodness.

"Good gods, this is good."

I weaved my way through the stands and quickly found a few baggy blouses and thick trousers to weather the elements aboard the ship. I spent the majority of my time trying to find a good pair of boots. I settled on a pair of leather ones that wrapped around my calves. The soles were thick with good traction, very important when the deck gets slippery. The vendors were happy as clams as I tossed them coins for my wears. Last, I needed a dagger.

I searched the stands till I came across a vendor with all the sharp things any girl could dream of, the metal of them glistening in the sun like beacons calling my name. It may have been shameful, the way I felt my face light up at the sight of them. The craftsmanship alone was stunning. Sprawled out in front of me was an assortment of fine weaponry; knives, short swords, broadswords, an ax or two, and quite the array of daggers. One in particular called to me from its cradle of velvet material.

The middle-aged man behind the stand gave me an odd look, stroking his long, graying beard thoughtfully. "Careful girl, you may cut yerself. Do you know how to handle one of these?"

I cut him a look that was as sharp as the blade I was currently examining. "With deadly accuracy."

The hilt had two mermaids carved into either side, inlaid with golden accents. A stunning gem laid in between them. This was a piece of art, indeed. A neat pearl was cradled in a golden claw on the top of it. Fine leather wrapped around the handle. I weighed it in my hand, balancing the blade on two extended fingers.

"How much?" I stared at it in wonder as I twirled it between my fingers, slowly inspecting the blade.

"Four pounds." He spoke as he stood by my side. I was startled by his stealth, but my face remained stoic.

"I will give ye three."

He looked at me as if he would argue, the golden-brown skin around his eyes crinkling, until we were interrupted.

"I was hoping I would catch ye again."

The hair on the nape of my neck bristled, recognizing Bran's voice behind me. I shifted slightly.

"Pity, I wouldn't say the same."

"Quite the tongue on ye, lass." His voice was thick with menace that made my fingers tighten till they were white on the hilt.

I turned back to the merchant, dropped three pieces in his hand, and took the dagger. Bran seemed to notice it then and sneered.

"Careful, lass, ye may hurt yourself."

I huffed, irritation brimming. "I don't know why everyone seems to think I cannot handle myself. If I recall properly, I did just fine last night."

I could see Bran practically seething where he stood and couldn't deny the joy that sight brought me. A smile tugged my lips; I was quite ready to be done with this constant thorn in my side that they had been from day one. Funny, I hadn't seen much of his towering other half around.

"Well, I best be off. Thank you for my pretty new toy." I waved to the merchant and nodded a dismissal to Bran.

Weaving my way through the market was quick work of losing him. If anything, the past year aboard had taught me that he was not quick on his feet.

I patted the satchel on my belt, reassuring myself it was there. My feet followed Casper's directions by memory, my gaze darting around casually every now and then to make sure I was going the right way. The thrum of voices from the town was silenced by the thrashing pulse in my ears. The blood roaring in them was deafening. Not too much longer. I noted the immense steepled building signaling the outskirts of the town beyond. A ragged breath left me that I was unaware I had been holding once the building was in front of me. My fingers trailed the cool stone for a moment, grounding myself. I turned left; Casper had said he would be waiting in the tree line about a hundred yards away. My pace quickened. I swallowed around the lump that formed in my throat as I took in his brooding figure, the silhouette of the horse beside him.

My mouth gaped as he came into clearer view. I thought Casper was tall. This beast must have been at least seven feet high. His white body gleamed in the rays bouncing off of it. Apparently, my gulp was auditory because Casper chuckled, patting his side softly.

"He won't hurt ye, lass."

My nose wrinkled in response, my heart a hummingbird in my chest. I wiped my moistened hands on my pants and cracked my knuckles as I edged closer. Casper patted the beast again before he greeted me in three long strides. He grasped my chin lightly between his forefinger and his thumb.

"Only a few more moments until our forever, my love." His lips lovingly caressed my temple.

I worked around the lump in my throat. "If I don't fall off this beast to my death beforehand."

I felt his laugh rumble through my chest. "If you have handled riding me, I have no doubt ye can ride this beast. Those thighs have a steel grip, lass."

Blush bloomed in my cheeks, even if pride swelled in my belly at the remark. I shook out my still trembling hands, cracking my knuckles again nervously.

"Ok, how do I get on this thing?"

A cough from behind startled us both. I shifted slightly to see who it was as Casper stepped in front of me. A shield that I, as well as Bran and Braxon, noted. My throat constricted in palpable fear. We were so close, so close to being gone.

No, no no this can't be happening.

"Now, just where do ye reckon ye be goin'?" Bran's voice was a low rumble, his mouth quirked to the side. I wanted to punch that grin right off his face.

"I am takin' the lass fer a ride. She has never been on a horse before," Casper's reply was smooth.

Bran turned his attention to me. "Again, I find Casper swooping in when I am trying to get to know ye. Doesn't seem mighty fair now, does it?"

I swallowed painfully, trying to get moisture back into my bone-dry mouth. "I thought I made it clear both times I was not interested."

Bran's face turned to hardened stone, his gaze sweeping slowly down me and lingering at my waist. "I would believe this was innocent if it weren't fer the bags strapped to yer belts. Both of yer belts. Seems the lass is more interested in other rides."

My stomach turned sour; I could feel my blood heating. "I don't know what you are intending to say, sir, but I do not appreciate your accusations."

I was too busy keeping a sweltering glower on Bran that, at first, I did not notice a third figure appear behind the two men. Not until they stepped to the side to reveal a much smaller frame. The mousy mop of brown hair caught the sun.

"Hello, Demi." Porter's voice was foreign to my ears, thick with distaste.

My heart shattered into pieces; I could feel it shuddering through every meager pump that rattled my chest.

"Porter?" My voice was barely a quivering whisper that left my lips.

Shock bloomed on both Bran and Braxon's faces before their smiles turned into bloodthirsty flashes of teeth. They had gained a better prize than they anticipated.

"Had we known ye were a wench, we may have treated ye better. At night, at least." Bran's voice was laced with a dark poison, enough that my flesh goose-pimpled even as my lip curled in a snarl.

Eyes locked on the men in front of us, I fumbled to get my satchel open, hunting for my dagger. I refused to go down without a fight.

"From your fighting skills, I could tell you wouldn't be a very fulfilling partner in the sack," I sneered as I felt the cool hilt in my hand blustering my confidence.

I felt Casper stiffen in front of me as the look on Bran's face darkened. Porter barked out a laugh.

"She's got ye there, mate."

Blood pounded in my ears. If he were not standing before me, I wouldn't have believed it.

"How could you? I thought we were friends," I muttered, spitting on the ground. My hand clutched the hilt so hard it bit into my skin. My heart was shattering as I willed myself not to crumble.

"Gotta look out fer number one mate."

Porter's cold reply was a slap to my face. As my mind whirled around, everything over those passed months clicked into place. How distant he was, the assignment to the medical unit when we had surgeons on board, Captain's direct orders. My blood ran cold, the color draining from my face. Fury laced through my veins.

"How long?" My voice went utterly quiet, the calm before the storm.

He smirked at me. "Who do ye think took your key? I needed proof. Even after I suspected as much, that little journal of yers did wonders."

My blood boiled. "You fucking prick!" I yelled, lunging forward. Casper's arm shot out, curling around my waist and keeping me there.

I seethed as my vision began to blur from unshed tears—tears of rage. Tears of betrayal.

"You were my only friend!" I thrust myself forward again, but Casper was pure steel beside me, unrelenting.

"That is no one's fault but yer own. Likely enough would have stayed that way if ye didn't start fuckin' him."

He spat toward Casper, who I could feel shaking at my side in barely contained fury.

"I am the first mate. Ye would be best holdin' yer fuckin' tongue. Ye do nah speak of her to me in that manner. I have killed fer less."

I looked up at Casper, seeing his face completely calm. The power coming off him would have made me piss myself if it were directed at me.

"Oh, please, no one likes you. The cap'n has lost faith in ye. Why do ye reckon I was able to sneak in to be his mouse?" I felt Casper bristle beside me.

"How do ye reckon the cap'n will react knowin' ye were about to maroon yer contract?"

"What makes you reckon he will believe a mouse?"

The tone in Casper's voice had me bracing in a fighting stance, dagger ready to party. My blood was singing with the call for revenge. To unleash this building fury on my so-called friend.

"I'm here on Cap'n's orders." Porter's smile was as deadly as a Siren's.

With that, Braxon charged at Casper and Bran rushed me. A few quick foot movements and I was dodging his attacks, Zig-zagging and ducking under his right hook. He left his side vulnerable; I took advantage, slashing my dagger across his ribs. Blood spewed out from my assault.

"You bitch!" Bran seethed, swinging harder than I could duck. His fist caught me across the jaw. I blinked away the stars that danced in my vision.

I spit blood on the ground. "You never were fast enough."

I slashed my dagger again, catching his bicep, crimson streamed down his arm. Blood was blooming the fabric of his shirt on his side. A wicked smile tore across my face at the sight. Bran lashed out again, his fist coming slower than before. I ducked left but didn't notice the glint of metal. The blade bit into my flesh. I hissed in pain as I felt blood trickle from my chest. I seized the moment to catch him unbalanced and swiped my leg out, taking him down. My pulse was racing in my chest as I hovered over him. I angled my dagger and plunged it into his throat. The crunch of his jugular satisfied some of my growing rage. Hearing his bloody gurgle was a symphony to my ears. Over a year's worth of agony aboard that ship, all brought by him.

"You got what you deserved." I spat on his face as he took his last fluttering breath, his death rattle.

Too bad I had been a little preoccupied with Bran to notice Porter behind me. That was till the thwack led me into blissful darkness.

I was back in my village, and gentle waves lapped at the boulders surrounding me. The ocean lay in front of me, glistening under the sun, the calm bringing me peace. I curled my toes in the sand, relishing in the warm squish between them. The melody flinted through my mind before I saw her golden-brown hair pop above the surface. Her emerald eyes shone bright; her lips curved into a welcoming smile.

"I knew I would see you again." It came out as a breath-less laugh. My heart filled with overwhelming joy.

"*Young one, I never doubted for a minute we would be reunited.*" Her melody caressed my mind, raising goose-flesh on my arms.

I didn't hesitate a moment more to run into the water to-ward her. Her arms enveloped me the moment she was close enough. The love that radiated from her spread warmth throughout me.

"Gods have I missed you," I sobbed into her shoulder.

"*I have missed you too young one.*" She pulled back just enough for her eyes to search my face. "*Has this life gone how you wished?*"

My eyebrows knitted at the question. "It isn't how I thought it would be. I went out looking for a purpose, a simple dream of being free. But what I found was so much more, Mother." I gulped in a heavy breath. "I found adventure, friendship, love."

I paused and drew back from her further, clasping her shoulders so hard I could see my fingers leaving marks.

"Mother, I found Casper. I didn't mean for it to happen. I knew it was dangerous, but I would die one thousand deaths if it meant I could find him again and we could share what we had for whatever amount of time we could."

"*Love finds us in unpredictable ways, my darling. Not when we are searching for it but when we need it the most.*" Her eyes held mine as she gently ran her hands up and down my arms, soothing me. These were the moments I longed for the most in my childhood—having a mother's nurturing comfort.

"He makes me feel alive in a way I never have before. As if the sea suddenly parted in the middle of chaos to find peace. He dared me to dream of a life I thought I had thrown away when I signed that contract. I was ready to leave it all behind. I was bound by nothing but the sea ahead of me."

My excited rush of words turned into ghostly whispers by the end. She watched me knowingly, her eyes crinkling at the corners.

"*But it was not enough.*" She stroked her nimble fingers through my hair, and I leaned into her palm. The emotion inside overwhelmed me as I spoke the words I never thought I would utter.

"No," I sobbed. "It was not enough."

She nodded slowly; her smile saddened.

"*It is not yet your time, young one.*" The voice in my head caressed me and she kissed me softly on the cheek.

"What do you mean?"

"*I will find you,*" she trilled. "*I will always find you.*"

I blinked, trying to clear the grogginess from my eyes. The splitting pain in my head brought tears immediately.

"Fuck," I muttered, bringing my hand gingerly to the wound; they came back sticky. My mouth was bone dry, only the taste of iron encased it. I smacked my lips, trying to get back some moisture.

I felt the movement before I realized I was back on *The Shadow*. More accurately, I was in one of the holding cells in the back of the berth. My stomach rolled, threatening to unleash whatever contents were still in my stomach. I tried to sit up, only for my head to spin relentlessly. Porter's blow must have left me concussed. I heard my father speak of sailors suffering from this when the boom wasn't secured properly, and they got hit in the head. Never did I imagine it would feel like this.

"Easy, love."

My head whipped to the sound of Casper's voice, which I instantly regretted as the pounding increased. I crawled over to the bars of our adjoining cells, ignoring the crunch of bones beneath me. Gooseflesh littered my skin at the thought of those who died in this very cage before me.

"Are you okay?" I whispered, reaching my arm between the bars to touch him. He scooted closer so I could palm the side of his face. He looked worse for wear, the skin around his right eye puckered—an ugly purple and green hue. There were a few gashes in his shirt the more my eyes roamed, spotting the blooms of dried brown blood. The more I took in his state, the more a raging fire grew in my belly.

"Ye should see Braxon." He grinned, showing his split lip, blood welling at the wound. "I didn't go down without a fight. But you be the only one to claim a life."

I gulped over the growing lump in my throat. "I killed Bran."

It was a statement, but Casper nodded, nonetheless. I recalled the feeling of taking his life, it was terrifying, how good it felt. Never in my life would I have thought I could kill a man. My satisfaction was short-lived as the gravity of our situation dawned on me.

"This is not going to end well for us, is it?" My voice trembled as I looked desperately into his eyes, pleading with him to give me hope, something to hold on to.

It was his turn to reach through the bars and comb the knotted strands of hair from my face. His face was grave as his eyes met mine, I could see my terror echoed in his own, somber acceptance.

"I am afraid nah, my love," he whispered as his thumb stroked over my lip. "I regret nothing. I made my choice when I found ye in that ship."

There was no point in holding back the tears as they streamed down my cheeks. Everything in my life boiled down to this moment. My mind spun in a whirlwind of thoughts. I held my regrets, the only one that mattered was I brought him down with me. My Casper, my everything.

"Shhh," Casper whispered as he wiped my tears with his thumb.

"I am so sorry. I should have stayed away," I sobbed, my shoulders heaving heavily. The weight threatened to crush me.

"Nonsense, I would cross the seven seas and face the stars to find you," Casper murmured, pressing his forehead against the cool bars. "I will love you till my last breath, Naida. In the afterlife, I will face Davy Jones to find you again. In every life, I will choose you. 'Twill always be you."

"It will always be you, Casper. I love you more than the sea itself."

I pressed my face against the bars, the metal biting into my skin, and our lips met gingerly. I savored the taste of him, even as it mixed with the taste of dried and fresh blood from his lip. Running my hands through his soft curls, I wanted to memorize the texture. The color was deeper than squid ink. My eyes fluttered open briefly to take in his golden-brown complexion. The arch of his thick brows. I pulled back slightly to take in the curve of his full plump lips, even if they were swollen. The glacial blue of his eyes was a strain to see in the dim lighting. I could tell by the way his eyes flickered across my face he was doing the same. Both our bodies shook as we mapped each other, holding on for dear life. I only had a taste of him, I wasn't ready to give that up—to give him up. It was selfish but he was the one light that remained in the dark.

"I will find you again, I will always find you," I murmured the same words my mother said in my dream.

Chapter 37

Cruel Twist of Fate

It had been a week, at least that is what I assumed, since Bill happily chucked a rock-hard loaf of bread at me each day. Seven days locked in a cell, with nothing but some musty hay, rotten bones, a bucket in each corner to relieve ourselves, and a poor attempt to hold each other throughout the night. My body was stiff from sleeping huddled in the corner just so I could touch Casper.

How were the bread stores already stale?

My stomach rumbled with its meager protests. Bill must have delighted in leaving it to sit out on purpose. I regretted pissing him off over a year ago, it seemed he still hadn't forgotten it. I could feel myself withering away. At least he tossed a slab of butter and hard cheese to Casper occasionally. It was a strain anymore to crawl across the cell to Casper. I couldn't recall a time I had felt this weak; even when Father had nothing in his net for dinner.

I missed warm food and walking around—hell, even swabbing the deck was better than this. The hunger had eaten away at my muscle mass, my shirt hung off me, limp and dirty. Glancing at Casper as he slept showed me the same. I never saw him look so frail. His shirt was coated in dry blood. His breaths came out ragged; even in sleep, his wounds carried the pain. My heart ached for him—for our situation.

Footsteps thumped heavily down the stairs, and I scooted to the far corner of my cell and tucked my head between my legs. I heard him spit before I felt the warmth on my neck. The work I did with these men for over a year was all forgotten now. The past week had shown that any remorse I hoped for was vacant from their rabid expressions. I had never felt more alone. At least before I had Porter, always standing by me. They enjoyed it like the savages they truly were, spitting on me, and flinging brutal slurs that cut worse than any cutlass would. I swiped the back of my neck, rubbing my hand stiffly against my trousers. I used what strength I had to flip him off as he walked away chuckling. That was not the worst I had gotten over the days.

I learned quickly to stay away from the edges of the cell; there were wandering hands in the night. They raked over me in ways that burned my flesh worse than the bite of a fire ever could. My blouse was in tatters from them ripping the fabric away from my chest. Scratch marks littered over my skin from their savage grip on me as I tried to tear them away. My throat became raw from my screams. I did not go without a fight. In the beginning, I almost took off a thumb before they slammed me against the bars, and I saw stars. I was a caged animal whose fight had been going out as the days lingered on.

Casper couldn't help me; they took him out every other day. I heard the whip crack through the air, yet he never screamed. Each time it cracked through the air, I cringed. How he managed not to scream I would never know. He was strong, and they knew it. Flashes of his punishment of Bran and Braxon haunted me. My chest ached when they eventually returned him to his cage. His ribboned flesh unleashed a bloodthirsty part of me—one I hadn't known could exist before ending Bran's sorry life. I tried the best I could to tend to his wounds, sacrificing my tankard of water a few times to wash the blood from him. Without proper care, infection would set in. If there would even be time for infection to take hold before our inevitable end. I craved blood in payment, the thought sent me absolutely feral.

I would slaughter them all.

I knew it was nothing but a lustful thought, they would kill me. Us. Tears pricked my eyes, and I buried my face in my arms. Nothing but an iron cage containing an animal slowly withering away. I bit my tongue hard enough I could taste blood, that would be enough to settle my poorly contained rage for now.

Casper groaned, I crawled over to him as I watched him try to move.

"Don't move too much," I whispered, reaching out to touch his shoulder gingerly. He answered me with a hiss as his back muscles spasmed. "How are you doing?"

A strangled laugh left him. "Never been better, lass."

"They need to bring the doctor in here to tend your wounds," I muttered angrily, looking over his back—some of the wounds scabbing, some weeping. The new crimson leaked through the material of his shirt

"To make me better just to kill me, anyway?"

My throat swelled with emotion, making it harder to breathe over the foreboding lump of what was to come. I would give my left arm to be able to properly hold and care for him. Waves of heartache crashed into me. They were getting stronger over the days and seemed to be the only thing growing besides my rage. Most days, the despair threatened to swallow me whole. Casper was the only thing keeping me tethered, keeping me from sharpening one of these bones and ending the misery myself. This waiting game was taking its toll.

"I'm sorry." My voice was barely audible.

Slowly, ever so slowly, he turned, wincing as he did to face me. "Never be sorry, lass."

My chest deflated as I unraveled into quiet sobs, shaking my entire body. The little hiccups of breath were the only sound carried through the berth. I cried until I fell into a restless sleep, like my body just gave out on me and succumbed to the darkness.

The sound of a lock unlatching was my wake-up call. I thought I had felt fear before. I was wrong. The terror I felt was only the beginning as burly hands wrapped around my arms. They drug me out of my cell, my feet trailing along the boards. My head hung limply, watching the floor move below me.

"No, no, no, no, no, no," was all I could mutter as my thoughts seized me.

This was the end.

Tears streamed down my face as I looked back at Casper, he was reaching his hand out to me. His voice was drowned out by the ringing in my ears. I was sobbing enough to heave. If there would have been any contents in my stomach, they would have met the floor. The crewmates carrying me grunted in irritation as they hauled me up the steps. My knees hit every single one. Agony radiated up my legs as my sobs turned into a low-pitched keening.

They dragged me painfully to the top deck. The sun scorched my eyes like an eternal flame, the first I had seen a glimpse of it in seven days. I tucked my head into my shoulder to shield myself from its unforgiving rays. The two men I recognized but could not name hauled me to the mass and tied my arms above my head. My body throbbed, my arms burning as I hung there limply.

I lifted my head, every inch sending bolts of lightning through my nerves. My eyes roamed over everyone standing around me. They crowded like a pack of sharks, and I was the bait. My throat constricted, even as I bared my teeth to them all. I spit at the ground by their feet. It was getting hard to breathe, but I would be damned if I showed them. Half the crowd turned around to look at something else. I strained against my binds to see them dragging a limp Casper between two of our burliest sailors. Rage flooded my veins again, white-hot and blinding.

"What are you doing to him?" I seethed, struggling harder against my restraints.

Porter appeared by my side. He lightly stroked my hair back with his hand. It was such a friendly gesture and I jerked away. "What he deserves Demi, what ye both deserve."

His words were a dagger to my heart, shredding the last hope I had for my friend. The one that cared for me at all. "Fuck you, Porter. May Davy Jones claim your rotten soul." I spit in his face.

He backhanded me across the face with such force my world spun. Little black spots dotted my vision.

"You wench!" He snarled. I did not recognize the man standing in front of me. He wiped the red spittle from his face with the back of his hand, wiping it on my trousers.

"Let him go!" I yanked against the rope, feeling it tear at my flesh. "You have me, take my life but please spare his. If the friendship we had once was ever true, please. Please spare him, Porter."

I loathed the desperate plea, even as it fled my trembling lips. Porter sneered at me, his mouth tugging up on one side. "I be following the captains' orders"

A sob raked through me as he turned away abruptly. The crowd parted for Porter as he made his way to Casper's side.

"I won't lie, I am going to enjoy every single bit of this." He yanked Casper by his hair to look him in the eye. I seethed, seeing him treat Casper that way boiled my blood like no other.

"If 'tis me time, I go to Davy Jones willingly," Casper rasped. "But when it comes yer time, I will be waitin' the first in line to welcome ye to the after life."

Porter reeled his fist back, landing a heavy blow to Casper's jaw. I heard the crack and cried out as if his pain were my own. It felt like my own. My heart pounded in my chest, raging against its constraints much like I was.

"Tie him to the anchor," Porter bellowed to the two sailors holding onto him. They shared a bloodthirsty grin, hoisting him up roughly.

They were going to Keelhaul him. The thought washed over me like an ice bath. They would tie him to the anchor and drop him into the water, dragging him along with the ship. It was one of the worst ways to go for a pirate—often the fitting punishment for mutiny if unsuccessful.

"Porter, I will find you. I will string you up and gut you like the fucking fish you are. Hear me! This is my vow." My voice cracked as I shouted at him.

Terrors cold claws sunk into me, leaving me frozen as I gaped at Casper. Our eyes met and held briefly before he was dragged to the side of the ship and tied. Silent tears fell down my face, blurring my vision. I fought with all my might against the ropes, but it was no use. They were tied too tight, and I had no energy to give. I felt the despair ripping up my throat, it begged to be set free.

"I love you, I always will."

Casper's words barely carried to me as they finished tying him. My mind couldn't process when they tossed over the anchor and him along with it. The splash rattled me to my core, a scream wrenched from me with a force I didn't think I possessed. My soul and my entire being shattered instantly.

My sobs grew to the strength I was hyperventilating, this time my stomach found bile to release all over the deck below me. The men surrounding me laughed menacingly as the trails of tears and snot streamed down my face. Porter sneered up at me, but I was too consumed in my despair to pay him any mind. Seeing Casper go over the edge had ruined me. My mind was still spiraling, trying to catch up—trying to understand that my end was coming just as quickly.

"Get her down lads and tie her up," Porter called and the crew swarmed their hands groping and ripping at me.

I wept without making a sound. What did it matter now? They tugged me down from the mast, and I collapsed in a heap on the deck. I clawed at the deck, forever marking it with my agony. A morbid thought popped into my head, at least I would be joining Marie. I hoped I haunted this ship just as she had. This would not be the last they saw of me. I had a vow to keep. More hands gripped me as they tugged me roughly to my feet. I kicked out in desperation, only to have more swarm around me and bind me tight. The only hope I held onto was that I would see Casper again soon. For him, I would meet my fate with open arms.

What had I done?

That was the only thought consuming my mind as I shuffled down the length of the plank. This was my personal brand of hell, carved out just for me. The whole 'walk the plank' thing wasn't typical for pirates; it was a folktale exaggerated throughout the years. How did I get so lucky as to experience it for myself? The crew grew restless, crowding behind me, cheering—actually cheering—spewing their vile thoughts about me. So much for brotherhood. What else did I expect? I knew the risks of this life, I just hadn't expected them to catch up to me so quickly. Thick jute ropes bound my body; I could only move in small shambles. The scrape of the cannon against the wood grated against my ears.

I felt the tip of a sword against my back, the cool metal biting into the cloth of my tattered shirt. Ice clutched my body; the fear of impending doom made my entire

being frigid and setting my body into pre-rigor mortis. I couldn't flex my fingers. Terror seeped through
the numbness that had overcome me. This was the
first time I looked at the sea below and panic barreled
through me, instead of the peace I usually claimed from
it. My heart shredded into a million jagged pieces, I felt
hollow. I gazed down into the murky expanse of open
water, gulping what was soon to be my last breaths.

"Move! Faster down the plank, yer fate awaits ye," Marduke bellowed, his voice booming like a gust of wind at
my back.

I winced reflexively and felt the sword nip at my flesh,
just enough to send a wave of pain down my spine. A little yelp escaped my shivering lips, and the crew roared
with laughter. The warm trickle of blood running down
my spine made me want to scratch it.

"Down goes the whore!" another crewmate yelled ferociously. Rage crept back in, locked in a deadly battle
with the panic seizing my soul.

My gasps quickened as I stared into the depths. No matter how hard I tried, my lungs wouldn't fill with sweet,
salty air. I worked around the lump in my throat, the
barrier for me to take in the oxygen I desperately needed. My knees trembled as I stood frozen, forever rooted

to the spot. This had not been my plan. Everything had gone wrong, so, so wrong.

How did I not see this coming?

The plank bowed beneath the captain's foot as he brought it crashing down with brute force. As the plank sprang back, I felt myself knocked off balance, then I plummeted to my awaiting doom. The drop was in slow motion; the choppy water lapped at the bottom of the ship, and dread raced up my spine as I plummeted into the sea's cold embrace. I was bound and helpless to their mercy.

The icy waters swallowed me whole. I sank rapidly, the weight of the ball and chain dragging me to my watery grave. An overwhelming pressure began to crush me as the sea sought to enter my lungs. Salt water burned my eyes. My body betrayed me, forcing me to cry out and allowing the last of my air to escape to the surface. A billowing trail of bubbles marked my path as I descended further into the depths.

Oh, how my lifetime friend has forsaken me.

A dark haze crept into my vision as black seeped into my peripheral. My lungs burned with the desperate need for oxygen; if I breathed in, I would drown. My body bucked against my binds in a desperate attempt to save itself. I gave myself over to the darkness wholeheartedly, welcoming the sweet embrace of death. With a final acceptance, I took a breath, ready for this to be over. Death was a sort of freedom, right? Only, it didn't come. My body seized and a change took hold. The soul-wrenching pain that overcame me was more imposing than the crushing of my lungs. The haze in my mind went up in flames, crashing into me in hot flashes like the waves of a relentless storm.

My lungs seemed to burst, yet I could breathe again. I took a deep, shuddering breath as I screamed in agony. My flesh cracked as if it were made of marble and peeled away from my body in rivets, revealing a murky gray complexion. I writhed and thrashed like a wild animal against the ropes that bound me. They seared into my legs, so hot my skin morphed around them. They glowed as they sank into my skin, lashing them together. A new silver skin formed around my binds, elongating into a joined tail. Fins pushed their way out of where my thighs had been, bulbs tipped the flared ends of them. My feet elongated, curving as they went. Spines formed and webbing bound them together into a large fin that dipped into two equal lengths. Little bulbs adorned each of the swooping ridges, glowing purple in the dark water.

Agony seared through my arms as spiked fins pushed out of my flesh, blending with the silver of my tail. My eyes were the last to morph; I could see into the darkness now...as clear as the waters of the Caribbean. I took a few ragged breaths, recovering from the pain my body had just endured. As if my body knew what to do by instinct, I flipped my tail, and rushed back up to the surface. I broke through the water, flipping my hair back and gasping for any air my lungs could swallow. My body was still in shock, pain rushing through me in currents. Slowly, the earth-shattering agony eased away; the bite of the cold water worked to numb it. I already noted the water didn't feel as chilling as it should have. I saw the ship sailing in the distance, a black mark on the horizon. She was one of the fastest ships in the sea.

"Fuck the lot of you!" I screamed, my voice coming out hoarse and alien to my ears.

I bobbed up and down with the movement of the ocean, my tail flicking languidly through the current to keep me upright. I noticed my fingers were webbed, and sharp claws took over my nail beds. I slid my hand through my wet hair. It was no longer golden-brown, as it had been, but the color of seaweed, such a dark green it was almost black. I looked over myself in wonder, feeling my new slippery skin. Silver scales glistened over my tail and fins.

What do I do now?

Just as the thought crossed my mind, heads rose out of the water. I looked around, astonished at the crowd of beings that looked like me. Their eyes glowed yellow against the dying light. I knew then, this was where I belonged. Slowly, they began going under one by one, without a sound, and I knew they wanted me to follow. Not by any thought of my own, only instinct to guide me, my body turned with them, and with a flip of my tail, I followed them into the depths below.

I was now one of the feared monsters that lurked in the deep. I was a Siren. If only my mother could see me. There were only two things I knew for certain: that I was home and I would have my vengeance if it were the last thing I did. Porter's life would be mine. I had much to do to prepare. There would be blood in the water.

Chapter 38

Lyra POV- Broken

I knew something was wrong, I could feel it in my bones. Call it a mother's instinct. I thought I had time. I had been away from the ship far too long, taking a break to rest after Devil's Port, one that was much needed with how scarce food had been out in the open sea. I was tired of feeding on bottom feeders, they tasted like death and grit. They were supposed to be docked for much longer, much to my surprise when I came back, and they weren't there. Panic took hold of me, its clutches making it hard to think straight.

I had been swimming for days trying to catch up, but the winds carried on stronger this last week. It called for times of change, the bringing of a new season. My heart ached, urging me to hurry. The currents caressed my tail, the temperature dropping the further I swam from the island. It has been a long time since I'd seen my sisters. A pang of homesickness curled tight inside my belly. I needed to return to them. Eventually, it would take its toll to keep away.

Soon, soon, I will return home.

I needed to check on Naida one more time, for my sake—at least that was what I kept telling myself. It was as if she reached me in a dream. I wasn't sure how it happened, I knew we had telepathic abilities but nothing like this. I would have to speak to the elders to see if this had happened before. I heard her voice; she spoke of how happy she was. Spoke of a boy, what was his name?

Casper.

Yes, that was it, Casper. She was in love. My heart thundered in my chest. Fresh memories of Dunstan and I falling in love blinded me. How he courted me. He brought me lilies of all different colors. I didn't know how to read so he would read to me, spinning beautiful tales of princesses, dragons, heroes, and villains. Every story had a happy ending, just not our own. I blinked away tears as I swam.

Faster, I must go faster.

I swam through the night into the next day. My body was throbbing, heavy with exhaustion. I was pushing myself to the brink, and I knew it. Nothing but deep blue waters had greeted me, not a soul in sight for days. No ships. Not even a shark, which I was mighty grateful for—those beastly things were a nuisance I did not need currently.

When I first saw the speck of black in the distance, I thought it was a hallucination. Maybe I had succumbed to the exhaustion and slept as I swam. No, I was certain that was the bottom of a ship far off. I willed every ounce of energy I had reserved into pushing myself forward.

I am almost there, Naida. Just a little longer.

I could hear commotion the closer I got, the shouts from aboard carrying into the water. I was but one hundred yards from the ship when a splash caught my attention, sending massive ripples through the water. My heart jumped into my throat. The sound carried through the water around me.

All I saw was a dark head of hair—that had me propelling forward in a shot of speed. I rushed to the ship to watch the anchor plummet to the ground below. Air bubbles floated up as it went. My tail flipped harder than it ever had before as I plunged through the water. My throat constricted as I went, my fear a melody as I called for help. Any help. My distress signal radiated around me; I was certain help would come. I just hoped it would come in time.

The sand below plumbed as the anchor hit bottom. Shaking the rocky bottom as sand shot up in a current that was blinding. As I approached, the figure tied to it was limp. My shaking fingers grasped the ropes, putting speedy work into undoing the knots. I cursed every sailor I could for these knots. Time was running out. I was glad for all those rescue missions, they made working under pressure easier. My panic was trying to drown me and swallow me whole. Curse these gods-forsaken knots.

Finally, with a desperate cry the last knot loosened, and I tugged the figure from its binds. I hoisted them over my shoulder, adjusting for their weight. Propelling myself to the surface in a mad rush, I sent my trill out again, calling for the help of any wildlife around.

A looming shape came into my peripheral, following my ascent. A giant sea turtle came to my call. My heart throbbed hopefully in my chest. We broke the surface, I pulled the turtle closer. Once we were out of the water, I was able to tow the body onto the turtle's shell, settling it as best as I could face up on the turtle's back. It was not Naida. It was a man, an actual man.

The face looked familiar, like the one Naida had spoken of. I had seen him on the ship from time to time when I checked on her.

"*Casper?*" My call into his mind was a desperate plea, I urged him to wake up. Using my command much like I did to get sailors to jump into the water with us.

Nothing. He wasn't responding. I drew up my arm, slapping him once across the face with enough sting to leave a red welt. His eyes flew open as he sputtered, coughing the ocean out of his lungs.

"Everything is alright, it will be fine my sweet." I caressed a soothing hand across his face, urging him to take even breaths.

His coughing ceased for a moment to take me in, I could see the questions crossing his face.

"All will be answered in time. You are safe."

"What about Naida?" He gasped, his voice hoarse from the assault of the seawater.

My heart seized in my chest, all thoughts becoming one singular question.

"*Where?*"

"They threw her overboard."

Take him to safety.

I communicated to the sea turtle and dove back into the water, heading to the ship. Naida was the singular thought that consumed me. I pounded harder against the current. My body shivered in protest against the exertion as I fought against the current.

Please, please not her too.

I could not bear the thought. Losing Dunstan was enough—it was all the heartbreak I could bear in this lifetime. My vision blurred with unshed tears as they whipped away in the water around me. My heart thrashed against my ribs painfully. Panic was rearing its ugly head again, harder this time. I shoved it down deep, choking on its suffocating hold on me. Now was not the time to give in. The ship came back into view, a still figure descending into the darkness. I pushed faster, but no air bubbles were floating to the top.

I was too late.

I could see the transformation taking hold—my daughter, my young one. The ropes fused to her flesh. Her hair turned seaweed green. The silver of her skin glinted off whatever light penetrated through the depths. The darkness consumed her and brought out a monster in her place.

She was gone. Naida was gone.

As quick as that, I experienced my second death. My heart, my Naida, was lost to me. A mournful trill left me, carrying my pain for all those to hear. My grief, my loss, my heart bled for all those who cared to witness my undoing. All I could do was stare from a distance as my daughter, my second love, was claimed by the sea. My second love, twisted and mutilated into the monster I had sworn to hate.

The End

...Or is it?

Epilogue

Porter

The tightness in my chest unraveled, even as the knot grew in my throat. This was always the plan, I had to remind myself. A bitter sourness filled my mouth with the thought of what I had done. Sacrificed my best friend. I shook off the feeling, turning my attention to the still cheering crew.

Bloodthirsty blokes.

"Alright, shows over. Get back to work!" I yelled, barely audible over the dying cheers.

The crew started to thin out, getting back to their duties. We would all be a little lost not having Casper barking orders left and right. The nagging thought that cursed me crept back in, why did he notice her? I had been trying to gain his favor for years, to no avail. Yet, she wiggled her way in and captured his heart. The watery grave serves him right.

I looked up, catching Marduke's eye. He nodded toward his quarters and I followed reverently. My fingers curled at my sides as I hurried my strides to him. As was my duty. I closed the heavy door behind me, feeling the wooden grain beneath my fingers. My heart fluttered in my chest.

"Ye did good," Marduke murmured, grabbing a tumbler for his stash of bourbon he kept on hand. I preened under the praise, lapping it up like a starving dog with scraps.

"Thank ye, sir." My footsteps were light as I made my way around his desk.

He glanced over at me, his steely gaze heavy as I perched on his desk.

"Now, without Casper, who be filling the first mate role?" I questioned, keeping my tone light and innocent the way he loved.

"Who would ye suggest?" He took his seat, arching a brow at me as he took a heavy swallow.

I tracked the movement all the way down, licking my bottom lip. Rubbing my hands on my trousers, I ran light, playful fingertips over his trinkets on the desk.

"If I'd be so bold." I looked at him through my lashes, a light grin playing on my lips. "I would suggest meself."

He tipped his head back, grimacing after another large swallow. "I think I like ye exactly where ye are. My little mouse."

My heart stuttered, the bitter taste filling my mouth once more. He glided his hands over my leg, picking one up behind the knee to place on one side of him.

"Come now, don't make that face, love," he murmured, pulling me roughly into his lap. "After all, I got rid of them fer ye."

Heat rose to my cheeks and raced to my core. He had a way of doing that to me. I took my time weaseling my way under his skin. When Casper wouldn't give me the time of day except to order me around, I made it my mission to go higher up. Lucky for me, Captain was weak to his primal urges. In return for keeping a diligent ear to the floor and keeping his bed warm, I got my needs met and secured safety on this ship. Demi wasn't the only one with secrets. I scratched at my head, little pinpricks driving me mad as I tugged at the wig.

"Aye, ya did. Promise me, when we get to port again, ye will secure me a proper wig." My voice was husky as I played lightly with his locks.

He pulled the wig off, and my long sandy blonde hair fell around my shoulders, curtaining us. Soon enough, his fingers threaded my hair, his rough grasp tugging at my scalp and sending a delightful spark of pain down my spine. I purred under his control, letting him guide me to his rough lips. I always had a thing for older guys; with age comes experience, like a fine wine. Oh, how I missed the taste of proper wine; I would make sure he picked me up a bottle or two while he was at it.

"Anything for you, my mouse. Now, let me taste ye."

I gave in to the growing warmth, letting him scoop me up and shift me over to his bed. A little giggle escaped me as he tossed me down, pinning me and clasping the cuffs he had hidden around my wrists. A thrill raced through me, my pulse spiking. He relished control, and I was fully willing to submit to him.

"Yes sir, tighter," I moaned, letting him have his fill.

Acknowledgements

My first thank you will be to my husband, Ed; thank you for believing in me even when I did not believe in myself. Thank you for never letting me quit on my dreams. Thank you for being cruelly blunt when you do not like something I write (even if I hate you for it at the moment).

Thank you to my mother for always encouraging my writing and for letting me escape into my books constantly. Without your support, I am not sure I could have continued writing.

Thank you to my 5th and 6th grade teacher for supporting my dreams and letting me share my stories in class. You were always such a big fan.

Thank you, Mr. Costa, for having a poetry club where I found a voice to share my work. You have always inspired me. Thank you for teaching me how to give constructive feedback, even in my own writing.

Thank you to my dear friends who have supported me my entire journey. Thank you for giving me inspiration for the worlds and characters I create. Your support and the joy you found in my writing gave me hope for my future.

Thank you to my sister, who wrote my stories down when I stunk at typing. Thank you for being a bright light even when your world was dark. I wish you could have seen one finally make it into the big world.

Thank you to my brother's who inspire me to live boldly and fully as myself each and every day. I hope you are as proud of me as I am of you.

Thank you to those new and old friends who helped beta-read my story. I couldn't have done it without you all.

Last but certainly not least, thank you to my editor who was such a pleasure to work with. All of your suggestions and help meant the world to me. As well as the Etheric design team for bringing my book to life with your amazing cover, interior and character art.

About the Author

Since you can't actually live in a fantasy realm, you will often find Cheyenne creating her own. Born and raised in Lancaster, PA, she often turned to books and writing as an escape from the mundane. Her animals, husband, and toddler make life quite interesting at home. If she is not wrangling the household, getting lost in her own worlds, or crafting something for her business, you'll be sure to find this dragon curled up on the couch devouring her hoard of books, tea, and chocolates.

Milton Keynes UK
Ingram Content Group UK Ltd.
UKHW030947140324
439440UK00001B/68